THE SCARY STATES
OF AMERICA

THE SCARY STATES OF AMERICA

Michael Teitelbaum

Delacorte Press

A Stonesong Press and Town Brook Press Book

Published by Delacorte Press
an imprint of Random House Children's Books
a division of Random House, Inc.
New York

Delacorte Press and colophon are registered trademarks of Random House, Inc.
A Stonesong Press and Town Brook Press Book

www.randomhouse.com/kids

Educators and librarians, for a variety of teaching tools, visit us at
www.randomhouse.com/teachers

Library of Congress Cataloging-in-Publication Data
Teitelbaum, Michael.
    The scary states of America / Michael Teitelbaum. — 1st ed.
        p.   cm.
    Summary: Twelve-year-old Jason Specter, self-proclaimed "clearing house for the weird,"
introduces and presents his favorite stories of the paranormal—one from each state of the
Union—submitted to the Web site he created after his own encounter with a ghost at
school three years earlier.
ISBN 978-0-385-73331-1 (trade)—ISBN 978-0-385-90348-6 (GLB)
1. Children's stories, American.   2. Haunted places—Juvenile fiction.   [1. Haunted
places—Fiction.   2. Supernatural—Fiction.   3. Ghosts—Fiction.   4. Occultism—Fiction.
5. Short stories.]   I. Title.
    PZ7.T233Sca 2007
    [Fic]—dc22
                                2006019357

Printed in the United States of America

10 9 8 7 6 5 4 3 2 1

First Edition

CONTENTS

THE SCARY STATES OF AMERICA

MEET JASON SPECTER

You're probably wondering how an ordinary kid like me came to be the official collector of all things weird and scary in the USA. With all the strange and unexplained stuff happening out there, you'd think we'd have a whole army of investigators trying to uncover the truth. But unless they're keeping a really low profile, I haven't seen any teams of ghostbusters or psychic detectives prowling my neighborhood. So I gave myself the job after a terrifying experience convinced me that someone needs to be keeping an eye on the paranormal in this country. This story, like the others in this book, is true.

So before we get into monsters and ghosts and UFOs, let's talk about something truly frightening—the fourth grade. Bullies, atomic wedgies, stolen lunch money . . . it was a real house of horrors.

Did I mention bullies?

Charlie and Steve were the cool kids, and they thought I was a total geek. Maybe it was my obsession with comic books, and collecting baseball cards, and watching every sci-fi show on TV. At nine years old, I wasn't too worried about my image. Now that I'm twelve, I think I've wised up a little (though I still like all that stuff).

Anyway, Charlie and Steve ended up in my gym class, and man, did I hate gym class. Some steroid-pumped ex-jock former marine commanding us to climb the rope, shoot the ball, lift the weight. They had the nerve to call that guy a teacher?

Mr. Rockwell was his name. He loved to shout at me. "Specter!" he would yell. "Get off your rear and gimme twenty, boy!"

So I was reading a comic book when I was supposed to be doing push-ups. What about reading being exercise for your brain?

And, of course, he treated Charlie and Steve like future Olympic champions. They were good at every sport. After Rockwell was done yelling at me, they'd take their turn in the locker room.

"Hey, shrimp, where's the rest of you?"

"Nice legs, Specter. Did you swallow a couple of broom-sticks?"

So I was small for my age. Sue me.

One day, I was the last to finish getting dressed after gym.

Or so I thought.

As I tied my shoes, Charlie and Steve suddenly appeared on either side of me.

"What's the matter, Specter?" Charlie cackled. "Forget how to dress yourself?"

Steve laughed his goony laugh.

"Well, I'm not lucky enough to have Steve here to dress me, like you," I replied, realizing it was a mistake as the words left my mouth. It's fun being a wisecracker, but you have to make sure you have an easy escape route. And I didn't.

Charlie grabbed me by the front of my shirt and slammed me into a bank of lockers. Pain shot down my back. Then Steve punched me in the stomach and I felt like I was going to barf.

"You think you're funny, huh, shrimp?" Charlie snarled, shoving me back into the line of metal doors. "How'd you like it if I smacked your head into one of these lockers? You think that would be funny?"

"Hey, Charlie, maybe he'd like to see locker six-fifteen," Steve said, giggling. "Up close!"

"Good idea," said Charlie. A sick smile spread across his stupid face.

I froze in terror. Every kid in the school knew about locker 615. That locker had some kind of evil history attached to it. I didn't really know what it was, or how far back it went. Everyone says the school covered it up pretty fast. They even replaced all the lockers in the boys' locker room, hoping that people would forget.

But something bad still happened to every kid who used 615—it was cursed.

One kid fell off the rope in gym and broke his leg on the first day he used 615. Another choked in the school cafeteria, also on the day he was assigned 615. Mr. Rockwell won't admit it, but he now goes out of his way not to give 615 to anyone. Even parents get a little superstitious when kids start getting injured at school.

I started to feel sick to my stomach. I tried to run but didn't get far. Charlie and Steve each grabbed one of my arms. I desperately struggled to break free.

"Leave me alone!" I shrieked, in a higher voice than I would've liked.

They lifted me off the ground. I kicked my feet wildly, hitting nothing but air as I twisted and squirmed. They hustled me toward locker 615.

"You guys are idiots, you know!" I screamed.

"You're not so funny now, are you, shrimp?" Charlie yelled back.

"Mr. Rockwell!" I bellowed, hoping the gym teacher was still around.

He wasn't.

Realizing I couldn't free myself, I hoped they would only slam me against the locker door, or maybe just shove my head inside.

No such luck!

Charlie wrapped me in a viselike bear hug while Steve grabbed the handle of locker 615. After a couple of unsuccessful yanks, he jerked the door open.

Instantly, a horrible stale smell, as if someone had left

a dead animal in there, made my eyes water. I started coughing. Charlie and Steve squeezed me inside the locker and slammed the door. Everything went dark. I heard the sound of a lock snapping shut, and then it got weirdly quiet.

"Let me out!" I screamed. Then I coughed uncontrollably as the foul stench burned my throat. *"Let me out of here!"*

Panic now mixed with the nausea. I was squeezed in so tight I could barely move an inch. I felt my throat closing as I breathed the stale, damp air. Shifting my position a little, I tried banging my shoulder into the side of the locker.

"Somebody let me out of here!"

"They won't come," a faint voice said. It was as if the person were standing right next to me. Then I heard someone inhale a tortured, wheezing breath.

I tried to turn my head to the right but ended up smashing my cheek into the side of the locker.

"Who said that?" I demanded. *"Is somebody out there?"*

"Nobody's there," the same strained voice replied, only it came from behind me now. Then I heard another painful gasp for air.

What's going on? I thought. *This locker barely fits me, let alone two people. I've only been in here for a second, but I must be totally losing my mind!*

"They never come!" the tormented voice gasped from somewhere inside the locker, followed by a raspy struggle for breath.

I was suddenly filled with exhaustion, totally drained of strength, and unable to move. It had only been a minute, but it felt as if I had been trapped in the locker for a week.

What's happening to me?

My throat began to tighten. I tried to breathe but had to fight to suck air into my lungs. *I can't breathe! I'm going to die!*

Then my eyes snapped open, and I found myself staring at a boy about my age. The boy was being dragged toward a locker—this locker—by a kid twice his size. I watched helplessly as the boy was shoved into the locker. Just before the door slammed, something small tumbled from his pocket.

"*No!*" he screamed. Or was I the one screaming?

"My inhaler!" the boy and I shrieked together, as if he had taken over my body and was controlling my voice. I felt his panic shoot through my veins.

Then everything went dark again. Because I was wedged in so tightly, I'd lost feeling in my feet and arms. I didn't have the energy to try to yell, bang the door, or change position. My wheezing was worsening and I was losing strength.

"I'm so tired. I'm so cold." I couldn't tell if the voice was my own or his. It didn't matter. I felt like I was dying.

A small hand closed around my throat. The last bits of life seeped from my body. "Brian Coles," the faint voice whispered as the phantom tightened its grip. "Don't forget about me."

Somewhere, far away, I heard the sharp snap of metal being cut. Then light flooded the locker.

"Specter!" cried a man's voice as two strong hands gripped my shoulders and pulled me from my stinking, dark prison. "How in God's name did you get in there?"

As Mr. Rockwell set me down on a bench, I looked back into the open locker and spotted the boy I had seen inside tumbling to the floor. He lay there motionless.

"Specter! Are you all right?" Rockwell's voice was far away.

I reached down for the dead boy. When I touched his lifeless body, images flooded my brain like a superspeed slide show.

The dead boy surrounded by kids in gym uniforms.

A man and a woman standing over him, crying.

Two policemen leading away the bigger boy who had locked the kid in the locker.

I took my hand off the boy's body and the images stopped. I felt my strength returning, and I could breathe normally again. I sat up, then noticed something on the floor next to locker 615. Reaching down to pick it up, I was shocked to discover that it was an inhaler. I slipped it into my pocket.

I had to tell Rockwell about Charlie and Steve. I didn't want them to have the chance to abuse anyone else. They were suspended from school. I was afraid they'd try to get me back, but then I realized I was more afraid of what had occurred inside the locker.

Instead of letting my fear take over, I was determined to figure out what had happened to me. I Googled "Brian Coles" but found only a music reviewer and a computer engineer. Then I checked out the back-issue database at our local newspaper. Bingo!

Brian Coles was a student at my school about ten years ago. Some jerk shoved him into a locker and locked him in. The kid didn't know that Brian had asthma. Brian had a serious attack and didn't have his inhaler. He was trapped in that locker for hours. When they finally opened it, Brian was dead.

I felt the hair on the back of my neck stand up as I turned the inhaler I had picked up over and over in my hands. I still keep it as a kind of talisman, to remind me of the day when I learned that the world we see every day is just the surface of all that's out there.

So that's how it all started for me. I was only nine. No matter how many times I replayed the events of that day in my head, I always came up with the same answer—I had met a ghost.

I started reading everything I could about the paranormal. I became positively obsessed. As I began checking out Web sites and blogs, I realized this stuff happens to lots of people, all over the country. But we needed a central hub. Someplace where kids like me could report their encounters and meet others who might have had similar experiences.

So I put up my Web site (www.scarystatesofamerica .com) and started collecting stories. People from all over the country contact me now, telling me the stuff that's happened to them. Some have turned to me for help. Others have helped me, pointing me to paranormal hot spots. I've even been lucky enough to visit a few. Now I'm kind of a clearinghouse for the weird.

I've made some friends doing this. Mostly other bloggers also obsessed with the paranormal. Most I've never met in person.

I figured this book would be another way to get the word out. I've picked one tale I uncovered in each state in the USA, or as I've started calling it, the Scary States of America.

These are my fifty favorites. Some are so scary that they'll keep you up at night, and some are just sick! Others will creep you out. But I've also learned that the paranormal world is not always a horrible place. Some spirits are actually kind, and some aliens have even saved lives. That's why I keep searching and collecting, learning all I can about the realm of the unexplained.

Welcome to my world!

Jason Specter

ALABAMA
The Hitchhiker

What I learned in history class: Man walked on the moon thanks to the state of Alabama. The rocket used by *Apollo 11* was designed, built, and tested at the Marshall Space Flight Center in Huntsville, Alabama.

A story you won't find in your textbook: Most of the stories I've collected have been sent to me by the people who experienced them or by my paranormal blogging buddies from all over the United States, who are always shooting me e-mails packed with weird stuff that's happened to them or people they know. But I have traveled a little, and wherever I've gone, I've looked for the strange and unexplained.

A few of those times, it's come looking for me. Like the time I was in Alabama visiting my cousin Rich.

◉◉

I really like my cousin Rich. He's a few years older than me, and we couldn't be more different. But he's always been nice to me when he's come to visit, and when I've gone to Alabama to spend some time with him.

Rich is a total jock. You know, captain of his high school football team, a big strong guy. All the things I'm not. But he's not a jerk like some of the jocks in my school. Maybe it's because he's my cousin, but we always have fun together.

Rich had just gotten his license the last time I'd visited, so he wanted to drive everywhere. We were tooling around in his beat-up bomb of a car when it started to get dark. It was raining pretty heavy so I figured we'd head for home, but Rich had other ideas.

Heavy rain beat steadily down on the windshield as we wound along the dark country roads. The thick forest creeps in close in Alabama. It got real hard to see between swipes of the windshield wipers.

"Can you see where you're going?" I asked.

"Sure," Rich said, squinting out the window. "Absolutely."

Yeah, I thought. *You've only been driving for a month and you think you're ready for NASCAR.* But I kept my mouth shut.

Suddenly, I saw the headlights flash across something on the side of the road.

"What's that?" I cried, squinting through the rain. "I think there's a person out there!"

"Where?" Rich asked, leaning forward in the driver's seat. "I can't see anything in this rain."

"Good thing you're driving, then, huh?" I said, pointing. "There! Look!"

On the side of the road, in front of what looked like an old factory, stood a tall figure with its thumb outstretched.

"Hey, you're right!" Rich exclaimed. "It's just a hitchhiker. Look at the poor guy. He's getting drenched. We should stop."

"Stop?" I cried. "What do you mean, stop? You mean pick him up? But what if he's dangerous? What if he's not even human?"

Okay, so I had recently read a story about a demon hitchhiker who drained the blood out of his victims.

"You believe all that junk?" Rich asked as he put on his right turn signal.

I felt my heart pound as the car slowed.

"That was funny when you were nine, Jason, but come on, dude, you're twelve. It's time to outgrow all that Halloween stuff," Rich said, poking me in the ribs. "Besides, look at him. He's just a kid."

Rich pulled over onto the shoulder and stopped. I did not like this scenario one bit. Even if the kid turned out to be normal, the "never pick up hitchhikers" rule was one I didn't want to break, thank you very much. Anyway, what the heck was a kid doing out on a night like this?

Rain beat down hard on the hood of the car. Steam rose

off the heated metal. I thought my heart was going to leap from my chest. My palms got all sweaty, and I started to breathe real fast.

The hitchhiker approached the car. With each step my panic grew, and images of serial killers flashed in my head. Would he have a gun or an ax? Or a *chain saw*? Would he kill us instantly or maybe torture us slowly and painfully?

He crept along the shoulder, passing in front of a rusty chain-link fence that surrounded the abandoned factory. Reaching our car, he slowly grabbed the handle of the back door. My nerves were on fire, and it took every ounce of restraint not to scream. I could almost count the raindrops splattering on the windshield. It felt like hours had passed since we'd stopped. *Who is this guy? Why's he moving so slowly?*

"Jason, just chill, would you?" Rich said. He must have sensed my fear, or maybe he'd heard my heart pounding.

I heard the metallic click of the handle, then the creaky whine of the back door opening. *This is it!* I thought, my mind racing with the image of a masked hitchhiker sawing off Rich's limbs.

With a sudden jerk, the hitchhiker thrust his head into the car. I spun around in the seat, ready to confront a demented psychopath. But Rich was right. The hitchhiker was a teenager, just a few years older than me. Maybe even the same age as Rich. He had short red hair and was wearing a blue shirt and black jeans.

"Thanks for stopping," he said, wiping the rain from his eyes. He was nervous and jittery, shifting from one foot to the other. "My name's Frank. Could you take me home? It's building seven, apartment fourteen, in the Carver Park housing project. I haven't seen my mom or my little brother in six weeks and I really miss them."

My weirdness meter shot up to the max. *Where has this kid been for six weeks that he hasn't seen his family? Why is he standing out here in the pouring rain?* I could sense that even Rich was getting creeped out by this guy.

"Sorry, we're not going all the way to Carver Park," Rich explained. "We're stopping up on Highland Avenue."

"Please!" the hitchhiker pleaded in a strained voice. "Please take me home. My mom is waiting for me. She's worried."

Just peel out, Rich! I thought, wishing he could read my mind. *Take off! Go!*

"I can take you as far as Highland Avenue," Rich said. "Maybe you can get another ride from there."

Are you nuts! *Maybe he's not a demon, but this guy has mass murderer written all over him!* I shot Rich a look. *This is no time to be brave, Mr. Tough Guy!*

The hitchhiker nodded, then slipped into the backseat.

Rich signaled left and pulled out onto the road. I stared straight ahead, trying to pretend there was no one in the backseat.

"So," Rich began. "What brings you out in the middle of nowhere on such a miserable night?"

"Take me home!" the hitchhiker insisted, ignoring the small talk. "My mom is waiting for me! I have to go home!"

His tone grew angry. Then he leaned forward in the backseat, and I smelled alcohol on his breath. From the expression on Rich's face I could tell that he did too.

The hitchhiker began to groan, as if he was in pain. His voice filled the car, so I heard nothing else—no rain, no engine, no radio—just a low animal moan, like a beast preparing to attack its prey.

I saw that Rich was finally realizing what a big mistake he'd made. I only hoped we both lived long enough for me to say "I told you so!"

"You okay, dude?" Rich asked nervously.

"I have to get home!" the hitchhiker shouted. "Take me home now or it will be too late!" Then he reached over and grabbed the shoulder of Rich's varsity jacket.

The car swerved as Rich flinched. The tires squealed on the wet roadway. Rich fought for control of the car. My strapping football-hero cousin was gripping the steering wheel so tightly, his thick knuckles were white. I'd never seen Rich scared of anything. Now his face was pale with fear.

Maintaining his grip on Rich's jacket, the hitchhiker reached his other hand into his own pocket, fumbling for something.

He's got a knife! Or a gun!

As the hitchhiker pulled the weapon from his pocket, Rich turned the steering wheel hard to the right and slammed on his brakes. We skidded onto the shoulder, screeching to a stop.

"That's it!" Rich shouted, balling his left hand into a beefy fist. "Get the hell out of my car!"

As Rich spun around to bash this guy's face in, the hitchhiker's weapon dropped on the front seat between us. I looked back.

To my shock, the seat was empty.

"Where did he go?" Rich asked, looking out the window.

The rain came down in sheets. There was no other noise—and no sign of the hitchhiker.

"Whoa!" Rich cried. "How could he have gotten out without opening the door?"

I inspected the backseat. Nothing. The guy had simply vanished.

"I don't get it," said Rich as the color returned to his face. "Guys don't just vanish."

Sometimes they do, I thought, but I figured this wasn't the time to educate my freaked-out cousin on the world of the paranormal. Then I remembered the weapon.

I looked down. On the front seat between us sat a half-empty bottle of whiskey.

"That guy was polluted," Rich said.

"Yeah," I agreed, a plan hatching in my mind.

We headed for Rich's house. I let a few minutes pass, then said, "We know where he lives, you know."

"Yeah, so?" Rich said sharply. "You wanna bring him back his booze?"

"No," I replied. "In fact, I think we should throw it out

now. It wouldn't look too good if you got stopped. I think we should pay the guy a visit tomorrow."

I never thought I'd feel braver than Rich, but it took a lot of convincing that night for him to agree to drive us out to Carver Park the next morning.

"This is nuts," Rich said as we found the apartment.

"Leave it to me," I said.

"Oh, great," Rich moaned.

I rang the bell.

A thin woman holding a young boy in her arms answered the door. "Yes?" she said. "Can I help you?"

"Are you Frank's mom?" I asked.

"Yes," she replied. "What do you want?"

"I'm looking for Frank," I said.

Tears welled up in her eyes. "I—I'm sorry," she stammered. "Frank is dead. My son was killed six weeks ago."

I felt the weird nervous rush I get when I know I've uncovered the paranormal. Now I knew the hitchhiker had been a ghost! I glanced past the woman into her apartment and, sure enough, spotted a photo of her, the boy, and a teenager with short red hair, wearing a blue shirt and black jeans.

"How did he die?" I managed to ask as I continued to stare at the photo.

"Frank was killed in a terrible car accident," the woman explained, unable now to fight back her tears. "The police said he had been drinking and lost control of his car."

"That's terrible," I said quietly. I could feel the hair on the back of my neck stand up. "Do you mind if I ask where it happened?"

"About twenty miles out of town," she said. "Right in front of some old factory."

I apologized to Frank's mom for bothering her, and Rich and I took off.

Rich was clearly shaken.

"Jason," he said as we climbed back into his car. "I'll never make fun of your freaky hobby again."

"Whatever, man," I said, knowing Rich and I would always make fun of each other. "Just don't stop for any hitchhikers on the way home."

ALASKA
Bigfoot Lives!

What I learned in history class: On March 30, 1867, Secretary of State William H. Seward agreed to purchase Alaska from Russia for $7 million. Nicknamed the Last Frontier, Alaska is the largest state in area and is the largest peninsula in the Western Hemisphere.

A story you won't find in your textbook: After my rude introduction to the paranormal a few years back, I found myself drawn deeper and deeper into the world of the unexplained. One of the first places I stumbled across when I started to check all this out was a Bigfoot chat room. I got totally into the stories, legends, and real-life sightings of this creature. A buddy of mine from the chat room, who calls himself Bigfoot (BF) Ed, IM'd me about something that happened to his uncle.

> **BF-Ed:** Jason, you're not gonna believe the story my uncle just sent me.
> **ParaGuy:** Try me.
> **BF-Ed:** He tracks bears in Alaska, and he had a real-life encounter with a Bigfoot. I'll forward the story to you, bro. It's unreal!!

Here's the tale Bigfoot Ed sent me, as told by his uncle, a nature photographer from Anchorage, Alaska, named Allen Mara.

◉◉

Hi, Ed. I know what a Bigfoot fan you are, but don't think I'm making this up just to humor you. I wish I were. I'm still traumatized by the whole thing, but I figured telling you would help—at least I know you'll believe me.

I was on another expedition to a wildlife sanctuary in Alaska to photograph brown bears in the wild, which you know I've been doing for years. The sanctuary, located at the northeast end of the Alaska Peninsula, was created to protect the world's largest gathering of bears. The Alaska Department of Fish and Game strictly limits access to the park. There are no roads in the sanctuary; the only way in or out is by light aircraft. Visitor permits are distributed through a lottery system and only about 250 people a year are allowed in. So when I received my permit, I considered myself one of the lucky ones.

After being flown in and dropped off, I set up camp right near the swiftly flowing river that winds through the sanctuary. I had a three-day supply of food, and I wouldn't see another human being until the pilot returned for me on the third day.

On the way back to my campsite at the end of my second day of shooting pictures of bears, I spotted a set of footprints. They were enormous, at least sixteen inches long, six inches wide, and square. The second toe was longer and larger than the first, while the other three toes were small and appeared to be webbed. In all my years of shooting wildlife photos, I had never seen an animal that could make tracks like these.

I took a few pictures, convinced that no one would believe me without evidence. With my mind racing about what could have made the tracks, I returned to my camp, built a fire, and started preparing dinner.

Like everyone else, I had heard tales of Bigfoot creatures. I know that in 1967, two men in Northern California named Roger Patterson and Robert Gimlin took the only known film footage of a Bigfoot. I'd seen still photos from the Patterson-Gimlin film in several books, but I never thought I'd ever actually see a Bigfoot track, if that's what these really were.

I was excited and not at all worried. All the reports I'd ever read described Bigfoot creatures as shy, likely to flee at the first sign of humans. In fact, my biggest fear was that I might *not* get a glimpse of the creature, if it even existed. This was before I knew what I know now. I had never read some of the older descriptions that referred to the creatures' tendency to break bodies into a thousand pieces and their taste for human flesh.

As the sky grew dark, I heard a rustling in the trees a short distance away. Grabbing my camera, I approached the edge of the woods. I heard a twig snap behind me and spun around to find myself staring up at a seven-foot-tall creature! It had a thick, muscular neck and a small cone-shaped head with heavy brow ridges above its piercing black eyes. Its long arms dangled by its sides, its knuckles scraping the ground as it hunched over.

My brain wasn't really processing what I was seeing, but my photographer's instincts took over. Glancing down, I saw the creature's enormous hairy feet. I raised my camera just as the beast snarled, revealing its fanged canine teeth.

As I focused my camera, the creature lunged toward me. I felt a powerful clawed hand clamp around my left shoulder. As searing pain shot down my left arm, my right hand clenched and I pressed the shutter release button.

Flash!

The camera's flash went off as I snapped the picture. The creature instantly released its grip, crying out and stumbling backward. Its enormous arms swung wildly, slapping the camera from my hand and into the snow.

Recovering, the creature bent over, picked up the camera,

and slammed it into a tree. It smashed into a million pieces, destroying the proof of my Bigfoot encounter, along with all the incredible bear shots I had taken. I started running for my life. I saw what Bigfoot had done to my camera and I didn't want my head to be next. The creature gave chase, lumbering awkwardly after me, clearly enraged.

I reached my campsite and looked down at the crackling fire, over which hung a pot of stew. Realizing that the bright light from my camera's flash had startled the beast, I quickly grabbed an extra shirt from my tent, wrapped it around my hand, and pulled a flaming log from the fire.

The creature kept coming.

When it was just a few feet away, it grabbed for me with its long arms. I swung the flaming log in front of the beast's eyes, and the Bigfoot howled, backing up. I continued to wave the burning log back and forth, sending embers fluttering into the gathering darkness. The creature growled, then turned and shuffled back into the woods, kicking up clouds of snow as it tromped away.

But I knew it would come back.

Catching my breath, I contemplated my next move. I realized now that the Bigfoot was also afraid of fire. Having gathered a large supply of firewood on my first day, I surveyed my remaining pile. I figured I had enough wood, so I got to work building a circle of campfires.

When I had about half a dozen fires going, I placed myself in the center of the blazing ring. The plane would be arriving early the next morning. All I had to do was make it through the night and hope I didn't run out of wood. I've spent a lot of time in the wild, but this was the first time I really thought I might not make it out alive.

I wrapped my sleeping bag around me, huddling against the cold Alaskan night. I had to stay awake and alert all night, to tend the fires. I couldn't afford to doze.

I thought about all I had lost. Two days' worth of irreplaceable photos of bears in the wild. Photos of actual Bigfoot tracks, and maybe even a shot of the creature itself. Not to mention my best camera. I pushed those thoughts aside and realized that this journey had become a mission of survival. I stood to lose a lot more than my photos if I couldn't keep the creature at bay for the rest of the night.

I heard rustling in the darkness, and then Bigfoot appeared at the edge of the flickering circle, its reddish brown fur highlighted by the fire's soft glow. As one of the fires died down, the creature moved slowly toward me. I scrambled to add more wood and stoke the flames. As the flames grew, Bigfoot backed away.

This cat-and-mouse game continued throughout the night. As the sun rose over the Alaskan mountains, I placed the last of the wood on a dying fire. This was it. I couldn't risk leaving the protective circle to get more wood. The creature stood waiting just beyond the circle, as if it knew it was only a matter of time before the flames died out and its prey was left unprotected. It growled and pawed at the ground with its foot, like a bull preparing to charge.

As the sun climbed into the sky, the fires finally burned down. Bigfoot slowly approached the circle of glowing embers.

I'm not going to make it! I thought, overwhelmed by hunger, cold, and terror. I was exhausted.

Now the fires were totally out. The last wisps of smoke rose into the brightening sky. Bigfoot advanced, baring its fangs.

It was hungry, too.

It no longer looked at the campfires but instead stared directly at me as it moved closer.

I'm not going to make it! I thought again, feeling slightly delirious. *I'm going to die here alone, eaten by Bigfoot.* Too weak to run, I collapsed into the snow and awaited my fate.

Then, as if in a dream, I heard the distant hum of an engine. Looking skyward, I saw the small plane that had dropped me off. As it drew closer, the creature turned and disappeared into the woods, scared off by the deafening roar of the engines.

I stumbled to the plane, feverish, but finally rescued. I told the pilot about my horrible ordeal, but he looked at me like I was a crazy person waking up from a nightmare. If only I had those photos.

Well, Ed, keep spreading the word. Bigfoot does exist, and he's no cuddly teddy bear!

ARIZONA
Human Guinea Pig

What I learned in history class: You know the nursery rhyme "London Bridge Is Falling Down." Well, the bridge actually *was* falling apart in 1962 because it was too weak to handle all the London traffic. It was sold and shipped in pieces to Lake Havasu City, Arizona, where it was carefully reconstructed and now stands as a major tourist attraction.

A story you won't find in your textbook:
From: RBarker@tuc.net
To: Jspecter@scarystatesofamerica.com
Subject: abduction

Jason,

I've read your blog for a while and I'm a big fan, especially of the stuff about aliens. I like the stories you put up about Massachusetts and Roswell, New Mexico. I wasn't sure they were true, though, until I had an unbelievable experience myself. Meeting aliens isn't cool. If you ever encounter them, Jason, run for your life. I know you'll be curious like I was, but it's not worth it. Can I send you my story?

Randy Barker

Of course, I e-mailed Randy right back, and here's what he sent me in his next e-mail.

◉◉

I was working as part of a crew repairing a two-lane road just outside of Tucson. Me and the rest of my five-man crew had been working since early morning. The day grew short, and as the sun began to set, I felt the evening chill creeping up.

Five o'clock finally arrived. Time to knock off and head for home. The sky began to darken as we made our way toward the truck. As we sped along the road leading around the mountain, my buddies and I made jokes, relaxing from the day's hard work.

My friend James was in the middle of a good joke about a possessed cactus when I spotted a bright light flickering through the trees, against the blackening sky.

"What the heck is that?" I asked, peering through the windshield.

The other guys shrugged and stared dumbfounded at the huge light, which appeared to move sideways across the sky. As the truck rounded a bend in the road and we slowed to a stop, the glowing object came into full view.

"Am I nuts?" I asked, trying to make sense of what I was seeing. "Or is that a flying saucer?"

The spacecraft hovered no more than twenty feet above our truck. Brilliant red spokes of light radiated from a large white central circle on the bottom of the ship. The saucer made no sound and didn't move. It just hung in the sky, lighting up the truck and the surrounding forest.

To this day, I still don't know what I was thinking when I jumped from the truck and ran forward until I was standing directly beneath the spacecraft. I guess I wasn't thinking at all—I felt like I was in a trance. My buddies were shouting at me from the truck, but their voices faded into the background of my consciousness. I was completely focused on the impossible vision above me.

Suddenly, a low rumble rang out from the ship, growing in volume and intensity by the second. The vibrations rattled my bones and shook the fillings in my teeth. At this point I regained enough sense to make a run for it, but I was completely unable to move. Some kind of force field was holding me in place.

A shaft of white light shot from the bottom of the saucer. The wide beam surrounded me, and jolts of energy tore through my body. The pain was unbearable; it felt like I had shoved my hand into a high-voltage transformer. I tried to scream, but my body was no longer under my command. I was blinded by the light as my arms and legs twisted in agony. I was slowly being electrocuted!

Then everything went dark.

I slowly opened my eyes. My skin burned like it was on fire. I reached out my fingers and felt cold metal. *I must be in the hospital*, I thought, *on some kind of medical table*. Then the memory of the ship and the blazing white light came rushing back. *Am I dead?* I wondered in terror.

I tried to sit up but was stopped by a metal restraint across my chest. My ankles were also pinned down.

That's when panic set in. *I can't move!*

I struggled against the restraints, but they cut into my chest. *This is no hospital!* I realized as my body shook with fear. Trying hard to fight back the terror, I turned my head and saw three small figures leaning over me.

This can't be happening! This can't be real! Wake up! Wake up!

But I was all too awake.

Sweat from my forehead rolled into my eyes. It stung, and blurred my vision. Squinting, I could just barely make out the figures staring down at me.

They had grainy gray skin, large heads, and oversized green eyes. The creatures stood perfectly still and said nothing. I knew instantly that these guys were not human.

I've been abducted by aliens. The thought slammed into

my brain like a hammer blow. "Who are you?" I shouted, panic rising in my throat. "What do you want with me?"

One of the aliens leaned down toward me and reached out a long thin arm. Through the blinding glare I could see that it held a curved metal tool that ended in a thin, sharp point. It was headed right for my face!

"Leave me alone, you monsters!" I screamed, whipping my head from side to side.

The creature with the tool backed away, then made some noises to one of the others. The second creature moved forward and slammed a metal restraint across my neck and face. It pressed against my windpipe so that any movement I made cut off my air supply, and my head was locked into position.

The alien again brought the tool closer. It was clear now that it was headed right for my eye. Because I couldn't move, I had to watch it come closer and closer. I started to hyperventilate.

"Noooo!" I screamed as the creature caught my left eyelid with the point of the tool and pulled it up against my eyebrow. My left eye was blinded by tears and pain as he poked and prodded my eyeball.

Then a third creature snatched my right lid with another sharp prong, pulling that eye open too.

"No! No! *Stop!*" I screamed. But I still couldn't move without choking myself to death.

They jabbed my right eyeball, and searing pain tore into my brain. I felt weak, unable now even to scream.

Finally they moved away, leaving my eyes pinned open.

I was grateful to find I could still see, but what I saw terrified me.

They were coming back carrying a device shaped like a pair of headphones. But these were no headphones. They placed the thing onto my head and tightened it. Sharp needles plunged into my temples. Electric jolts shot into my head. I opened my mouth to scream, but they gagged me with a thick, smooth cloth.

I knew I was on the verge of unconsciousness, maybe even death. My mind flooded with images, flashing at high speed.

A series of circuits and gauges.

Brain waves dancing up and down like lines on a graph.

A strange red landscape, barren and rocky, with no sign of life.

My bedroom at home.

The farm I grew up on.

The gleaming exterior of the spaceship.

Finally, they yanked the needles from my head, and the pictures stopped shooting through my brain.

Is it over?

Six tiny but powerful gray hands tore at my shirt, shredding it and leaving my chest exposed. Then the aliens lowered a long knife toward my heart.

I trembled. My mind raced. I was a dead man.

"*Yiiiiii!*" I shrieked in pain as the huge, razor-sharp knife plunged through my breastbone. Then I blacked out.

I woke up slowly. Once again I wondered if I was dead. I opened my eyes and saw only darkness. *Were the aliens nearby?* Lifting my head uncertainly, I realized that I was lying facedown on the side of a road. *A road!* I thought, breathing hard.

I rolled onto my back. A stabbing pain on the left side of my chest made me gasp for air. My eyes stung as I was bathed in a bright white light.

No! Not again!

But the light vanished, leaving only the faint outline of a silver disc, growing smaller and smaller until it disappeared in the star-filled sky.

I struggled to my feet. My legs felt weak and rubbery, my head throbbed, and I ached all over. I touched the place where the knife had pierced me, but there was no wound, only a terrible pain. Unsteady and dazed, I fumbled for my cell phone, turned it on, and called my best friend on the work crew, Harris.

At first Harris thought I was a prankster, someone who had heard about the abduction and was calling as a joke. But within a few minutes I was able to convince him it was really me. Half an hour later, he arrived in his pickup truck and helped me climb slowly into the passenger seat. He stared at me in disbelief.

"You look awful, buddy. What happened to you? One second you were there and the next you were gone. We've been trying to convince everyone it was a UFO, but they say you must have just run off, you were so spooked," Harris explained urgently. "We didn't know if you were gone forever."

"It was horrible," I said weakly. "They . . . they . . ." I

shook my head and closed my eyes. It was too soon to talk about it; I only remembered the pain. Everything was so vague—too terrifying—to remember now.

"Well, you're back, and that's the important thing," Harris said.

"How many hours was I gone?" I asked.

My friend turned to me in wide-eyed disbelief. "Randy," he said. "You've been missing for *five days!*"

ARKANSAS
Living Shadows

What I learned in history class: The forty-second president of the United States, William Jefferson Clinton, was born in Hope, Arkansas, on August 19, 1946. In 1978, at the age of thirty-two, he became the youngest governor in the history of Arkansas and the nation.

A story you won't find in your textbook: It's amazing how many other kids across the country are into the paranormal. Once I started writing my blog, I began hearing from kids who seemed to be just as into all this stuff as me (well, almost as much). I traded stories with these other paranormal junkies, and one of the first friends I made was

FreakBoy479 from Helena, Arkansas. Here's an e-mail he sent me:

From: FreakBoy479@anet.net
To: Jspecter@scarystatesofamerica.com
Subject: shadow people!

Hey, j.

Dude, u gotta check out the shadow people. Have u ever seen one? Like, u catch something moving out of the corner of your eye, then u look at the spot where u thought u saw it, only to see there's nothing there? Or u see a dark shape moving across the wall and u wonder who in your family is making the shadow. And then u remember that u r home alone? Anyway, I helped my friend Tyler write down this experience he had so we could send it to you. Don't worry, I made him promise he wasn't making any of it up, so it's legit for your site.

Peace out,
FB479

◉◉

My friend Aaron (who I guess you know as FreakBoy?) made me swear on my mother's life that this story is true and promised to beat me up if it turns out to be a hoax, so you can trust me.

I was babysitting my three-year-old brother, Wesley, not too long ago. My folks were out for the evening. I was hanging out in my room, listening to my iPod, when I started to feel like someone was watching me. It was so weird. I didn't see anything, I just had this totally creeped-out feeling.

I popped my earphones out and slid down to the foot of the bed. I turned my head slowly, looking back over my shoulder. I could swear I saw something move in the corner. I blinked hard a couple of times and rubbed my eyes. When I opened them again, whatever I thought I had seen was gone.

That was really weird, I thought. But as I went to slip my earphones back in, I heard a noise out in the hall. It sounded like something was banging on the walls.

"What the heck!" I said out loud. "If that's Wesley causing trouble . . ."

I slid off my bed, stood up, and pressed my back against the wall of my room, inching slowly toward the door. I knew I'd feel silly if it was my brother banging around in the hall, but I still had that creepy feeling. I took two deep breaths, then swung out into the hallway.

Boy, did I feel dumb. There was no one there. *Nice going, Tyler,* I thought. *You can't even be home without Mom and Dad for a couple of hours without freaking out.*

I shook my head and went back into my room. That's when I saw it again, this time out of the corner of my eye. A short, dark figure crouched beside my bed.

I backed away, staring at the shadow. "Who are you?" I cried. I couldn't be sure it even had the shape of a person.

For a second it looked like an ordinary shadow. But in the next second it morphed into a swirling mist.

Again I backed toward the door, keeping my eyes locked on the thing near my bed. Then it moved, coming toward me slowly, flowing like smoke. I turned and bolted from my room, but the thing—whatever it was—flashed by above my head and streaked across the ceiling. I stopped short as I entered the hall in time to see it fly down the stairs.

I peered over the hallway railing but saw nothing. I waited for what felt like hours before I moved; then I paced the hallway, afraid to go back into my room and afraid to go downstairs. *What was that thing? Could I have imagined it all?* I glanced at the closed door of my brother's room. At least whatever it was hadn't gone in there.

Grabbing a baseball bat from my room, I slowly made my way downstairs, my eyes wide open. At the bottom of the stairs, I held my breath and stepped into the living room with the bat raised, ready to strike. Nothing. *Maybe it left the house?*

Squee! Squee! Squee!

I jumped into the air at the sound of my parakeet, Groucho, squawking like a maniac from his cage in the family room. *Could the thing be in there?* I slowly walked toward the entrance to the room. It was dark, and I sure wasn't going in there blind. Reaching my hand into the room, I switched on the light.

Groucho was quiet now. I scanned the room, looking

for any sign of the intruder, but it was empty. I was about to head upstairs when our cat, Lincoln, dashed into the den and began hissing. His fur stood on end, and his tail puffed up like he was ready for a fight. But still I saw nothing.

"What is it, Lincoln, buddy?" I said, kneeling down to pet him. "What do you see?"

He hissed at me and ran from the room.

Then I caught a glimpse of a speeding black shape ducking out of the den. I hurried to the door, stepped out of the den, and found myself staring at the shadowy figure, which hovered just inches from my face.

I froze, the bat hanging limply at my side. I had the strange sensation of making eye contact with the thing, even though it had no eyes or any kind of discernible face. As I stood there, it seemed to be sizing me up, plotting its next move.

We stayed frozen in place, the floating black shape and me, for about twenty seconds. Then the thing seemed to panic. It dashed along the wall and climbed up toward the ceiling. Then it floated back up the stairs.

It's after Wesley!

I rushed after the thing, no longer worried about my own safety; I could only think of what it might do to my little brother. At the top of the stairs, the shadow figure turned back toward me. It seemed to grow bold then, and it locked me in its blank, eyeless gaze. Once again I was frozen where I stood.

As the creature stared at me, I felt a growing sense of menace, as if the shadow being now meant to do me harm.

This was no mere curiosity. It was the longest thirty seconds of my life.

The shadow thing started toward me. Panic flooded my guts. I began sweating, trying to get my feet to move, but they wouldn't obey. It was going to get me, and after that, it would go for Wesley. If only I could lift the bat . . . but I wasn't sure hitting this thing would do any good.

That's when Lincoln tore up the stairs and ran right past me, hissing and spitting.

At the sight of the cat, the shadow creature released me from its stare and sprinted along the wall toward the window at the far end of the hallway. It paused at the window, turned, and looked back at me. Then it vanished.

Was it gone? Would it come back?

"Tyler?" a little voice said behind me.

Oh, no. How much had Wesley seen?

"I need a glass of water, Tyler," Wesley said, rubbing his eyes with one hand and clutching his stuffed bunny in the other.

"Water," I said, breaking into a smile. "You got it, Wes. You go back to bed. I'll bring it right in."

A little while later my folks came home.

"Everything okay, Ty?" Mom asked.

"Sure!" I said, a bit too enthusiastically. "Why wouldn't it be?" She kissed me and headed upstairs to check on Wesley.

"Ty!" she called a few minutes later.

Uh-oh! Maybe Wes did see something!

"Come up here and look at this," Mom said.

I hurried up the stairs and found her standing at the window at the end of the hallway.

"How did this happen?" she asked. "It was clean this morning."

My eyes opened wide at the sight of two small handprints on the hallway window.

CALIFORNIA
The Ghost in Aisle 15C

What I learned in history class: California boasts both the highest and lowest points in the continental United States. Mount Whitney is 14,495 feet above sea level, and Bad Water in Death Valley is 282 feet below sea level. The two places are within 150 miles of each other.

A story you won't find in your textbook: Amanda Walker's not a fellow paranormal nerd like me and my blogging buddies. She's just a regular girl who ended up with a totally sucky summer job in Sunnyvale, California. If you take a job in a toy store, you might expect to deal with bratty kids or stressed-out parents—but an ax-wielding freak in one of the aisles? She deserves a lot more than minimum wage!

Here's what she e-mailed me.

◉◉

My name is Amanda Walker. A friend told me about your site. You have a ton of haunting stories on there but nothing like mine. I still have nightmares about what happened to me the summer after my sophomore year in high school.

I took a job at a large toy store in Sunnyvale. I'm not even sure where you're from, Jason, but Sunnyvale probably wouldn't fit your image of California. There aren't any palm trees, or beaches, or celebrities driving around in convertibles. It's pretty much just a regular boring suburb. Anyway, the store was pretty close to my house, and since I'm a vegetarian, it beat working at McDonald's, my other great summer-job offer.

The creepy stuff started on my first day. The other kids working at the store told me that all new employees started over in aisle 15C, as a kind of initiation. I just shrugged. "Whatever. Doesn't matter to me." Hey, I was only going to be there for two months. I could deal with some lame pranks.

So I got to work, stacking boxes and boxes of dolls on the shelves. Bo-ring! About ten minutes into it, though, I felt someone tap me on the shoulder. I figured it was just someone who was going to give me something else to do, or maybe even ask me if I wanted to join them for lunch, since it was my first day and I didn't know anybody. I turned around, but no one was there. I went back to my work, and then it happened again. I was positive I felt a finger tap my shoulder, but again, nobody was anywhere near me.

All right, who's the comedian? I thought. *Is this your version of "initiate the rookie"?*

I'd gone back to stacking boxes when suddenly a blast of cold, rank-smelling air hit me right in the face.

Whoa! I thought, coughing and waving my hand in front of my face. *Did something crawl into the air-conditioning ducts and die?*

I took a step back, and the temperature rose instantly. The smell of new plastic replaced the stench of rotten flesh. I was now officially freaked out! Not wanting anyone to think I was crazy, though, and mostly not wanting to get fired on my first day, I just went back to work.

I pulled over a ladder and climbed to the highest rung so I could stack dolls on the top shelf. As I reached up to put a doll in place, I felt fingers running through my hair. My hair's pretty long and I'm kinda proud of it, so it really freaked me out to think that some stranger was touching it. Then I remembered that I was on the top rung of a ladder.

I shrieked, and lost my grip on both the ladder and the doll I was holding. The doll fell to the floor, and I was sure I was about to follow.

Reaching out at the last second, my fingers gripped one side of the ladder just as my feet slipped from the rung. Struggling with all my strength, I grasped the other side of the ladder and regained my foothold. As I caught my breath, the adrenaline still coursing through my veins, I looked down at the doll that had fallen.

The doll's unblinking eyes stared up at me, its tiny plastic lips curled into a frown, and a small tear escaped from its left eye. "Help me," it cried. "Help me find Elizabeth!"

The first thing I have to do is get off this ladder, I thought, fighting to hold back the wave of terror sweeping through my body.

"Help me!" the doll cried again.

Stay focused, Amanda, I told myself, concentrating intensely to find a foothold on the next rung down. I lowered myself rung by rung at what felt like a snail's pace. *One foot after the other. That's it, girl. Gotta get to the floor.*

And then I was down.

Stepping around the doll, I hauled butt to the ladies' room.

Gotta calm down! I thought, leaning over the sink and shaking with fear. Turning on the faucet, I splashed water on my face, again and again. *Okay, that's better.*

I turned off the faucet and grabbed a paper towel. *There's got to be a perfectly logical explanation for all this,* I thought as I patted my face dry. What that explanation might be escaped me at that moment.

Taking two deep yet shaky breaths, I headed for the door. Suddenly, the faucet came on again full blast, splashing water over the edge of the sink.

"I turned the water off!" I screamed, as if the sink itself could offer some answer.

I stepped back toward the sink and turned off the faucet. When I reached the door, I heard the water come on again. I didn't even turn around. I just ran from the bathroom.

Either someone at the store was pulling pranks on me, or I was losing my mind. I kept one eye over my shoulder for the rest of the day, but nothing else happened. I finished my work and went home.

The next morning, I arrived at work and looked into the eyes of my fellow employees. People nodded politely but no one gave any hint that they were aware of the creepy stuff that had gone on the day before. If someone had been playing tricks on me, they were doing a really good job of keeping a poker face. I had almost convinced myself that I had dreamed it all, when I turned into aisle 15C.

"Who did this?" I screamed, upset beyond belief. The dolls I had so carefully stacked the day before were scattered all over the floor, as if some jerk had spent the night yanking each one from its place on the shelf.

This little game has gone too far! I thought. I hurried down the aisle toward the employee lounge in search of my obviously demented coworkers. I no longer cared if they thought I was crazy or even if I got fired.

I swung around the end-cap display of toy trucks and turned into aisle 14. There, spread out across the floor, were fifty skateboards arranged into letters that spelled out a single word—*Elizabeth.*

I turned and ran, a cold sweat pouring down my face. As I passed the toy trucks again, they came flying off the shelves, one after the other. I ducked, covering my head with my arms. The trucks slammed into me, almost breaking my wrist and elbow.

I ran, faster now, scooting past a group of large, colorful rubber balls that were all bouncing up and down by themselves. The employee lounge was just ahead. But as I reached the door, a glint of metal caught my eye.

I stopped dead in my tracks, my eyes locked on an image that made my heart freeze. The picture haunts my nightmares to this day. Not more than a few feet away from me stood a man wearing overalls and a red flannel shirt. A bushy brown beard covered his dirty face. In his left hand he gripped an ax. Its blade dripped with fresh blood. Where his right foot should have been, there was a jagged stump, bleeding all over the linoleum floor.

"Elizabeth," the man whispered, reaching his right hand out toward me and staring me in the eye. "Help me find Elizabeth!"

Stifling a scream, I yanked open the lounge door, ducked inside, and slammed the door, imagining the cold blade of the ax slicing through the door behind me. Once inside, I found a group of my coworkers staring at me.

"You lasted longer than most, Amanda," said Todd, who had worked at the store for about five years. "I was surprised you even showed up today. But it should get better. They usually only bother the new people."

Still wide-eyed with fright, I managed to stammer, "T-T-Todd, what's going on here? There's a man with an ax covered in blood right outside the door!"

Then Todd told me the story. One hundred and fifty years ago, the land on which the store was built was a working ranch. A man named Johnny Johnson, a traveling preacher, moved out to California to work as a hired hand on the ranch. He fell in love with a young woman in the area named Elizabeth Yuba Murphy Tafee, only to discover that she was engaged to an East Coast lawyer. Elizabeth soon left the ranch, leaving Johnson with a broken heart. A short time after that, he accidentally cut off his right foot while chopping wood and bled to death.

His spirit has haunted this land ever since. In the 1970s, a famous psychic named Bertha Silver held a séance at the store and made contact with the spirit of Johnson, who still pines for his beloved Elizabeth.

It turned out that everyone who ever worked at the store knew about this. Some stayed, and some left. Maybe it did get better after you worked there for a while, but I wasn't going to stick around to find out. When Todd finished his story, I rushed out of the store as quickly as I could, not daring to look and see whether Johnson was still there. The rational part of my brain told me that I didn't believe in ghosts, but the events of the past two days felt all too real.

No job was worth putting up with that. I decided right then and there that even though I was a vegetarian, next summer I would take a job at McDonald's. At least the only thing there that scared me was the food!

COLORADO
"Here I am! Please find me!"

What I learned in history class: The International Olympic Committee awarded the 1976 Winter Games to Denver, Colorado, but the people of Colorado voted to ban the use of public funds to finance the games. The Winter Games were held in Innsbruck, Austria, instead.

A story you won't find in your textbook: Psychics love my site. I think some of them use it to drum up business, contacting people they think could use their help. I don't mind, really. Sure, there are a lot of fakes out there, but there are also a lot of people who have a gift and want to use it for good.

I'd been IM'ing back and forth with a psychic named Gina McArthur, of Durango, Colorado, who is so well known and accepted in her community that the police often use her to help them with "impossible to solve" crimes. I asked her to e-mail me the case she was proudest to have solved.

Here is her story.

◉◉

I work closely with the police, so I can't say I solved this all by myself. Plus, I like to think that the victim is the one who gives us the help—I'm just the vehicle to communicate messages from the other side.

Twenty-seven-year-old Marilyn Tilbett had lived in Durango her entire life. She had worked for a local insurance company and had lived in a modest apartment. Then, one day five years ago, Marilyn vanished without a trace. After days of searching, the police still had no clues as to her whereabouts. They did, however, have a suspect.

Marilyn's former boyfriend, Stewart Traynor, had a criminal record, including several convictions for assault. In the months leading up to her disappearance, Marilyn had made several calls to the police emergency line to report incidents of domestic violence. Marilyn's friends described Traynor as an abusive individual who was prone to outbursts of rage.

Finally, two weeks before her disappearance, Marilyn had broken up with Traynor and gotten a restraining order preventing him from coming within a hundred yards of her.

Traynor's friends told the police that he was enraged by the order and had threatened to make Marilyn pay for it.

Several eyewitnesses also said that on the day Marilyn disappeared, they had seen Traynor leaving the apartment building where she lived. The police arrested Traynor, but they feared that without Marilyn's body, they wouldn't have enough evidence to prove he was guilty.

And so, as a last resort, the Durango police chief contacted me. I'm always the police's last resort, but I don't mind. They would be out of a job if they came to me first with every case!

I asked them to take me to Marilyn Tilbett's apartment so that I could try to receive psychic signals from the woman by surrounding myself with her possessions. Now, not all police officers are on the psychic bandwagon, and I always hear a lot of sarcastic comments about my abilities. Durango detective Harvey Otis was definitely a nonbeliever.

"I think this is all a load of bull, ma'am, but I've got my orders," Detective Otis said as he held the apartment door open for me.

"I understand, Detective." It's best not to argue with a nonbeliever. They change their tune pretty quickly once "impossible cases" are solved.

The apartment was dark and musty, with a depressive air that overwhelmed me. As I walked from room to room, opening drawers and closets and holding Marilyn's clothing, jewelry, books, and trinkets, I had to stop myself from bursting into tears. In all my years of psychic work, I had never felt a victim's pain and hopelessness quite like this.

Marilyn, I said to myself, *I'm here to help you. You're still afraid, and so sad, but that can all go away if you let me help you. Where are you? Help me find you, and you will finally be at peace.*

I turned the corner into the kitchen, and the sadness and fear disappeared. What happened next is difficult for me to describe; psychic visions always are. It was as if I were on an emotional roller coaster. I leaned against the doorframe with my eyes closed, and images flashed before me at fantastic speed. One second I felt panicked, then desperate, and then terrified. And the next moment, *nothing*. It was as if I were dead. I had never experienced that type of feeling, and I hope to God I never feel that way again.

I never know how long these psychic states will last, but when I opened my eyes, I was lying on the floor, surrounded by the police.

"Get an ambulance!" I heard one cop shout to another. "And some water!"

"Gentlemen," I said as calmly as I could. "Please help me to the table and get me some paper and a pen as quickly as possible. I'm perfectly all right. No need to worry."

After calling off the ambulance, the officers sat me down at the kitchen table and I began to transcribe every roller-coaster moment. I scribbled the words *road, water, knee, decapitate,* and *church* as quickly as I could. I noticed one of the policemen look at his fellow officer and make the cuckoo sign near his head.

"Detective Otis," I said when I had finished, "I have some things that might be of use to the case."

The detective took the piece of paper and looked at it for a moment before turning to stare at me.

"These things don't just arrive as easy, prepackaged solutions," I said, getting up from my chair. "They come in bits and pieces. Now, let me tell you what they mean."

I began to recite the following list. When I opened my mouth, I spoke in a voice completely different from my own.

"I will be found near a main road. I will be lying near an embankment, a creek, and a bridge. A church will have something to do with locating me, as will salt. There are leaves all around me. I am missing my leg. My head is no longer attached to my body. A man with a bad knee will find me, and the first initial S will be involved in some way."

Detective Otis wrote down everything I said, but I couldn't help noticing the skeptical look on his face. He thanked me for my time and had an officer drive me home.

The police chief later told me that Detective Otis had returned to the station that night and, using every available officer, focused the search on creeks that intersected main roads.

He told his officers to search bridge embankments, at the points where roads crossed the creeks. He also mentioned the church and the salt, although he wasn't sure what role either would play. He told his officers to look for a body buried under leaves rather than in a grave with freshly dug dirt.

Two days after my vision, one of Durango's officers was exploring Route 160, which intersects Lightner Creek in a few spots. He had already checked out several bridge embankments along the route, with no success.

At one spot along the route, where a bridge crossed over Lightner Creek, the officer had begun exploring the leaf-covered embankments when he happened to glance across the creek. There, in full view, was a salt storage facility, where the highway department stored its salt for use on the roads in winter.

Recalling that I, or should I say Marilyn, had said that salt would have something to do with the location of her body, the officer pulled out his checklist. His heart skipped a beat as he reread the list, which included the mention of a church as well. He had thought nothing of it at the time, but about a half mile up the road he had passed a kids' camp that was run by a local church.

Continuing down the list, he had nearly fainted when he read the last two items. The officer's name was Stephen Sacks, and he had injured his knee playing basketball the previous weekend. Officer Sacks quickly radioed the others on the search and asked for help exploring the area. Within minutes, twenty officers arrived and a detailed search of the embankment began.

As it turned out, Officer Sacks himself found the body, covered with leaves and lying in a shallow grave. Marilyn's left leg was missing, and her head was discovered some fifteen yards away from the body.

Traces of Stewart Traynor's DNA on the body later confirmed his guilt, and he was eventually convicted of the murder.

Marilyn really wanted to be found. She wanted justice, and she wanted to be released from the pain and terror she continued to feel in the spirit world. The incredibly strong psychic signals she had sent were her way of saying, "Here I am! Please find me!"

Marilyn's spirit could not rest until her body was found, so that her killer could be brought to justice.

CONNECTICUT

Dudleytown:
The Scariest Place in New England

What I learned in history class: The author of the first American dictionary, Noah Webster, was born in West Hartford, Connecticut. *An American Dictionary of the English Language* was published in 1828. Webster learned more than twenty-five languages to research this history of America's English dialect.

A story you won't find in your textbook:
From: DStark@ctnn.com
To: Jspecter@scarystatesofamerica.com
Subject: Dudleytown, CT

Jason,

My name is Doug Stark. I read on your Web site about haunted buildings, curses on families, and attacks by strange creatures. Well, there's an evil forest in northwestern Connecticut that combines all those things. My buddy Andy Barlin and I knew about the 400-year-old family curse, the weird lightning strikes, the sightings of dark spirits, the glowing lights, the scary creatures, the bizarre phenomena of nature, madness, death, and insanity, and the lives destroyed by the Dudleytown forest. We just never thought any of that would happen to us.

◉◉

Andy and I grew up in Ellsworth, Connecticut, the best of buds. Every Halloween we talked about spending the night in the creepy Dudleytown forest. When you grow up in Connecticut, you get used to playing in the woods, but everyone talked about how there was something sinister about the trees in Dudleytown, and how the place was always dark.

Of course, no one ever actually spent Halloween there. Even after Andy and I were in high school and could drive, fear always won out over our curiosity. Well, fear and girls. You ever notice how girls like to wear skimpy outfits on Halloween, even when it's really cold out?

So our senior year finally came. We were each going to different colleges and this would be our last Halloween together for a while.

"It's now or never, dude," I said to Andy two weeks before Halloween. "Are we really going to do this, or are we going to spend the rest of our lives e-mailing each other about how we really should have done it when we had the chance?"

Andy rubbed his chin for a moment, weighing the choice between really cool bragging rights and hanging out with our friends.

"Yeah," he replied, shrugging. "This *is* our last shot. Let's go for it!"

Bragging rights won.

Andy and I took his car on Halloween night and headed toward Dudleytown. I think back on that moment every day. My life would be completely different now if we had just gone to a party that night or maybe TP'd someone's house instead.

The sun was starting to set as we drove the half hour to Dark Entry Road.

"Dark Entry Road! Man, if this were a movie, people would be laughing. Could it be any more obvious?" Andy said, laughing.

"It is cursed, you know. It's the only forest I've ever heard about that's actually evil," I said.

"Yeah, I know. All that stuff that happened in England. Henry the Eighth was pissed Edmund Dudley tried to overthrow him, so he chopped off his head and cursed the whole Dudley clan. Horror! Death! Insanity! Hemorrhoids!" Andy joked. "One of the Dudley kids thought he could escape the curse by coming here in the 1700s, but he just brought the curse with him."

"Remember the dude who bought the place after the

Dudleys bolted? His whole family got some weird sickness and croaked. Then there was the general in the Revolutionary War whose wife got struck by lightning . . . even though it was a clear sky! That dude went mental," I said, trying to remember even more crazy stories I'd heard over the years.

"Uh-oh!" Andy cried. "We're leaving out Dr. Clark's nutcase wife! Remember, he bought the place in the 1920s? He had to go to New York City for two days and when he got back, his wife was flipping out about a dark creature who ran out of the forest and attacked her. She went mental too, and they put her in the nuthouse!"

"Duh, lady, don't you know Bigfoot when you see him?" I said.

Even though we continued to laugh at all the horror stories we knew, I was starting to get a little scared. I couldn't admit it to Andy, but by the time we reached Dark Entry Road—which, despite its name, is actually an idyllic-looking lane that leads into Dudleytown forest—I was thinking about bagging the whole idea and turning back. Unfortunately for us, Andy parked the car and started to get out.

"Doug, come on. Let's go," he said.

"We could just go back and hang out with Mike and Jordan instead. Tell them we got lost on the way," I suggested.

"*What?* Dude, one, we drove all the way here and, two, we would get so much grief from them about being complete

chickens. I'm gonna see me some *demons tonight, baby!*"
he yelled.

There was no use arguing with him. His reputation was
at stake. We had to go through with it.

We left the car at the start of the road, since we'd told
everyone we'd go into the forest on foot with nothing to
protect us except our own wits. The sun was dropping low
in the sky and it was starting to get dark.

Almost immediately I noticed the total lack of sound.
Whereas a second earlier I could hear the wind in the trees,
the chirping of birds, and the scurrying of squirrels and
chipmunks among the fallen leaves, now . . . nothing. Not
a peep.

"Did it suddenly get colder?" Andy asked, turning up
his collar and zipping up his jacket.

"Now that you mention it," I replied, "the temperature
did seem to drop when we stepped in here. And is it just
me, or is there no sound whatsoever? Where's the wind?
Why don't I hear animals?"

"They're probably all *possessed! Muhahahahaha!*" Andy
shouted, doing the world's worst Count Dracula impression.

We continued on in silence.

About half a mile in, we heard a weird scratching noise
behind us. We looked around but couldn't see anything.

"What's that?" Andy whispered tensely, pointing to the
ground behind him.

There, carved into the soft dirt, were the words *Never
return!—Satan*

"Shut up. You just did that. I'm not a moron," I said, punching Andy in the arm. "The Satan part is a little over-the-top, man."

"Doug," Andy said seriously. "You and I both heard that noise, and I've been standing right next to you the whole time. I didn't do that, dude."

"Fine," I said. "Someone put that there to freak out people like us who were coming here to check it out."

"I don't know," said Andy. "It looks like it was only scratched into the ground a minute ago. Look at the mounds of dirt around each letter. If this had been here for a while, they would have blown away in the wind."

"Come on," I said, surprised to find myself being the brave one. "There are supposed to be some ruins of old Dudleytown houses at the end of this road. Maybe we can spend the night there."

As we left Dark Entry Road and entered the dense forest, the final crimson rays of sunlight faded to gray behind the stone foundation of an eighteenth-century house.

"There's nothing left of this place but some stones," Andy said, peering over the edge of the foundation.

Suddenly, a white circle of light moved across the trees.

"Don't turn the flashlight on yet," I said. "Let's wait until it's really dark."

"Uh, Doug, I—I didn't turn on my flashlight," Andy stammered. "That wasn't you?"

I felt the hair on the back of my neck stand up.

"No," I whispered.

"Then what's that?" Andy said, pointing at three glowing white orbs dancing among the trees.

Not waiting for my reply, Andy took off, running deeper into the woods.

"Wait for me, dude!" I shouted, following my friend. We had Satan telling us never to return, and now weird orbs were flying around. It was not the time for the two of us to separate.

Andy stopped running and I practically crashed into him.

"It's really dark," he said, trying to catch his breath. "I'm going to put my flashlight on so we can find our way back."

"What about those white floating things?" I asked nervously.

"I don't see them anymore," Andy replied, clicking on his light. "But I think we should head back."

"Yeah," I agreed. "We're totally telling Mike and Jordan we got lost. I don't care how much grief I get. Now let's get the heck out of here."

Andy's eyes suddenly opened wide. Looking down, he began grabbing at his shirt and pants. "Doug, get them off me!" he shouted. "Get them off!"

I shined my light on Andy's body but I saw nothing.

"Get *what* off you?" I asked, alarmed by the terror in my friend's eyes. "There's nothing on you, Andy!"

"The bugs!" Andy screamed, clawing at his clothes, his face contorted into a mask of horror. "They're crawling all over me. Get them off me! *They're eating me alive! Doug, help!*"

"They're not real, Andy!" I screamed, recalling stories I had heard about people in Dudleytown who had suffered from hallucinations. "It's just in your mind. Dude, you have to focus on me. Andy, focus!"

Andy dropped to his knees and began yanking at his hair. He actually tore a bloody clump of hair from his head. "Get them off!"

I grabbed him by his shoulders, forced him to his feet, and shook him hard. "Andy!" I shouted, slapping him right in the face. "Andy!"

Andy jerked backward. Breathing hard, he looked down the length of his body. "Oh my God, Doug," he cried. "It was so real. I saw big, disgusting bugs crawling over every inch of my body. I felt them! I felt them bite me!"

He clawed at his clothes, looking for bite marks and for the creatures that had just tormented him.

"Come on," I said, grabbing Andy's arm and handing him a bandanna to hold against his bleeding head. "We're leaving before anything else happens."

With each step, the gnawing sense of doom inside me grew. Someone . . . no, *something* was watching us. Waiting. Small shapes darted through the darkness on either side of us. The perfect silence was broken by high-pitched shrieks echoing in the trees. I felt my chest tightening as we retraced our path. Andy clutched his head and breathed hard. I wanted to assure him that we'd be okay. Dark Entry Road was just ahead, I noticed as we approached the foundation. I was about to say, "We're going to get home safe," but before I could speak, a flash of movement caught my eye.

We both froze in terror at the sight of a swirling black blob rising from the foundation. The expanding blob changed shape, its inky blackness so thick that it stood out against the night sky.

"I can't move," Andy groaned through his clenched jaw. "I'm trying to force one leg to go in front of the other, but I just can't move."

Before I could respond, the shape enveloped me.

I gasped for breath. The very life was being sucked from my body. I felt like I was about to pass out; then images began to fill my mind. Mutilated, maggot-filled corpses lay strewn around me. I knew I would soon be one of them.

Then I blacked out.

Soft rays of sunshine woke me. Andy was sprawled out on the forest floor next to me. The corpses were gone.

"Andy? Wake up." I shook him gently.

He opened his eyes with a start and jumped to his feet. Without saying a word to me, he headed toward Dark Entry Road.

"Wait up!" I shouted.

Andy turned and peered at me with a look of fear on his face.

"Never return," he croaked.

Those were the last words my best friend ever spoke to me.

We made it back home that morning. We had spent the night in Dudleytown and survived.

But from that day on, Andy never spoke another word to anyone. The doctors at the institution have tried shock treatment to see if he'll at least cry out in pain, but he's like a walking dead man.

As for me, pre-Dudleytown I had always been a pretty happy kid. Post-Dudleytown's another story. The voices and visions start each day around sunset and torture me throughout the night. Yeah, I'm not in a mental hospital like Andy, but I don't exactly get out much.

Why didn't we just stay away?

DELAWARE
A Very-Long-Distance Call

What I learned in history class: Delaware's nickname is the
First State, because it was the first state to ratify the United
States Constitution. It did so on December 7, 1787.

A story you won't find in your textbook: SpookseekerDE is a
fellow paranormal blogger, but while I've gone national, he
only collects stories that happen in his own state. For a
small state, Delaware sure seems to host a lot of strange occurrences. SpookseekerDE's specialty is visits from the
dead. While most of the stories he has collected manage to
scare the heck out of me, my favorite is the one his neighbor Rick Ulman posted on the site. It still chokes me up
when I hear Rick's story. I hope you don't mind that I

borrowed it for this book, SpookseekerDE! If I hear from any freaked-out Delawarians with a tale to tell, I'll be sure to refer them to you.

◉◉

My mom and dad both worked full-time, so my maternal grandma practically raised me. Almost every fond memory I have from my childhood involves her and her big rambling Victorian house. I remember staying home sick from school and Grandma making me chicken soup, which I'd eat in her big sleigh bed. Or all the times we sat on her wraparound front porch as she shucked corn, shelled peas, or peeled an apple for us to share. She told me stories about growing up in Wilmington, and tales of all the people who had lived in her hundred-year-old house.

When I was a teenager, I was still close to her. Sure, I went to football games, dated, and went to parties, but I always made time for Grandma. Her health had begun to go downhill once I turned sixteen, and by the time I graduated from high school, she was completely deaf. But she never stopped living on her own in the house she treasured.

Soon after I turned eighteen, my dad got offered a job in Ohio. My mom didn't want to move until she knew Grandma would be safe, so they looked into putting her in a nursing home. Well, that idea didn't go over well with me or my grandma.

"I'm deaf, not dead!" she shouted at my mom after Mom proposed the idea on paper for Grandma to read.

"I'll move in with Grandma and take care of her," I promised. "She'll stay in her house as long as she's alive."

So my parents moved away, and I moved in with Grandma. We made a great team. She still had the energy to cook and clean, and I took care of all the outdoor chores and heavy lifting. Back then I was an aspiring musician and spent lots of time in different friends' basements— jamming, practicing, and working hard to put together a band.

I worried about Grandma when I was away but we devised a good system for her to get in touch with me if she ever needed to. This was 1990 and no one had even heard of cell phones back then, so Grandma kept a list of phone numbers of my best friends' homes. If she needed my help, she would dial the first number on the list, wait a minute for the person to pick up, and then say, "If Rick is there, please tell him to come home now." She would repeat this phrase a few times before hanging up. Then she'd call the next number on the list, until she had dialed all the places where I was most likely to be.

Even though Grandma was deaf, this system worked. My friends knew about it, so if she happened to call one of them and I wasn't there, they would do their best to track me down. I'd get the message and hurry home to help her. She only did this when she really needed my help, like the time she twisted her ankle and could barely walk. I never minded the interruptions. I would do anything for Grandma.

The year I turned twenty-one, Grandma died in her sleep at the age of eighty-nine. I missed her so much, and for months not a day went by that I didn't cry. She left her house to me and I continued to live there, but, man, it was really hard coming home and not hearing her singing in the kitchen or seeing her knitting by the fireplace.

Luckily, my band, The Witch's Dorothy, began to take off and we started touring regularly, which helped to ease the loss. Soon we signed a record contract and were in the studio recording our first CD. I truly wished that my grandmother could have lived long enough to share in my success. She would have been so proud. As silly as it might sound, when I went home at night after the recording sessions, I sat by the fire and talked to her. I told her about my day, the CD, and how much I missed her. I somehow got the feeling that she was there, listening and looking out for me, just like she did when she was alive.

Late one night I was at home listening to a copy of a song I wrote for that first CD.

"Something's not right," I said aloud. "I need to get back in the studio and give this some finishing touches."

I hadn't scheduled any studio time, but I took a chance and called the engineer to see if the studio was free and if I could come by to work. He said yes, so I called the band and told them to meet me there in half an hour.

Later at the studio we were all concentrating so hard on the song that we almost didn't hear the recording booth phone ring. I hadn't given the private studio number to anyone, and the guys in my band were all already there, so I didn't pay any attention.

"What?" I heard the engineer say. "Lady, you'll have to

speak up." I saw him shake his head and hang up the phone. "Crazy old bat," he murmured.

"I think that bass line is too loud," the drummer, Mike, said. "If we give it another listen, you'll see that—"

The phone started ringing again.

"Hello?" the engineer answered loudly, obviously annoyed. "Say that again. Who are you looking for? You want Rick?"

What? I thought. *But no one knows I'm here.*

"Rick, there's an old woman on the phone," the engineer said. "She sounds like she's talking into a tin can so I can barely hear her, but I think she said she wants you to come home."

The guys gave me a surprised look.

"Is someone messing with you, dude?" Mike said.

I grabbed the phone angrily, ready to chew out anyone who would pull such a sick and messed-up prank on me. I began to yell into the phone, but I quickly lost my breath as I heard the voice on the other end of the line.

"If Rick is there, please tell him to come home now."

"Grandma?" I gasped. "Grandma, can you hear me? Grandma, is that *you?*"

But there was no response.

I hung up the phone and grabbed the edge of the engineering console to steady myself. It was Grandma. Somehow, impossibly, it was her, calling from beyond the grave. There was no mistaking that voice, which I knew so well and missed so terribly.

"Listen," I said in a trembling voice. "I'll—I'll be right back. I've got to go home."

"Rick, your grandmother died, didn't she?" our lead singer, Vinnie, asked quietly.

"I have to go home. I'm sorry!"

As I sped home, my brain tried to come up with some logical explanation for the phone call, but I could find none. That was my grandma on the phone. This was real, and something told me I'd better get home as soon as possible.

As I rounded the corner onto my street, I half expected to see her there on the porch. Screeching to a stop in the driveway, I flew from my car and dashed up the front stairs. As I stepped inside, I called out, "Grandma?"

But there was no answer.

I went from room to room searching for some sign, something that would explain the call.

I collapsed into the armchair next to the fireplace where Grandma had always done her knitting and ran my hand through my hair. I reached over for a long fireplace match and was about to strike it when I smelled something weird.

Could that be . . . gas? I wondered.

Panicked, I jumped from my seat, ran to the cellar door, threw it open, and gagged at the overwhelming smell of gas wafting up from below. I bolted down the stairs and discovered a major gas leak in the basement pipes.

Later that night as the gas company's emergency crew was leaving, the guy in charge turned to me at the front door and said, "You sure are lucky, son. A few minutes more and the flame from your hot-water heater would have set off an explosion. It would have taken the whole house down."

"Yeah," I said. "I am lucky."

I looked up at a portrait of my grandma as a young woman that hung in the foyer.

"Thanks, Grandma," I whispered as I closed the front door.

And the portrait seemed to smile back at me.

FLORIDA
Skunk Ape Encounter

What I learned in history class: In 1513, Spanish explorer Juan Ponce de León led the first known European expedition to reach Florida. Some believe he named the land Pascua de Florida (Feast of Flowers) because he first spotted the land during the Easter season.

A story you won't find in your textbook: Fifteen-year-old Cheryl Groves never thought she'd have to deal with anything scarier than a killer wave threatening to wipe her out on her surfboard. Then she came face to face with a genuine Florida Skunk Ape near her town of Coral Gables. This legendary creature stood eight feet tall and looked like a humanoid primate, with shaggy brown fur, a bright blue face, and piercing yellow eyes punctuated by jet black pupils. Just one whiff of its stench could knock you over. Here's the story Cheryl e-mailed me.

◉◉

Okay, first off, why couldn't my parents take me on a normal vacation, like on a tour of the best surfing spots in Hawaii or something? No, we had to stay in Florida. And not only that, we weren't even going to be near the ocean!

I know I live near the ocean, but still. A camping trip to the Ocala National Forest? Bo-ring!

"Where you headed?" Mr. Jeffries, our nosy next-door neighbor, asked as I started carrying stuff out to the van.

"Camping in the Ocala National Forest."

"Watch out for the Skunk Ape," Mr. Jeffries said, picking his teeth with a toothpick and spitting out of the side of his mouth.

Lovely.

"The what?" I asked.

"Never heard of the Skunk Ape?" he said, shifting his toothpick to the other side. "It's an old Florida legend. Big hairy monster with a blue face. Smells like it hasn't washed in years. Stink'll knock you right over."

"Yeah, well, if I see one, I'll be sure to send your regards," I said as I went back to loading the van. What a loon. My parents and I got into the van and we took off for the forest. Whoopee.

We got to the campsite in the late afternoon and set up our tents. At least I had my own tent, separate from my parents. We cooked some dinner, like beans or something gross like that, over an open campfire as the sun went down. The s'mores were good, though. After my fourth s'more, I said good night and slipped into my tent. But how was I going to fall asleep? I mean, I was practically outside, exposed to the elements. How totally uncivilized can you get?

Soon I heard my parents climb into their tent, and a short while later the campsite was silent, except for the crickets—they were *sooo* loud. Like, how is anyone supposed to sleep with that racket?

Then, wouldn't you know it, I had to pee. As quietly as I could, I crawled out from my tent, gripping my flashlight tightly. Switching on the light, I followed its beam along one of the marked hiking trails that led away from the campsite. I wanted to get far enough away not to disturb my folks—I hate when anyone can hear me pee.

The trail grew narrower, and the woods got darker. I figured I'd gone far enough. I finished my business and turned around to return to the campsite. My flashlight beam slid across the tree trunks, then lit up what appeared to be a hairy foot poking out from behind the thick trunk of a tree. Startled, I shrieked and dropped my flashlight, which went dark when it hit the ground.

Oh, God! What was that?

Then the smell hit me. Actually, it assaulted my senses like a sledgehammer. Imagine a mix of rotten cabbage, decaying flesh, and a dead skunk. Only worse. The stench was unreal. It made my eyes water, and I swear I thought I was gonna puke s'mores all over the forest floor. Then I got dizzy from what felt like a lack of oxygen. Dropping to my knees, I was barely able to breathe.

I heard a shuffling sound and could just make out something walking toward me—something very tall. The thing emitted a low growl as it got closer.

I was completely overcome by terror but paralyzed by the horrible smell. The thing was huge and could have reached out with one long arm to grab me if I tried to run away. I was trapped, moments away from a certain, horrible death. Sweat crept down my face as the creature shuffled closer.

"Help!" I tried to scream—like anyone would even be able to hear me. My parents were too far away and I was surrounded by thick woods. The cry came out as a choked whimper.

I covered my head with one arm, trying to protect myself but knowing I was seconds away from blacking out. Then I'd be completely at this thing's mercy. *This is it. I really am gonna die!*

Then my hand brushed against something hard and metallic on the ground—*the flashlight!* I fumbled in the darkness for the switch. *Come on, come on!* Glancing up, I saw the outline of an enormous, hairy creature staring down at me. Its growling grew louder. *Got it!*

Click!

My flashlight beam revealed a sight more hideous than I could ever have imagined. The apelike beast was more than seven feet tall, and its body was covered with thick, shaggy fur. Its face was remarkably human except for the blue tint of its skin, and its enormous hands ended in sharp claws. Gleaming nostrils expelled jets of steam with every foul breath. Ropes of saliva dangled from its jagged yellow teeth.

Another wave of noxious odor slammed into my nostrils, and my eyes stung. Through blurry tears, I saw the shaggy thing moving closer.

Don't just sit here and die! Get up! Do something!

I stood up quickly, and the flashlight beam struck the creature's face, illuminating its wrinkled blue skin. As my beam caught the beast's sickly yellow eyes, the monster let out a shriek.

The light! I thought. *It doesn't like the light!*

I aimed the flashlight directly into its eyes. The creature let out an unearthly howl, then turned and bolted back into the woods. I raced back to the campsite, followed by a cloud of the horrible stench.

I didn't sleep that night—I mean, duh! I stayed up listening for the monster's approach until dawn. I got out of my tent and waited for my folks to get up, vowing at that moment never to go camping again. I didn't know if they'd believe my story, but at least my stench would convince them I wasn't very good company on a camping trip!

GEORGIA
"My house is bleeding!"

What I learned in history class: Franklin D. Roosevelt first went to Warm Springs, Georgia, in 1924, seeking relief from polio. The springs' naturally hot water was thought to be curative. In 1932, during his run for the presidency, FDR built a cottage in Warm Springs that was later dubbed the Little White House. He died there of a cerebral hemorrhage on April 12, 1945.

A story you won't find in your textbook: An hour after I mentioned in my blog that I'd be away for a few days, visiting relatives in Atlanta, I got an e-mail from a couple named Judy and Russell Wilson. They sent me the details about their house, desperately searching for answers. I knew I had to see this house and talk to them. Needless to say, it was a wild experience. Here's the story I wrote when I got back.

◉◉

Russell and Judy Wilson of Atlanta saw an ad in the local paper announcing an auction for houses taken away from owners who hadn't paid their taxes.

The Wilsons went to the auction and found a modest house that normally would have been out of their price range. But at the auction price, they could make it work. They moved in and enjoyed fixing up and decorating this first home of their own. It was dirty and in disrepair, but with some hard work and imagination, the Wilsons transformed it into a nice place.

They celebrated their first Thanksgiving in their new home and were making plans to decorate the house for the upcoming holidays when the bizarre event took place.

On the evening of December fifth, Judy came home from work and went upstairs to take a bath. Russell was in the basement, working on a project in the small woodworking shop he had set up for himself, when he heard a piercing scream coming from upstairs. He dropped his drill and dashed up the two flights of stairs, reaching the master bathroom in a matter of seconds. He heard another shriek as he flung open the door. What greeted his eyes was beyond comprehension.

Red liquid dripped down the tile walls, running in thin scarlet rivulets before pooling on the floor. It was thick and dark—it could only be blood! Indeed, the strong smell of blood filled the room. Judy stood in the tub with a towel wrapped around her and a look of terror in her eyes.

"What happened?" Russell shouted. "Are you hurt?"

"I'm not," Judy cried. "I was just lying in the tub. One stream of red appeared, then another and another, until it was pouring down! Russell, what is going on?"

Blood continued to stream down the walls, splattering as it hit the tile floor. Russell stepped across the growing crimson puddle and helped Judy from the tub. Placing his arm around his wife's shoulders, he led her out of the blood-soaked bathroom, down the hall, and into their bedroom. Judy sat on the edge of their bed wiping the blood from her feet and trying to regain some composure. Then, glancing down, she screamed again.

"Oh my God! What's happening?" she shrieked, pointing at Russell's feet.

Blood spurted up from the floor as if from a sprinkler.

"This is insane!" Russell wailed. "Where is it coming from?"

Judy threw on some clothes and followed Russell downstairs. There they were greeted by a waterfall of blood cascading down the living room wall.

"It's everywhere!" Judy cried. "The whole house!"

A sickening noise drew their attention to the kitchen.

Blurp bloop bloop blurp . . .

The sink bubbled up with blood, which overflowed and splashed onto the linoleum floor.

Overwhelmed with fear and confusion, Russell and Judy ran from the house and called 911 on Judy's cell phone.

"What is your emergency?" the operator asked.

"My house is bleeding!" Russell shouted into the phone.

"I'm sorry," the operator replied. "I'm not sure I heard you correctly. Do you mean that someone at your house is bleeding?"

"No!" Russell screamed. "My *house* is bleeding. Please send someone."

The operator must have believed that Russell was truly panicked and confused and not just pulling a prank. A police car arrived at the Wilsons' home a few minutes later. The Wilsons met two officers on the front lawn.

"Is somebody here hurt?" one of the officers asked.

"Just please come inside," Russell pleaded.

The officers were stunned by what they found. Blood now seeped from walls in the downstairs hallway and the guest bedroom. The blood in the kitchen, bathroom, and master bedroom had stopped running but still coated the floors in a thick, sticky, reddish brown layer. An odor of death filled the house.

"You say no one was hurt here?" one officer asked, scratching his head.

"I'm not bleeding," Russell said, trying to remain calm. "My wife is not bleeding. No one else is in the house, and we have no pets. Like I said on the phone, my house is bleeding!"

As one officer filled out a report, the bleeding finally stopped. His partner took samples of blood from each of the rooms, promising to have them analyzed. "Would you mind if we looked behind one of the walls?" he asked.

"Let's do it," Judy replied. Russell headed down to the basement and retrieved a few of his tools. Then he and the officers cracked open a large hole in the upstairs bathroom wall, where the bloodbath had started. Peeking behind the tile and Sheetrock, they saw nothing but the basic construction material of the house. There was no sign of anything that might have caused the bleeding.

"There's not much more I can do," one officer said apologetically. "We'll let you know the lab results in a couple of days."

Over the next week, Russell and Judy Wilson slowly took on the daunting task of cleaning the blood from their house. One evening, as they were busy scrubbing, the phone rang. It was one of the officers who had come to their house on the night of the grisly event.

"We got the results back from the Georgia State crime lab," he began. "That was definitely human blood. And, even stranger, the blood from each room was a different type. We just can't explain it."

The officer went on to tell them that all he could do was list the incident as an unusual circumstance, since there was no apparent cause, no rational explanation, and no sign of a body.

The Wilsons were frustrated and suspected that the police might dismiss their whole terrifying ordeal as some kind of hoax. The only thing they could do was keep cleaning and not give up on the home they had worked so hard to make.

So when I showed up at their house a few weeks after this happened, they were relieved that someone was going to look into this mystery further.

"Nice to meet you, Jason," Russell said when I arrived. "After the incident, I started looking at Web sites that dealt with the paranormal. It's the only thing I could think of to explain what happened. I really liked your site."

He invited me in. Looking around the house, I saw that they had worked hard to clean the place up. You'd never know that anything strange had ever happened there.

Except for the bathroom. The Wilsons hadn't had a chance to repair the hole in the wall that Russell and the police officer had opened.

"Got a flashlight?" I asked, looking up at the hole, which was about a foot and a half above my head.

Russell left and returned a few minutes later with the flashlight.

"Give me a boost," I said, switching on the flashlight.

I placed my foot in Russell's clasped hands and he lifted me up. I just managed to squeeze through the hole and drop down on the other side of the wall. There I noticed writing scrawled on the back of the bathroom wall.

"This is really strange," I said. Sweeping the light along the back of the wall, I saw what appeared to be a list of names, scribbled sloppily in red paint. "It looks like a list of names. Harry Wiles, Andrea Backman, Sarah Marsh. Those are the first three. Mean anything to you?"

Russell repeated the names. "No," he said. "Never heard of any of those people."

"Me neither," Judy added.

"I'll keep going down the list," I said, squatting and leaning my hand against the wall. The instant my hand touched one of the painted names, I heard a disturbing sound.

Thwush!

It was like someone had turned on a faucet inside the tiny space between the walls. Red liquid poured from the letters that formed the list of names—and it wasn't paint, either. It was blood!

Before I could move, the blood was up over my ankles. I tried to turn and get out, but the blood was as thick as glue and it held my feet in place.

"Jason, what's going on?" I heard Judy scream.

But I couldn't speak. Terror gripped my throat like a powerful claw.

The gushing torrent of blood climbed up past my waist. I mustered the strength to pound on the wall, but I was completely trapped. I couldn't even reach the hole above me. I looked up and saw Judy looking through the hole. She reached out her arm for me, but it was no use. The blood was coming too fast.

I'm gonna drown! I thought. *I'm gonna drown in blood.* Then the blood reached my neck. I squeezed my eyes shut and took a deep breath, certain it would be my last.

Bash!

The sound of the wall splitting forced my eyes open. The blade of an ax was mere inches from my face!

The blood began to drain out, flowing from between the walls. I could move again, and I hurried back out into the bathroom. I saw Russell holding a bloody ax. Blood covered the bathroom floor.

"Oh my God, Jason, are you all right?" Judy gasped, handing me a towel.

"Those names were written in blood!" I cried, trying to catch my breath. "Those people have something to do with why your house is bleeding."

Russell led me to the guest bathroom, where I took a shower while Judy washed my clothes in the laundry room downstairs.

A short while later, I joined the Wilsons in their den. I was totally freaked out by what had just happened, but I couldn't abandon them now. "Where's your computer?" I asked. They sat me down in front of their desktop. "Now what were those names again?"

I entered "Harry Wiles, Andrea Backman, Sarah Marsh," wondering what they had in common and what they had to do with this house. It didn't take long to get my answer.

"They were all victims of the same serial killer," I said, reading from the story I'd found on the site of a local newspaper. "A guy named Mark Fredrickson committed a ton of bloody murders over a period of years in Atlanta, until he was finally caught, tried, and executed."

I entered "Mark Fredrickson" next and scanned the articles about him. I practically fell off the chair.

"Recognize Fredrickson's address?" I asked, pointing to one listing.

"That's our address!" Russell boomed. "That's this house! We never knew who owned it before us because we bought it at an auction."

"On what date did you say the walls first bled?" I asked next.

"December fifth," Judy replied.

"Look," I said. "That's the day Mark Fredrickson was put to death last year."

The Wilsons stared at the screen, completely stunned.

"I think your walls were bleeding with the blood of Fredrickson's victims on the day he died," I said. "That would explain all the different blood types the cops found— and the names scrawled on the wall."

A short time later I left the house, followed closely by Russell and Judy Wilson, who were carrying their suitcases.

HAWAII
Night Marchers

What I learned in history class: On December 7, 1941, the Japanese attacked U.S. military and naval facilities at Pearl Harbor, on the Hawaiian island of Oahu. The next day, December 8, the United States declared war on Japan, thereby entering the Second World War.

A story you won't find in your textbook: The volcanic cliffs of Hawaii are home to a lot of local legends. But sometimes, as I've discovered firsthand, legends can turn out to be true. Rachel Kaikunano, a fourteen-year-old girl who lives on Oahu, sent me an e-mail after her terrifying experience.

From: RKai@hawaiinet.com
To: Jspecter@scarystatesofamerica.com
Subject: Night Marchers

Hi, Jason.

I know that the stories on your Web site are true and that's
why I had to tell you my own. The legend of the night
marchers is known all over Hawaii. Adults like to use it to
scare little kids and freak out the tourists. I have to tell you,
though, that the night marchers are for real. I hope you believe
me. Here's what happened.

◉◉

Every kid who grows up in Hawaii knows about the night
marchers. Long ago, their leader, King Kamehameha, defeated the chieftain of Oahu in the famous Battle of the
Nuuanu Pali. Nuuanu Pali is a high, volcanically formed
cliff. It's said that the king and his warriors threw their enemies off the cliff at Pali Lookout, sending them to a bloody
death on the jagged rocks below. As some sort of karmic revenge, the night marchers were condemned to walk the
earth forever. Every night, they march along the cliffs of
Oahu, banging their drums as if heading into battle.

"Oh, please!" I always said. My friends and I laughed
about the night marchers and really never gave the story
much thought.

A week after my next-door neighbor and best friend,
Lika, got her driver's license, our moms let us drive to the
mall alone. They made us promise that we would head

home before it got dark. Well, of course we ended up talking to these guys from Lika's class, and before we knew it, we were late for dinner.

"My mom is going to kick my butt," Lika said as we ran to the car and tore out of the mall parking lot. It was almost dark, and a thick fog was drifting in from the ocean.

"Should you call your mom and let her know we're on our way?" I asked.

"No way. You think I want her screaming at me? I'll just deal with her when I get home. You can call your mom, though," Lika said. "She won't freak out like my mom will."

I flipped open my phone, but the battery was dead.

"I forgot to charge it again. Lemme use yours," I said, reaching into the backseat for Lika's purse.

"Rachel, let's just chill. We'll make it home on time once we lose this fog. It'll lighten up as we drive inland," Lika assured me, turning the radio up and dancing in her seat to the music.

But the fog didn't lift. On Highway 61, it was as thick as pea soup.

Suddenly, there was a loud boom and the car swerved violently to the right.

"Oh my God! What's wrong with the car?" I screamed.

"We blew a tire!" Lika cried as she struggled to hold the wheel steady. "We can't stop in the middle of the road in this fog. Someone might plow into us!"

Up ahead, I barely made out the sign for Nuuanu Pali Lookout.

"Can you make it to Nuuanu Pali? We can pull off there," I said, pointing to the exit.

A minute later, Lika managed to park the car at the edge of the deserted parking lot. The fog had let up just enough to reveal the outlines of the valley below.

"I'm calling home. There's no way I'm trying to change a tire." Lika grabbed her purse and started digging through it for her cell. "Where the heck is my phone?"

"Probably on your dresser. Again." I sighed. "I have no battery, and you have no phone. We better head toward Sixty-one and see if we can flag someone down."

"We can't go in this fog. We'll get run over. Let's just sit on the hood and wait it out," Lika said.

Trying not to think about how much trouble we'd be in, we sat on the hood of the car and attempted to make out the dried lava landscape before us. It seemed even more unearthly than usual.

"I'll never be allowed to drive again," Lika moaned. "Why didn't I leave on time? Why didn't I remember to take my stupid phone? Why is there so much damn fog tonight?" She dropped her head in her hands and whimpered.

Then I heard a noise in the distance.

"Shut up," I whispered. "Did you hear that?"

"No," Lika said, raising her eyes. "But you just want me to stop complaining. I get it. I'll shut up now."

"I'm not kidding," I said. "Just be quiet for a sec."

Lika and I sat perfectly still. The faint sound—a crunching noise—grew louder.

"What *is* that?" Lika asked.

"It sounds like footsteps," I whispered. "A lot of them."

The snapping and crunching of dried lava under the tread of what sounded like hundreds of feet marching in unison became louder by the second. The fog grew thicker as the sound drew nearer and nearer.

"Oh my God, Lika. We're at Nuuanu Pali. Is it the night marchers?"

"You're nuts!" Lika responded. But I could tell she was scared. My heart felt like it was in my throat.

Boom! Boom! Boom!

"What's that?" Lika shrieked, scrambling to her feet.

A sharp chill shot down the back of my neck and my hands grew cold despite the warm breeze. "The drums," I whispered, hardly believing my own words. "The night marchers always announce their arrival by pounding war drums."

Boom! Boom! Boom!

Again they sounded.

Boom! Boom! Boom!

Closer and closer.

The pounding of the drums fell into a perfect rhythm with the crunch of bony skeleton feet on the brittle lava. The sounds grew louder. The fog swirled into a thick haze. I could barely see my hand in front of my face. The night marchers were coming toward us, here on Pali Lookout, where they had tossed the bodies of their enemies to a horrible, twisted, bone-shattering death below!

I fought the panic welling up inside me. Lika and I were

paralyzed by fear. I had to do something. Before I knew I was even moving, I had jumped off the hood of the car. I heard Lika do the same and crouch beside me. I took a deep breath. "Don't run," I whispered. "We'll lose each other in the fog."

Boom! Boom! Boom!

Louder now. Closer. So very close!

That's when I saw the torches. Hundreds of dim, ghostly lights flickered through the fog, approaching quickly.

The legend was all coming true. The footsteps, the drums, and the torches. The same story I'd heard as a kid. But now . . .

"Let's get back into the car until they pass," I whispered to Lika.

But why had we waited so long? It was too late.

We froze. The bright blaze of a hundred torches was right before us. I gasped as the faces of the long-dead warriors emerged through the fog in the glittering flames. Sharp-boned skeletons with empty, soulless eyes, determined to reach their destination and slaughter again.

Suddenly, Lika tore from my grasp and went running for the highway.

I got up and tackled her to the ground, just a few feet away from the advancing procession of skeletons.

Crunch! Crunch! Crunch!

Boom! Boom! Boom!

The footsteps stopped. The drumming stopped. The night wind howled.

They had heard us.

I cupped my hands tightly over Lika's mouth and whispered quickly into her ear.

"Remember the legend. Keep your eyes shut tight. Whatever you do—do not look at them! If you make eye contact with a night marcher, he will steal your soul and you'll die. Now play dead. It's our only chance!"

I let my body fall limp next to Lika's. A single pair of feet scratched its way toward us. Lava dust filled my nose.

Don't sneeze! Don't sneeze! Don't sneeze!

I squeezed my eyes shut and kept my body completely motionless. I heard the spirit warrior's body creak. Then I heard a low hiss as he exhaled, and the stench of death nearly overwhelmed me.

He must be kneeling down, I thought. *Don't move, Lika, please!*

I heard a scraping sound and felt Lika's body being pulled away from mine. Even with my eyes closed, I knew that the night marcher was rolling her over, checking to see if she was alive.

I smelled the musty burning of his torch, which he must have held over us to get a better look. The night marcher waited. I heard his sickly hiss again, smelled his hot putrid breath. Minute after tortured minute, the dead thing poked and shook Lika.

Then, after an eternity, I heard the skeleton's creaky, ghostly bones as he stood up and crunched his way back to the rest of his troops.

Crunch! Crunch! Crunch!
Boom! Boom! Boom!

The marching and drumming resumed. I remained perfectly still, afraid to speak, reluctant to breathe. I listened as the army of death marched further along, the sound of their footsteps becoming faint, then vanishing into the misty night.

"Lika, are you okay?" I asked, opening my eyes and getting to my feet.

She nodded bravely, but a half second later was choking through tears. "I don't care if my mom has to drive me everywhere from now on. I hate driving. I want to go home," she sobbed.

We started the long trek through the fog, back toward the highway, hoping to flag down help. I strained my ears for the sound of the night marchers, but they were gone— for now.

Needless to say, I've never gone back to Nuuanu Pali. But on really still nights, the sound of drums in the distance can keep me awake in fear for hours.

Thanks for reading, Jason. Be careful out there!

Rachel

IDAHO

A Cry in the Night

What I learned in history class: Idaho is known as the potato capital of the world. In 2004, potato farmers in Idaho produced 13.2 billion pounds of potatoes.

A story you won't find in your textbook: *"Do you believe me?"* If I had a dollar for every time I read that in an e-mail or an IM, I'd be one rich guy. I don't believe every story I get. I'm not naive. There are a lot of people pulling pranks out there, and some ghost stories are just that—stories. But sometimes I get a message from someone who so desperately wants to be believed, I just know they're telling the truth. Too bad for Barbara in Boise that I seem to be the only person who feels that way.

From: BMoulton@bnet.com
To: Jspecter@scarystatesofamerica.com
Subject: believe me?

Jason,

I need someone to believe me. I wish I didn't see what I saw,
but I did, and now I have no home. Will you listen to my story
and not judge me?

Barbara

I wrote her back and told her that I'm not a judge,
just a collector of the paranormal. Here's what she wrote
back.

◉◉

Thanks for getting back to me and offering to hear my
story. I'm thirteen, and my name's Barbara Moulton. I read
your blog all the time. Well, ever since *it* happened. So I
figured you might believe me. My parents sure don't. That's
why I'm living with my friend Madison and her family.
That, and the fact that I will not go back to that house, no
matter what anyone says.

I hate thinking about it. From the day my family moved
into the 110-year-old farmhouse, I felt there was something
weird about the place. I always had the feeling that I was
being watched.

I hated going upstairs. I just knew that someone or
something was up there. My parents told me it was just my

imagination. I was only eleven when we moved in, but I knew that something wasn't right.

Then things started going missing from my room. The weird thing was that *my* stuff—my clothes, hairbrushes, dolls, and other toys—wasn't touched. What was taken were things I had for my dolls: baby bottles, clothes, tiny combs and brushes, even a small crib where I kept my favorite doll. The doll wasn't taken, just the crib, and the tiny quilt that was in the crib, and the other baby-sized stuff.

Then one night about a year after we moved in, I heard a noise that woke me up from a sound sleep. At first it sounded like a soft sobbing. But as I lay awake, my mind racing, I clearly heard the sound of a baby crying. I jumped from my bed and ran along the upstairs hallway.

The sound seemed to be coming from somewhere in the hall, but it also felt like I was surrounded by it. My whole body was overcome by grief, which I couldn't explain. I started to weep, sitting right there on the hallway floor, a huge weight of sadness pressing on my shoulders.

Forcing myself to stand, I ran into my parents' room and woke them. But by the time we all stepped back out into the hall, the crying had stopped. They told me I'd had a bad dream and sent me back to bed.

But the same thing happened again the next night. And the night after that.

After a while, I stopped waking up my parents. They had started to become pretty upset with me and thought I was turning into the girl who cried wolf. So I'd stay in bed listening to the baby crying, panicked and wondering if I was going crazy or if there really was something out there.

A few months ago, I made the discovery. My parents had been renovating one part of the house or another since the day we moved in. At this point, they were working on the upstairs hallway, scraping off layers and layers of old wallpaper. One day, when I was home alone, I happened to notice that several layers of wallpaper had been scraped from the center of the hallway wall. But it looked like one more layer remained. The corner had been started on the last layer, and I just couldn't resist reaching up, grabbing it, and pulling it away from the wall. I wish now that I never had.

I tore away the final layer of wallpaper, and what I saw left me standing there in total shock. Hidden under layers of wallpaper was a *door*! I was *so* curious. But I was also totally scared. Finally, though, I ripped away the remaining pieces of paper to fully expose the door.

Why would someone hide a door behind wallpaper, to make it seem as if the door never existed? I wondered. And more importantly, what was behind that door?

The door had no doorknob, so it could remain flat and hidden. I pushed on the door, but it was locked.

It was making me crazy. I had to know what was behind that door!

Racing to my father's tool cabinet, I grabbed a screwdriver. Slowly, I unscrewed the hinges. Then I yanked the door open to reveal a small room.

I stepped halfway inside the room and a rush of freezing

air poured through the door. My chest got tight and I couldn't take a full breath. My fingers stiffened and immediately started to turn blue. I felt light-headed, like I was about to faint. I stumbled back into the hallway, and all the weird sensations went away.

I should have run, but some part of me still had to get to the bottom of this mystery. I took a deep breath, then stepped all the way into the room.

No freezing air. I looked around uncertainly and saw a very old crib, some old toys, and rolls of wallpaper patterned with cartoon animals. It was definitely the kind of wallpaper someone would use in a baby's room. My heart almost stopped when I looked in the corner of the windowless room. My stuff!

"What the heck?" I said out loud. How could these things end up in a locked room, sealed behind a hundred years of wallpaper? Then I noticed a large metal box on the floor next to the crib. My heart beat faster as I slowly opened the box, its rusty hinges creaking ominously. Inside I found a baby's bonnet, a pair of handmade baby shoes, and a lace christening gown. I pulled a yellowed newspaper clipping out from the folds of the gown. Looking closely, I realized that it was an obituary—an obituary for a baby!

Her name was Elizabeth Macintosh. She had lived for only three months in the year 1915 and had been sick for her entire short life. The address listed in the clipping was my address!

The freezing air returned as I set down the clipping;

this time it gripped me like an icy claw. My whole body shivered violently. I fell to my knees and started crying. Then my throat began to close. I gasped for breath.

In a last desperate attempt to live, I flung myself out of the room and lay sprawled on the hallway floor. My breath returned, and the chills passed. Then the truth of what happened came into sharp focus.

This was to have been baby Elizabeth's room, but she never lived to see it completed. The family must have suffered such sadness that they couldn't bear to see the room, so they sealed the door behind the wallpaper and boarded up the window from the inside. No evidence that a window had ever existed remained on the outside, either. But someone or something—maybe it was the ghost of Elizabeth herself—still wanted to prepare the room for a baby.

Scrambling to my feet, I ran downstairs and stepped outside. I glanced back at the house, looking up at the spot where the room would have been. I saw a window where the day before there hadn't been one. In the window I saw a woman dressed in old-fashioned clothes, crying and holding a motionless baby in her arms.

I kept running and haven't been back to the house since.

My folks are upset. They don't believe me. They said I should stay with my friend until I stop lying and want to come home. What kills me is that they know the room is there. They just don't believe that I heard the baby or got the chills when I went into the room. They say I made up seeing the woman with the dead baby. They even say I put my doll things in there myself.

I hate that house. The Macintoshes lost their little girl when they lived there, and now my parents don't even realize they're losing their own daughter, too.

You do believe me, Jason, don't you?

ILLINOIS
Fire in the Mind

What I learned in history class: The Sears Tower in Chicago, Illinois, is the tallest building in the United States at 1,450 feet. When you include its antennas, the measurement increases to 1,725 feet. The Sears Tower has the most floor space of any structure in the United States except the Pentagon. It even has its own zip code.

A story you won't find in your textbook: My good bud Cub-Maniac1908 from Chicago is not only a serious baseball fan but also a huge freak about the paranormal. He e-mailed me a story about a twelve-year-old girl named Megan Faren who contacted him through his blog. Megan and her dad, Pete, live in Chicago now. But the story she told

CubManiac1908 happened to her in a small Illinois farm town called Macomb. Here is the story Megan told him.

◉◉

Everything bad started when my mom got sick and died about a year ago. My mom, dad, and I used to live in Chicago. I really liked it there. I had lots of friends, and I liked my school. Things were okay. My dad and I are back there now, but for a while after Mom died, we went to live with Dad's brother, my uncle Bob, on his farm in Macomb. That's when all the trouble started.

I think my dad just needed a break from the city, but I hated life on the farm. There was nothing to do. The only kids around were my cousins—eight-year-old Jenny and six-year-old Scott. I felt like a babysitter when I hung out with them. I missed my friends. But mostly I really missed my mom.

I couldn't figure out how to live without her. I was sad all the time. Sad that Mom wasn't there anymore. And my headaches got worse—much worse. I've always had headaches since I can remember. But not like these.

One night Dad, Uncle Bob, and Aunt Angela went into town. They left me to watch Jenny and Scott, as usual. Jenny pulled out one of her little-kid board games and the three of us began to play.

Then Jenny started asking me about my mom. Maybe she was curious about what it was like for me when my mom died, or maybe she was scared, afraid her own mom could die. Whatever she was thinking, I wasn't ready to talk about it.

As soon as she brought it up, the headache hit me like a knife in my skull. It was horrible. I fell off my chair and struggled to get back to my feet. Then I stumbled into the kitchen, screaming from the pain. I fell to my knees, squeezing my eyes shut and holding my head in my hands, wishing the pain would go away—and wishing my mom was there to hold me.

That's when it happened.

Smoke began to creep over the wall directly in front of me. A smoldering brown patch ate into the wallpaper. No flames, just smoke. The kitchen smelled like burning paper, and Jenny and Scott, who were peeking in from the next room, started crying. As the brown spot grew, my headache got worse.

I forced myself to stand up, fighting through the head-splitting pain. I dragged myself up to my room, fell into bed, and collapsed into a fitful sleep.

The next morning I felt awful. The pain in my head was different, though—like a dull soreness rather than a stabbing knife. I came downstairs for breakfast. Dad and Uncle Bob were waiting for me.

"What happened here last night, Megan?" Uncle Bob asked, pointing at the brown spot on the wall. It was about the size of a book.

"I don't know," I said, feeling frightened. And I really didn't know. Had I made it happen? How? "I got a terrible headache, and the next thing I knew, the wall was turning brown."

Uncle Bob looked at Dad, like maybe he was checking to see if Dad thought I was lying. Dad believed that I really didn't know. Uncle Bob smiled and said not to worry about it, but I could see in his eyes that he was worried.

Things only got worse from there.

A few weeks later I was alone in my room, reading one of my favorite books. It was one my mom used to read to me. I got so sad thinking about her sitting on the edge of my bed, letting me turn the pages. I put the book down and picked up my favorite picture of Mom, which I keep beside my bed. I thought it might make me feel better.

I stared into her eyes and looked at her big smile. But instead of feeling better, I got sadder. And then the headache returned.

It came from all sides, like a bunch of fists punching my head. I tumbled off my bed and rolled toward the window, finally stopping at the bottom of the curtains.

I tried to fight the pain, but it became hard to breathe, hard to see. So again I squeezed my eyes shut.

That's when I smelled smoke. My eyes flew open and I saw that the curtains were on fire! Flames tore up the sheer lace, climbing quickly toward the ceiling. I could see that if the wooden window trim caught or if the flames managed to reach the ceiling, the whole house might be lost.

"Uncle Bob!" I shrieked through the relentless pounding in my head.

The door of my room burst open and Uncle Bob looked

in. He ran out into the hall and returned a second later with a fire extinguisher. He sprayed the curtains and stopped the flames.

"What in the world happened here, Megan?" he asked. I could see that this time he was really upset.

"I don't know," I said. "I'm not lying, I swear. I didn't start this. I had another headache, and the next thing I knew, the room was on fire."

But how do I really know that I didn't start it? Another headache. Another fire.

Uncle Bob shook his head and left my room. He said he was going to call my dad. Slowly, the pain eased and I fell back onto my bed. My mind raced. Was Uncle Bob going to ask us to leave? Would I be responsible for getting us kicked out?

The door of my room swung open and Dad walked in. "You okay, honey?" he asked.

I nodded. Now I was lying.

I saw Dad look around at the charred curtains. He didn't say a word. I guess he could tell I was pretty freaked out. Then he noticed the book and Mom's picture.

"You miss her a lot, I know," he said softly. "I miss her too."

He kissed me and left the room. I tried to sleep, but I stayed awake all night wondering what was wrong with me. What kind of freak had I turned into?

As it turned out, Uncle Bob didn't kick us out. Now I wish that he had. Everything would have been much better—for everyone.

A few nights later, as everyone in the house slept, I had an incredibly real dream. I was with Mom, and we were in Grant Park, my favorite spot in Chicago. We were running around the fountain, laughing. I felt a rush of happiness, like I could take off into the sky and fly around the whole city.

I woke up suddenly, ripped from my beautiful dream by the most severe headache I'd ever had. My perfect day with Mom was just a dream. She was dead, and nothing was going to change that. Moaning and weeping in my bed, I wished with all my might that the pain would go away, but it only got worse.

As I writhed in pain, screaming for it to stop, I saw bubbling brown spots appear on the walls and ceiling all over my room. This time, the smoking patches burst into flames. Within seconds, my room was a blazing inferno.

I sat up in bed and wrapped my arms around my knees. There was no way out. I was going to die. Maybe that was okay. Maybe I would be with Mom again. For some reason, I was calm. I felt I was no longer in any danger.

Every smoke alarm in the house was screeching. The door of my room flew open and, to my horror, I could see that the rest of the house was on fire too.

"You get out!" Dad shouted over his shoulder to the others. "I'll get Megan!"

He stepped into my room and his face sank at the sight of me in my bed, surrounded by the flames. Several times he stepped toward me, hoping to find a path through the blaze, but each time, his hands and face were scorched and he turned away.

Still strangely calm, I slipped from my bed and walked through the blaze toward my father.

"Megan, no!" Dad shouted.

As he watched in amazement, I slowly made my way across the blazing room. The flames parted as I moved, creating a safe path. *Did I do this, too?* I wondered.

I reached him, and then all the calm I had been feeling shot right out of my body. Panic gripped me, and all I wanted to do was get out of there.

"Come on, Megan, faster!" Dad cried, grabbing my hand and pulling me toward the stairs. "Faster!" The flames chased us down the long wooden staircase.

We heard a sickening crack.

"Jump!" Dad screamed when we still had four stairs to go.

I leaped, and the staircase fell away behind me. Dad pulled me to my feet and we ran from the house.

Joining the others outside, I could only look up through my tears at the burning house and wonder if all this was my fault. Of course it was. What other explanation could there be?

The fire department eventually arrived, but they were too late. The house couldn't be saved. Fortunately, no one was hurt, but Dad and I left to go home to the city a few days later. We never heard from Uncle Bob again.

The doctors here tell me that I'm still angry about my

mother leaving me. They say that terrible grief can push the mind to extremes. I like the doctors here. They're nice. They let me talk about Mom as much as I want.

Dad visits me every day, and we talk about what we'll do when I get out of here. When visiting hours are over, the nurses come and let Dad out of my fireproof room.

INDIANA
Edna Collins Bridge

What I learned in history class: Held every Memorial Day, the Indianapolis 500 covers 200 laps around the 2.5-mile Indianapolis Motor Speedway. The Speedway, or Brickyard as it is sometimes called, has 250,000 seats, making it the largest sports venue in the world.

A story you won't find in your textbook: I'm not sure what it is about ghosts and bridges, but it seems that in every state there's a strong connection between the two. A number of people from Indiana have written to me about the Edna Collins Bridge in Clinton Falls, but Andrew Mackenzie told it the best. Here's the story he sent me.

◉◉

I wouldn't be surprised if you've heard this story before, Jason. Everyone in Putnam County knows the Edna Collins story. I even gave a class presentation on it in the fifth grade. Here's the background: Edna was a happy ten-year-old girl who lived with her parents in Clinton Falls in the 1920s. She was a free spirit, a real tomboy, who loved nothing more than to explore the rivers and woods with her dog, Tippy.

Edna's parents made frequent trips to nearby Greencastle in their brand-new car, to go shopping. When she was very young, Edna looked forward to these trips. She enjoyed exploring the stores with her folks. But soon her sense of adventure and her love of nature came to outweigh her interest in shopping. And so she and her parents worked out an arrangement.

On the way from Clinton Falls to Greencastle, the family would drop Edna and Tippy off on the far side of the covered bridge they had to cross. She was allowed to play along the edge of the river and to hike into the neighboring woods, but she had to remain in earshot of the road. When her parents reached the bridge on their way back, they would stop and honk their horn three times—the signal for Edna to rejoin them for the ride home.

This worked fine for many months. Edna enjoyed her time exploring the woods and river with Tippy, and her parents were pleased to foster their daughter's sense of independence and trustworthiness. They honked, and she appeared.

Except for the last time.

One afternoon, Edna's parents dropped her off as usual on the far side of the covered bridge and then headed off for their day in Greencastle. On the return trip, they stopped at the bridge and honked three times.

No sign of Edna.

They waited a few minutes, then honked three more times.

Still no Edna.

After the third round of honking, Tippy came scrambling up the riverbank, dripping wet and barking frantically. Hurrying from their car, Mr. and Mrs. Collins followed the agitated dog down the bank and along the river.

A few hundred yards away, they spotted a piece of red material caught on a branch, dangling over the raging river. Snatching the material from the branch, Mr. Collins was horrified when he recognized it as a piece of Edna's jacket.

A massive search was organized, but the little girl's body was never found. It was concluded that despite being a good swimmer, she had gotten caught in the powerful river current and had been swept away.

Her parents, who had no other children, never recovered.

The entire community was devastated. For months after Edna's death, drivers would pause at the bridge and honk their horns three times. They did this partly as a tribute to Edna, and partly in the irrational hope that the little girl might hear the horn, as she had so many times before, and come running to the car. Eventually, the town board voted to name the bridge after Edna Collins.

Shortly after the naming ceremony, a couple driving across the bridge honked their horn three times. Glancing in their rearview mirror, they saw what appeared to be a little girl scrambling up the riverbank, stepping onto the bridge, and waving at them. She was soaking wet and wearing a red jacket with a large section torn away. Leaping from their car, the couple raced across the bridge, but the girl had disappeared.

This phenomenon has recurred again and again, for decades, the girl appearing to various locals. I drove over that bridge hundreds of times with my parents, and then by myself once I got my license. It was like a ritual. You stopped, you honked, you waited, you drove off. Nothing ever happened, and I always felt like a moron sitting there waiting for a dead girl to show up.

Okay, so here comes the creepy part. I swear, Jason, this was no hoax. I love your Web site, and I wouldn't waste your time with a phony story.

One night last summer, I was driving around in my truck with my friend Jack and his cousin, Matthew, who was visiting from Alabama. We were supposed to meet these girls and go to the movies. Jack started bragging to Matthew about the bridge and how terrifying it is. Matthew wasn't impressed. He said they had a bridge in his town called Cry Baby Bridge and even though it was supposed to be haunted, Matthew had been there hundreds of times and had never seen a thing.

"I have to agree with him, Jack," I said. "People who say they've seen a ghost are either lying or insane."

"Okay," said Jack. "Then let's go out there and put Edna to the test."

"Jack, we're meeting the girls," I said. "I don't want to be late. I don't want to miss the start of the movie."

Matthew agreed, but Jack just wouldn't let it go. I don't know what's wrong with him sometimes.

Finally, we drove out there and I stopped my truck in the middle of the bridge, turned off the engine, rolled down all the windows, and honked three times. Nothing happened. I honked again. Still nothing.

"I told you this was stupid," I said to Jack in the seat next to me. "Now let's get out of here. We're going to be late."

"One more time, c'mon!" said Jack. "For Edna!" Then he leaned over and pressed hard on the horn, letting out three long blasts.

Hooonk! Hooonk! Hooonk!

In my rearview mirror I saw motion. I stared into the mirror and watched as a small figure rose up from the river-bank and climbed onto the bridge. I whipped around in my seat and saw that Jack was already peering out the back window.

"You two boneheads are in on this together," Matthew said, shaking his head. "Scare the rube from Alabama. Nice try."

"Turn around, Matt," Jack whispered.

Matthew swung his head around to look, and gasped.

Through the truck's back window, we could all see a little girl, about ten years old. She was wearing a torn red coat. Water dripped from her clothes and hair. I swear she smiled right at me. She waved like she was happy to see us. Then it got even weirder.

"Mommy! Daddy!" she cried out. She started running toward the truck. "Here I am. Right on time."

"You see her, right?" I asked Jack. "You see her?"

"I see her, Andrew. Let's get the hell out of here!"

"Daddy!" the girl screeched. Her face turned red; tears streamed from her eyes. "Why won't you come for me?"

That was it. I fumbled for the ignition, then turned the key, but the truck didn't start.

"It's time to go home, Mommy!" the girl shouted through her sobbing. She was right behind the truck now. "Where's Tippy? I can't find Tippy!"

I was really scared, and a little embarrassed. I mean, she was just a little girl. But I swear she was the ghost everyone always talked about, and she was so . . . real.

Again I tried to start the truck. It coughed and sputtered but wouldn't kick over. I looked up and jumped in my seat. The little girl's face was right at my window. She was pressed against my door. Blood trickled down her face.

"Daddy!" she bellowed, sobbing hysterically.

Chik-chik-chik-throoom!

The engine started up with a roar. I put the car in gear and took off. Then I glanced out my rearview mirror.

The girl was gone.

"Why didn't you give her a ride home, Daddy?" Matthew said, laughing. "Man, you guys pull some really elaborate stunts up here."

"Shut up, Matt," Jack snapped. "That was not a stunt. It was that Edna girl. Her ghost. I—I'll swear on Grandma's grave, okay?"

That must have been some family signal, because both of them got real quiet. I focused on the road and at the same time tried to wipe the sweat from my face and hands.

When we pulled into the local diner for a late-night snack, I was stunned by what I saw when we stepped from the truck.

Standing in the back of the truck with her arms open wide, blood still streaming down her face, was Edna.

"Daddy!" she cried, staring right at me. "Take me home!"

IOWA
Circles in the Fields

What I learned in history class: Meredith Willson, a native of Mason City, Iowa, was the author and composer of *The Music Man*, which premiered on Broadway in 1957. One of the famous numbers from the musical is "Iowa Stubborn," which describes the ways Iowans can be obstinate but always charitable.

A story you won't find in your textbook: If there's one thing I really hate, it's when people fake spooky stuff as a joke or to rip others off. Lots of people fake crop circles. I get stories all the time from my fellow paranormal aficionados who have been called out to farms to investigate so-called extraterrestrial-created circles. They get there only to find some crudely stamped-down corn, obviously the work of imposters. But a good IM buddy of mine who specializes in crop circle stories told me about a story he personally verified.

> **CircleFan:** Got a live one for ya, Specter!
>
> **ParaGuy:** What, more people with ropes and boards making fake crop circles?
>
> **CircleFan:** No, dude! I'm talking real crop circles, alien visitors, the whole enchilada!
>
> **ParaGuy:** Is this really CircleFan, the guy who told me 99.9 percent of all crop circles are fake? The guy who knows every method for pulling off crop circle hoaxes? What happened to Mr. Cynical?
>
> **CircleFan:** I know, and I was skeptical too. But this one is real. Come and see for yourself, dude. We'll check it out together.

I'd told CircleFan, whose real name is Ben, that my family was taking a road trip through the Midwest later in the summer, so he was eager for me to visit him and the Machen farm near Iowa City—the site of these so-called authentic crop circles. So I met up with Ben, who turned out to be seventeen and had just gotten his license. He picked me up at my aunt's house, and on the way out to the Machen farm, he filled me in on the details.

◉◉

"Ben, I'm trying to keep an open mind here," I said as we headed out of Iowa City, zipping through a sea of cornfields on our way to the Machen farm. "We've been IM buds long enough that you know I'm open to all kinds of really strange stuff."

"Specter, you just don't buy that crop circles could be anything but fakes, right?" he asked. "Well, that's why I waited to check this farm out until you got here. I'm a skeptic too, but I know smart people who've seen these circles and they swear they're real."

"Okay."

"I've been doing more reading, and some of these circles are really starting to check out," Ben continued. "I read about scientists who studied one Iowa field where the plants were bent in a teardrop-shaped depression. They discovered that those plants had been exposed to what they called a complex energy burst, like a microwave oven. You know, microwaves cook food from the inside out. Well, all these plants were drained of all moisture from the inside, while remaining unburned on the outside."

"That still doesn't mean extraterrestrials are behind it," I said, enjoying giving him a hard time.

"All right, Specter, think about it. In this other case,

two huge crop circles show up in a field overnight. No way anyone would have had time to fake those. Then, the following year, when soybeans were planted in the fields, only the seeds planted within the circles sprouted. The rest of the field stayed brown."

I kept giving Ben a hard time, but I was sort of excited. By the time we got to the Machen farm, I had agreed to keep an open mind. And what I found was unreal!

"Thanks for coming, guys," said a fifteen-year-old boy who introduced himself as Charlie Machen. His dad owned the farm.

"Hey, Charlie, I'm CircleFan," Ben said, shaking the boy's hand. "You can call me Ben. This is my buddy Jason Specter. He also has a Web site."

"Hey, thanks for letting us come out here," I said, shaking Charlie's hand.

"Charlie got in touch with me at my CircleFan Web site when the weird stuff started happening on his dad's farm," Ben explained as we started walking into the enormous cornfield.

"CircleFa—I mean Ben—told me you don't believe crop circles are real," Charlie said to me. "But if this one's fake, I have no idea who could have faked it."

"This is what I'm saying, dude!" Ben said, putting his face right up to mine.

The three of us made our way through the perfectly straight rows of corn, which towered over my head. Then, out of nowhere, the field opened up into a huge circle.

There was no path leading to or from the circle. It was just there, as if a giant with a round foot had stepped on the field.

But the cornstalks weren't broken! They were only bent over, as if someone had gently folded each one, careful not to snap them. The circle was enormous, measuring about forty-five feet in diameter. The bent corn spiraled to the center of the circle.

"My family's been farming this land for five generations," Charlie told us as we stood in the middle of the circle. "My dad's the head of the local farmers' co-op. My grandfather even ran for city council. Everyone in the area knows my family. We're not ones to start believing in ghosts or UFOs. I mean, no offense, I know you write about all this stuff on your Web site. But that's just not who we are."

"It's okay," I said. "I didn't believe in this stuff either, until I had a firsthand experience myself."

I walked back to the edge of the circle and grabbed a cornstalk. I tried to bend it gently without breaking it, but it snapped in half in my hands. I tried again, bending another one even more slowly, but again the stalk snapped in two.

"I can't figure out how someone could bend each of these cornstalks without breaking them," I said.

"Told ya," Ben said, smiling a goofy smile. *Sometimes people are way cooler online than in person*, I thought.

"We had investigators visit the farm," Charlie continued. "They ruled out all the hoaxes they knew about, and they've seen a bunch. They couldn't explain it, so they just left it at that. My dad had a friend who worked in a lab in Iowa City, so he borrowed a meter for measuring radiation from this guy. We scanned the crop circle and sent the results to the lab. My dad's friend said that the meter was picking up traces of energy, similar to microwaves. Called it plasma energy, whatever that is."

Ben glanced over at me with an "I told you so" look.

"But the real show starts after dark," Charlie explained as we walked along the outside of the enormous circle.

"What do you mean?" I asked.

"That's when the glowing begins," he said matter-of-factly.

Glowing? I thought. *This I have to see!*

"Why don't you guys stay for dinner?" Charlie said. "Then I can show you."

"Thanks," I said, pulling out my cell phone. I called my aunt's house and asked permission to stay for dinner. Ben did the same.

"Cool. Thanks for the invite," I said after hanging up.

"Ditto," said Ben.

After a dinner of fresh corn and chicken, we sat with Charlie and his parents on the porch, watching the sun set. Stars appeared, slowly filling the vast Iowa sky as it turned from dark blue to black.

"Come on," Charlie said after a while. "It should be dark enough."

After grabbing a flashlight and the borrowed radiation meter, he led us back out to the cornfield. His folks stayed behind. "They've already seen this too many times for their liking," he told us.

As we approached the circle, it seemed the sky was getting brighter. *What's going on?* I thought. *It should be getting darker out here away from the house, not lighter.*

Then I saw it. The glow came from the crop circle. Bright white light rose toward the sky and formed a perfect wall around the circle, like a sheer curtain of radiant energy.

"I don't think you could fake this," I said, getting that creepy but thrilling sensation I always get in the presence of the truly paranormal.

"Yes!" Ben yelped. "This is so cool! Oh man, this is the real deal. And Specter's here to see it!"

I caught a glimmer of movement out of the corner of my eye. Glancing up, I saw a brilliant white light streaking across the sky on the other side of the field.

"What's that?" I nearly shouted, pointing at the sky.

"I have no idea," Charlie replied. "I've never seen *that* before." Then he hurried across the field, away from the circle, toward the light in the sky.

When we reached the far side of the field, the glow of the circle dimmed, and the light moved slowly down toward us. As it hovered overhead, I noted its tubular shape and brilliant glow. I couldn't tell if it was a solid vehicle or some kind of energy phenomenon.

That's when Charlie switched on the radiation meter. He held it over his head, pointing the device right at the glow in the sky. The meter flashed and beeped.

"Hold my flashlight," Charlie said, handing it to me.

I shined the beam onto the face of the meter.

"I'm no scientist," he said. "But I have seen these readings before. The readings coming from that light are the same as that plasma stuff—exactly the same as what was coming from the crop circle."

The needle on the meter shot up to maximum and seemed to be pressing higher. Smoke poured from the device. Startled, Charlie dropped the meter, and it hit the ground in a shower of sparks and flames.

At that moment, the light in the sky swooped down even closer. We began running back toward the house, but we were no match for the streaking orb. As the light grew nearer, I heard a loud humming in my ears.

My skin began to tingle, like an electrical current was coursing through my body. My hair stood straight up and started smoking, and my fingernails began to glow bright red.

"Specter!" Ben cried.

My body was burning up. I was being fried to a crisp! I fell to the ground as a cooling force from the direction of the crop circle washed over me. The burning stopped, but my entire field of vision went white.

"I can't see!" I screamed. "I can't see!"

Everything flashed before me. Every ghost, creature, or UFO I'd ever encountered or even read about. For a brief second, I was back in that horrible locker in fourth grade, unable to breathe, trapped with a dead boy. I cursed myself for ever getting into all this. And now . . . now I was blind!

Then suddenly, I could see again. I jumped to my feet in time to see the white orb streak into the sky. It stopped and hovered right above the crop circle.

In a brilliant flash that made the ground shake, the light of the circle seemed to engulf the glowing orb, pulling it toward the ground.

And then all was still and quiet. Smoke rose from the circle, which was now nothing more than an area of charred earth. The crop circle had healed and protected me—but from what? Some sort of cosmic battle was being fought right here in Iowa. I felt like an innocent bystander who had been struck by shrapnel but lived to tell the tale. I checked my body for any scars or burns, but the skin on my arms was smooth.

"You saw it, Jason," Ben shouted when he saw that I was all right. "You know it was real!"

The Machen crop circle became just one more farmer's story. But I knew better. I knew it was real. I had seen and felt it. And it took over a month for my hair to grow back!

KANSAS
Ghost in the Heartland

What I learned in history class: The first African American woman to win an Academy Award was Hattie McDaniel. The Wichita, Kansas, native won the Oscar for Best Supporting Actress for her role as Mammy in *Gone with the Wind*.

A story you won't find in your textbook: I pride myself on being a member of every state's paranormal society. I even have membership cards for some of them (and no, I don't carry them around in my wallet. I realize that would be crossing a nerd line). I recently joined the Kansas society and sent an e-mail blast out to members, asking for their stories. Maybe I should have laid off all the sarcastic *Wizard* *of Oz* comments, because I got a lot of snide responses. I guess Julie Bonham found me amusing, because she sent me back a reply.

◉◉

Hi, Jason. Yes, Kansas is known for Dorothy and Toto, but Oz has got *nothing* on Atchison. This place is a hotbed for restless spirits. Doors open and slam by themselves; radios, TVs, and lights switch on and off mysteriously; and gleaming balls of light have been sighted floating from room to room.

But the most famous ghost in our town is little Sallie Isabel Hall, who will forever be known as Sallie the Heartland Ghost.

In 1905, six-year-old Sallie complained to her mother in the middle of the night of terrible abdominal pain. Sallie's mother rushed her to the doctor's house, where he diagnosed her as having a case of severe appendicitis. The little girl required immediate surgery, which he would perform right there in his upstairs office.

Sallie was terrified, and panicked at the sight of the surgical tools the doctor was preparing. He struggled to hold the girl down while he gave her ether, which was used in those days as an anesthetic. Sallie calmed down and eventually closed her eyes and drifted into unconsciousness.

But the doctor didn't wait long enough before making the first incision. The ether hadn't fully taken effect, and Sallie was not in a deep enough sleep. She bolted awake, screaming in agony from the pain of the cutting. She grabbed the doctor's hand, battling him as he tried to calm her down, as all the while the blood drained from her body.

The doctor couldn't save her. He couldn't calm her down enough to put her out again, and he couldn't repair the damage done by his incision and her struggling. Just before she died, Sallie looked up at him with terror and disgust in her blue eyes.

"I hate you!" she shrieked. "Forever!" Then she was gone.

But not really. Her spirit remains in the doctor's house to this day. How do I know? Because I lived in that house. My husband, Tom, our daughter, Sarah, and I experienced Sallie's angry spirit firsthand.

The really strange stuff started as soon as Tom and I moved in. Sarah was still an infant. We loved the house, and we were thrilled that Sarah had her own room. Until one night when we were awakened by her cries.

I hurried into Sarah's room to find the radio blaring. The knob had been turned . . . but who could have done it? Sarah was too small to even reach it. I flipped off the radio switch, held Sarah until she quieted, and then went to bed.

The same thing happened the next night, and then again a week later. I came into Sarah's room one morning to find pictures tossed to the floor and toys scattered everywhere.

"Tom!" I cried.

"What happened?" Tom yelled, racing into Sarah's room.

"Who did this?" I asked, shaking my head and pointing to the mess on the floor.

"It looks like an earthquake hit in here."

As we began cleaning up, I got a strange, uncomfortable feeling that I was being watched.

We tried to put these weird events behind us and get on with our lives. Being new parents, we took a lot of pictures of Sarah. When the first roll of film came back, every image of Sarah was covered with blurry blobs of light and distorted swirls of color. The rest of the photos were normal. It was like someone had deliberately tried to wipe our daughter from the photos.

We tried different cameras and different types of film, shooting in bright daylight or with a flash at night, but the result was always the same. Even digital shots showed up on the screen a second after we took them with Sarah pixelated out.

Then the strange noises began—footsteps and whispers at first, then growls, and finally the clear sound of a little girl's cry for help.

But all this was just the beginning.

One evening, Sarah was asleep, and Tom and I were downstairs watching TV. Suddenly, I smelled smoke. As I dashed upstairs, the smoke thickened. Smoke was pouring out from under Sarah's door. I flung the door open and was horrified to see flames spreading across the room.

"Tom!" I screamed, rushing into the room and grabbing Sarah from her crib just as Tom burst in with the fire extinguisher. He ran past me as I carried Sarah downstairs, and he hosed down the room. In a few minutes the fire was out.

"Why didn't the smoke detector go off?" Tom wondered, pulling the device open.

The battery was gone.

"I just put a new battery in that thing two weeks ago," Tom said.

Things stayed quiet for about a month, until one day, as Tom was painting the hallway, he felt the temperature drop suddenly. Frigid air surrounded him. He dropped his paintbrush and clutched his chest with both hands. When he removed his hands, they were covered in blood.

Tom cried out in pain. He looked down and saw a deep cut across his chest. Huge red welts appeared on his arms.

The assaults on Tom continued. Painful scratches, cuts, and welts appeared on his back, chest, and arms. These attacks were always preceded by a sudden blast of frigid air that surrounded him, cutting him like a knife and scarring his body.

The final straw for us came a few weeks later. I was at work, and Tom was home with Sarah. As she napped, Tom was repairing the railing at the top of the stairs on the second floor. As he leaned over it, the temperature dropped. Fear gripped him as he anticipated another cut or welt, but this time he heard a terrified, high-pitched voice scream out.

"I hate you!" it shrieked. "Forever!"

Suddenly, Tom felt a shove from behind. He tumbled over the railing. Reaching up at the last second, he grabbed two rails and stopped his fall. He dangled there, looking down at the long plunge to the hardwood floor below.

Tugging with all his strength, he managed to pull himself up and over the railing. He crashed onto the second-floor landing, trembling and breathing hard. As he rolled over onto his stomach, he stared at the bottom of the doorway to Sarah's room. As he lay there in pain, an image flashed into his mind—the image of a doctor's office and of a little girl bleeding to death. Later, we discovered that Sarah's room was the very room the doctor had used for surgery back in 1905, on the night that Sallie Isabel Hall had died.

I came home to find Tom lying on the landing with two broken ribs. That was it for me. We moved out shortly after that and eventually sold the place, though the new owners won't reveal whether anything strange has happened to them.

But they don't have a little girl sleeping in the room where Sallie died all those years ago.

KENTUCKY
Peering into the Past

What I learned in history class: Nicknamed the Bluegrass State, Kentucky gets its name from the Iroquoian word *Kentahten*, meaning "land of tomorrow."

A story you won't find in your textbook: A kid named Dan Treatch from Louisville, Kentucky, sent an e-mail to my Web site with a bizarre story about something that happened to him and his sister.

From: Dtreatch11@kycom.net
To: Jspecter@scarystatesofamerica.com
Subject: portals

Hi, Jason.

I came across your awesome site when I started to look up stuff about the paranormal after this, well, this *thing* happened to me and my sister. I gotta tell someone. Is that okay?

DT

Is that okay? It's what I live for! Which is what I told him when I wrote back. Here's the strange story he sent me.

◉◉

I'm eleven. My sister, Karen, is nine. We live with my mom and dad in a small house in Louisville, Kentucky. About a month ago, Karen started telling me that she believed there was a monster living under her bed.

"Give me a break!" I said, being my usual compassionate big brother self. "That stuff is for babies. When are you going to grow up?"

"Danny," she whined. "I heard a strange noise. I was sure it came from under my bed, so I stuck my head down there and it was like I was looking at a picture or a movie of another place. It was all white and snowy, and someone was walking through the snow. Then I saw the monster, like a big dog, growling. And—Danny, stop laughing at me!"

I couldn't help it. It just sounded so weird. My sister was pretty frightened by scary movies and stuff like that, and I knew she had a vivid imagination. But this was way wilder than anything I had ever heard her say.

"If I see it again, can I knock on the wall?" she asked, not letting it go.

"Sure," I said, smiling. This was the signal we had used since we were little kids. Whenever Karen got scared at night, she would knock on the wall and I'd come into her room and stay until she wasn't scared anymore.

The next night, I was awakened by a knock on my wall. I slipped out of my bed and headed quietly into Karen's room. Our folks were downstairs with some people and I didn't want them to know that we were still awake.

Stepping into Karen's room, I found her leaning over the edge of her bed. She tightly gripped the blanket, which draped over the side of the bed. "It's back!" she whispered, as if the creature she believed to be under her bed might hear her.

I knelt down beside the bed. "Go ahead," I said, rolling my eyes.

She pulled the blanket up, then hung her head over the edge of the bed. I flattened myself onto my stomach and stuck my head under the bed.

I'm only eleven, but this was the weirdest thing that had ever happened to me.

It's hard to explain. It was as if the small space between the bottom of the mattress and the floor had opened up into a vast arctic scene. It was not so much like watching a movie as like poking my head through a hole into another place and time.

With Karen's head upside down next to mine, I

watched as a man in a soldier's uniform trudged through the snowy wasteland.

"This is exactly what I saw last night," Karen explained. "It's like a movie that keeps playing. The monster should show up any second now."

Sure enough, a few moments later we heard growling; then suddenly, a four-legged beast came tearing through the snow. It had thick white fur and long teeth. Its face and teeth were drenched in blood, fresh from a kill.

"It's a wolf!" I said. "An arctic wolf." I'm an animal lover and I can identify animals from around the world. This one was pretty obvious.

The soldier stared at the beast with terror in his eyes. Then the weirdest thing happened. The wolf turned and looked right at me. I swear! Our eyes locked, and the wolf snarled as if it meant to charge me. Then it turned back and attacked the soldier, its teeth sinking into the man's leg.

"Make it stop, Danny!" Karen screamed.

I yanked the blanket down to cover the scene. When I peeked again a second later, the snowy scene was gone. There were only toys under Karen's bed.

Then I heard someone downstairs sobbing. It didn't sound like my mom or dad, so I went back to bed. The next morning, I asked my mom if everything was okay, and she explained that her visitors were sad because their son had died.

A week later, my folks had company again, a woman I

didn't know. Then, an hour after I went to bed, Karen knocked on the wall. I scooted into her room.

"It's happening again, Danny!" she cried, pointing under the bed.

I ducked my head under and once again peered into some kind of opening. I saw a man running down a dark, deserted, rainy street. It looked like a city scene, but it was hard to tell. The man kept glancing back over his shoulder as he ran.

Suddenly, another man bolted onto the scene. He was much larger than the first man. His brown hair was disheveled and he had a wild look in his eyes. The second man quickly gained on the first and within a few seconds had caught up to him, tackling him to the ground.

"What's going on?" Karen asked.

"Shhh!" I said. "Just watch."

The larger man had the first man pinned to the ground. He reached into his long overcoat and pulled out something that flashed in the streetlight.

"He's got a knife!" Karen whispered urgently.

Down came the knife, again and again, into the first man's chest. It made a sickening slicing sound with each stab.

"He killed that guy!" Karen shouted as tears poured down her face.

The murderer stopped as if he had heard Karen's shout. He turned and looked right at us, the bloody knife still dripping in his hand.

"Now, you two kids didn't see anything, did you?" he asked, standing up.

"Danny, he sees us!" Karen cried, grabbing the sleeve of my pajamas.

Still clutching the knife in his black-gloved hand, the murderer slowly walked toward us, his boots sloshing in the puddles on the pavement.

"I asked you a question!" he shouted, picking up his pace and coming closer. His eyes glowed with rage. "Did you see anything?"

His body filled the entire portal now, as if he were just a few inches away. We froze in terror.

"What's the matter?" he snarled. "Cat got your tongue?"

Karen grabbed my other arm. The killer kept coming. I could feel the dampness of the rain and the power of the man's anger pouring through the portal.

"Well, maybe I'll just cut *out* that tongue!" he barked, reaching through the opening and grabbing Karen's hand.

"Help!" she screamed. "Get him off! Get him off!"

The killer's arm and shoulder were in the room now. His huge hand closed around Karen's wrist. Then he began pulling her toward the portal.

"You're coming with me!" he shouted.

"Danny! Help me!" Karen screamed hysterically.

I scooted behind her, wrapped my arms around her waist, and yanked with all my might. We both fell backward onto the bedroom floor.

Then the portal snapped shut.

"Ahhhhh!" Karen screamed, completely freaked out.

"Stop screaming!" I yelled. "He's gone!"

She stopped yelling, but a horrified scream continued from downstairs.

"What's going on?" Karen shouted, running for the door.

She yanked open her bedroom door and jumped back, startled. A large figure filled the doorway, then stepped into the room.

"Dad!" I said, relieved. "What's going on down there?"

"I thought the screaming might frighten you," he said as Karen climbed up into his arms. "I came to check on you guys. That's a client of ours downstairs. She's very upset."

"What kind of client?" I asked.

"Do you know what a séance is?" Dad asked me.

"Well, duh, Dad, everyone does," I replied.

"Your mother and I conduct séances for people trying to find out what happened to missing loved ones," Dad explained. "We just helped our client find out that her husband was killed. The poor woman's so shook up. We were able to identify the murderer as a large man with wild eyes and red hair."

"Actually, Dad," I said, "his hair was brown."

LOUISIANA
Voodoo Priestess

What I learned in history class: The word *Dixie* refers to the most common currency used in the South after the Civil War. The Bank of New Orleans, which used the French language back then, issued a ten-dollar bill called a *dix* note (*dix* is French for "ten"), which soon became known as a Dixie note. Eventually, New Orleans and the South became known as the land of Dixies, or Dixie Land.

A story you won't find in your textbook: Spirits, ghosts, and magic are as much a part of Louisiana as Cajun food and jazz. Demons lurk in old houses and hotels, not to mention in the swamps of the bayou. So it's not surprising that one of my steadiest suppliers of firsthand paranormal accounts would live in that ghost-infested state. My IM pal Bayou-Bet has lived in Louisiana all her life, and she sent me a bunch of really scary stories. But this latest one is hands down the creepiest!

BayouBet: Got a winner for you, Jason! Real scary!

ParaGuy: Wait, wait! Lemme guess— haunted hotel?

BayouBet: Nope.

ParaGuy: Swamp monster?

BayouBet: You're getting . . . colder.

ParaGuy: The ghost of a famous jazz musician?

BayouBet: Lame! I said scary!!

ParaGuy: OK, OK! No more guessing. Tell me, tell me!

BayouBet: A voodoo priestess and a dead girlfriend!

ParaGuy: Don't tell me they walk into a bar . . .

BayouBet: Not funny. Bad joke. Now stop typing and start reading! I got this story from a kid named Steve, who lives around here.

◉◉

Sara was my first love. Right now it feels like she'll be my only love. People tell me I'll meet other girls. After all, I'm only seventeen.

Sara would have been seventeen next month.

With her death still fresh in my mind and filling my soul with darkness, it feels like I'll never love again. She's been gone six months, and I miss her so much, I'd do anything to get her back.

Which is why I turned to Madame LaRue.

Everyone in my town knows Madame LaRue. She's a crazy old woman who lives in a creepy, run-down shack deep in the swamp. Some people call her a gypsy, some call her a witch. Others say she's just an eccentric, harmless hermit. But for years, there have been rumors about strange rituals, human sacrifice, and black magic in her part of the swamp.

Then there are those who believe that Madame LaRue is a voodoo priestess, capable of bringing the dead back to life. It was with these stories in mind that I set off after school one day to find her.

Looking back now, I can see it was stupid, but I was a little crazy with grief. All I could think of was that somehow I could be with Sara again; see her one more time, hold her hands, kiss her lips. I was desperate. How could I live with all this hurt inside me?

The late-afternoon sun was starting to set as I made my way along narrow dry paths into the swamp. I'd played here with my friends years ago, but stories about the witch who lived there always chased us from the dark woods of the swamp's interior before nightfall. Now I was plunging into the darkening forest, searching for that witch.

The trees closed in like enormous rough-skinned arms

enveloping me, pulling me in deeper, hugging me tighter. The wind picked up, and the hooting of a distant owl startled me. I looked over my shoulder, unable to shake the feeling that someone was following me, watching my every move. But I wasn't going to leave. Madame LaRue was my last hope.

I came to a stream and sloshed across it, soaking my sneakers, slipping once or twice, then fighting to regain my balance. The sound of the rushing water seemed to speak to me, but its voice was muffled.

Was it a warning?

I continued on to the other side of the stream, and the wind-whipped trees swayed back and forth, waving me forward, signaling that I had passed the point of no return.

Zipping up my jacket against the fierce wind, I pushed forward, small branches slapping me on the arms and back.

And then I caught sight of it. Little more than a hut, the tiny house might have looked good at some point, but that was hard to imagine. Graying, rotted clapboard hung at all angles, blown up and down by the wind, straining against the few nails that still held the boards to the house. The slate roof was stained with years of moss and bird droppings, and the cracked front door looked like it could fly off its hinges at any moment.

As I approached, time slowed. I could hear my heart beating loudly, urging me forward. What if I really could see Sara again? But my brain kept telling me that this was a *really* bad idea.

I stepped onto the porch and the ancient floorboards

creaked a shrill warning. Then everything grew silent. I could hear the blood coursing through my veins.

Tap, tap, tap.

I knocked softly on the ramshackle front door. No response.

Rap, rap, rap.

I knocked louder now and heard a low moan coming from inside. Every instinct told me to turn and flee, but I fought the urge.

"The door is unlocked," a voice called from within. "I fear no one, for the spirits of the night and the souls of the dead protect me. You may enter, stranger."

I swallowed hard, then grasped the rusty metal doorknob and popped the door open. It squeaked out a mournful cry as it swung inward, and I stepped through the doorway.

I didn't see her at first. It was very dark inside except for the dozens of candles scattered throughout the cramped room. They flickered, tossing tiny fingers of light on the woven wall hangings. Images of demons and monsters and ancient scenes of evil and death covered the fabric.

Then I saw her, seated in a large, thronelike chair in the far corner of the room. The candlelight sent an eerie glow over Madame LaRue's ancient, wrinkled face. It was a face as old as time, lined with a thousand stories. Her robes flowed from her neck, draping over her feet. An elaborate headdress enveloped her head, the folds of its fabric swirling upward like the wind itself.

I felt my hands shaking. My lower lip trembled uncontrollably.

"You bring pain into my home," Madame LaRue said before I could muster the courage to speak.

"How did you know?" I said, gasping in disbelief. "I mean, yes, that's true. That's why I came here. I mean, to see you. To see if you can help me." I felt like a bumbling, nervous fool.

"You seek to be reunited with one who is gone," the witch stated with certainty. She had to be a witch. How else could she know why I was here?

"This can be done," she said.

I thought I was going to burst into tears. I struggled hard to hold it together. "How much?" I asked. The words popped out of my mouth and I instantly felt rude. "I mean, how?"

"I do not seek money from you," Madame LaRue said. "I am a priestess, descended from a thousand years of great spiritual women. I offer comfort to those in pain. Do not believe all the things you hear about me."

She never smiled. Her face remained composed, like a primitive mask come to life. "You must, however, be very precise in telling me what you want," she continued.

"I want to see Sara again," I blurted. "My girlfriend, I want her to be alive!"

"Very well, then here is what you must do," the witch began. "Bring a picture of Sara to her grave tomorrow night when the moon is full. You must then repeat this sentence five times: 'Ancient spirits, lift the one who is gone and cut the pain from my soul.' When you have repeated the sentence for the fifth and final time, she will be revealed."

"Thank you, Madame LaRue," I said, somehow totally believing her. Then I bowed (don't ask me why, it seemed like the right thing to do) and slowly backed out of the house.

"Remember," she said as I reached the door. "You will get precisely what you asked."

I ran from the house, crashing back into the woods. Darkness had almost completely fallen. I tripped over roots and smacked into branches as I stumbled my way back through the swamp. My mind was racing. *Could what she said be true? Is it possible I'll see Sara again? How can that be? Is the witch a fraud? But then, she did know I was in pain . . .*

By the time I made it home, it was pitch-black out. I was more tight-lipped than usual at dinner, but I guess my folks had gotten used to that since Sara died. After dinner, I scrolled through all the shots I had saved of her on my computer, but I knew before I started which one I wanted to bring with me. Sara in her yellow dress the night of the formal. She's holding the corsage I bought her, looking so pretty. Her smile just shines in that shot. I started to cry.

Would I really be seeing her tomorrow night?

I printed out a copy of the photo and clutched it to my chest. Then I climbed into bed, knowing full well that I wouldn't be able to doze off.

After sleepwalking through school the next day, I headed to the cemetery, Sara's picture gripped tightly in my fist. It grew dark and the clouds parted, revealing the bright full moon. Slipping past the cemetery gates, I made my way along the now all-too-familiar route to Sara's grave. I had come here dozens of times in the months since her death. But tonight I felt scared and excited and maybe just a little bit insane.

Reaching the grave, I stood on the soft grass, looking down at the headstone. Then, staring at the photo, I said the words for the first time:

"Ancient spirits, lift the one who is gone and cut the pain from my soul."

Nothing happened. Was this all a cruel joke? Was Madame LaRue a fake?

Then, without warning, the ground beneath my feet began to move. I glanced down, and the grass was being sucked into the earth by its roots. The dark, fresh soil shifted beneath my feet, bubbling up like boiling water.

Oh my God! She's alive! She's coming to me!

"Ancient spirits, lift the one who is gone and cut the pain from my soul," I shouted, for the second time.

A horrible wailing moan filled the silent cemetery, sending chills through my bones. I was terrified and deliriously happy all at once.

"Sara!" I cried out. "Sara, is that you?"

"Owwwww!"

The moans turned to cries of pain, and I felt sick to my stomach.

"Ancient spirits, lift the one who is gone and cut the pain from my soul."

As I finished the sentence for the third time, the stench of rotting flesh battered my nostrils. The odor was horrible. I choked and coughed, then puked my guts out.

What if this isn't the Sara I know coming back? What if it's some kind of rotting creature?

Still clinging to some small shred of hope, I repeated the phrase for the fourth time.

"Ancient spirits, lift the one who is gone and cut the pain from my soul."

The unmistakable crunching of footsteps on leaves threaded its way through the still night air. *She's coming! Sara is coming back to me.* I looked all around, hoping to catch a glimpse of her in the moonlight.

But the smell got worse as the footsteps drew closer. Then I remembered Madame LaRue's words:

You will get precisely what you asked for.

When you have repeated the phrase for the fifth and final time, she will be revealed.

Revealed? A horrible image flashed into my head. Sara in her beautiful yellow dress, now torn to shreds and covered in dirt, her decaying flesh hanging in clumps from her exposed skeleton.

You will get precisely what you asked for.

I'd asked to see Sara again. I'd asked for her to be alive. But I'd forgotten to say "alive as she was in life!" I had brought Sara back, but not as the beautiful girl I loved. She would be nothing but a rotten corpse walking the earth as the living dead! And now she was walking toward me.

"No!" I screamed. "This is all wrong!"

She will be revealed.

"No, I won't say it a fifth time. I don't want her to be revealed. I don't want to see Sara like this!"

I turned and hurried from the grave, glancing down at the picture in my hand. This is how I want to remember her. Beautiful and fully alive. As I reached the cemetery gate, I heard a soft sobbing.

Sara! I would recognize her crying anywhere. But I couldn't look back. I gently kissed the photograph and forced myself to keep walking.

The cemetery fell silent once again.

MAINE
Haunted Movie Theater

What I learned in history class: In 1839, there was a border dispute between Maine and New Brunswick, Canada. Known as the Aroostook War, the conflict was an undeclared and bloodless confrontation that heightened tensions between the United States and Great Britain. The issue was eventually determined by the Webster-Ashburton Treaty of 1842.

A story you won't find in your textbook: My parents' idea of a fun time on vacation is visiting every single gallery and boutique in town. When we visited Portland, Maine, I begged them to let me hang out in town solo. There were a ton of comic book stores I wanted to check out, plus I was dying to see a movie. Okay, "dying to see a movie" might not be the best expression to use before telling this story!

◉◉

I first noticed the weird woman across the aisle from me in the old Strand Theater while I was checking out the amazing mural painted on the theater's wall. It depicted scenes from the early part of the twentieth century in a New England town, which I guess could have been Portland itself. I imagined myself traveling back in time and walking around in the old town. After a few minutes, I came back to my senses. That's when I saw the woman.

She looked to be twenty or thirty years old, and she was dressed in the clothing of the period shown in the mural. She wore a long black dress, high boots, and a ruffled blouse that buttoned up to her neck. Her hair was wrapped into a tight bun on top of her head.

It was kind of eerie, like she had just stepped out of the painting on the wall. I know, I have an active imagination, and the idea of someone stepping out of a painting is a little silly. Still, there was something odd about her.

"It's Portland, you know," she said softly.

Who was she talking to? I glanced over my shoulder. There was only a handful of people in the theater, and nobody else seemed to notice her. I turned back, and she was staring right at me.

"Excuse me?" I said.

"The mural," she said again, softly. "It's Portland, about a hundred years ago."

She'd obviously noticed me observing the painting.

"Thanks," I said. I can be pretty bold, but I stopped myself from asking why she was wearing weird clothes. Not everything strange is supernatural . . . some people are just crazy!

"Would you like to see it?" she asked. "Portland, one hundred years ago, I mean."

Well, that explains the clothing, I thought. *This woman is nuts!*

"How would we do that?" I asked as politely as I could.

"The movie set," she replied. "Haven't you seen it?"

I shook my head.

"Just a few blocks from here is a re-creation of Portland from the early twentieth century," she explained. "For the film."

Now it made sense. They were shooting a film here that was set in the town a hundred years ago. And she was an actor playing a role in the movie.

"Sure," I said, thinking that a tour of a movie set with one of the actors would be pretty cool.

"My name is Gertrude Watts," the woman said as we left the theater and stepped out into the bright sunshine.

"Jason Specter," I said, shaking her hand. "I'm not from around here."

"I could tell," she said, smiling.

She led me to the end of Hancock Street. We turned the corner, and I could hardly believe my eyes. It was like stepping back in time. An amazing re-creation of the town of Portland one hundred years ago stretched out before us.

We walked past a general store, a barbershop, a bank, and a hotel before coming to a stop in front of the Hancock Tavern.

"Take a look," Gertrude said.

Using my sleeve to wipe the dust off the window, I peered inside. The place was a scene of loud, bustling activity. A piano player in a red-striped shirt with a handlebar mustache played a lively rag. Waitresses carrying trays full of beer hurried past tables filled with poker players smoking big cigars. The bar was packed, a haze of smoke hung over the sawdust-covered floor, and the crowd seemed to be having a great time.

"Very cool," I said, impressed by the attention to every detail. "They must be filming right now, huh? I guess you're not in this scene."

Gertrude smiled, and we continued down the street. In the dry-goods store, a woman dressed in the same style as Gertrude bought a bolt of fabric. A man in the hardware store wearing an old-time suit bought a long, wooden-handled shovel. At the end of the block, the stable was filled with horses.

"This is pretty amazing!" I said, watching a blacksmith put a shoe on one of the horses. "I never saw a movie being filmed before."

The tour ended and Gertrude headed back toward the theater. I walked beside her.

"When do you shoot your scenes?" I asked.

"Oh, my scenes are all finished," she replied. "I've given my last performance."

Again, I was embarrassed to ask her why she still had her costume on if she was finished filming.

When we reached the Strand, Gertrude smiled, waved, and then stepped back into the theater. "Thanks," I called out as she disappeared into the darkened building. "That was fun."

I turned to a man standing outside the theater. "I just got a tour of the movie set," I told him. "They did an awesome job. Do you know when they'll be done filming?"

The man looked at me strangely. "They finished filming here five years ago," he said. "We just left the set up as a tourist attraction."

"Oh, so now you hire actors to dress up and give tours, and act out the roles of people in the old-time town and stuff?" I asked.

"No," he replied. "There's no one in the old town. It's just a set."

"What about Gertrude?" I asked, growing curious and a little concerned.

"Gertrude? Do you mean Gertrude Watts?" he asked.

"Yeah, exactly," I replied. "She just gave me a tour of the movie set, and the place was wild! There were people all over the set in costumes acting out scenes."

The man smiled to himself and shook his head.

"Son, you did get to experience something pretty cool. Now, don't be scared, but Gertrude Watts was my great-great-grandmother," the man explained. "She was an actress who performed here at the Strand a hundred years ago, back when they did live plays. During a performance, a stage light fell on her and killed her. Her ghost has been haunting the Strand ever since."

I dashed inside the theater and looked around, but saw no sign of Gertrude.

"Oh, you won't find her," the man said when I hurried back outside. "She finds you."

I ran back to the movie set, my mind racing and my paranormal sensors on overload. Pulling open the door of the Hancock Tavern, I stepped inside. Only, there was no one inside—no poker players, no waitresses, no sawdust, not even a floor! The front of the tavern was just a wooden flat supported by braces. I stepped through and found myself looking at the back of a modern building, just behind the set.

Apparently, the man at the Strand was right. Gertrude Watts *had* found me and showed me a glimpse of the world she had lived in one hundred years ago.

As weird and freaky as the whole experience was, it sure beat hanging out with my parents!

MARYLAND
The True Story Behind
The Exorcist

What I learned in history class: Francis Scott Key wrote "The Star-Spangled Banner" during the War of 1812. In what would later be known as the Battle of Baltimore, the British began attacking Fort McHenry on September 13, 1814. The bombardment lasted through the night. At dawn, Key was thrilled to see that the fort was still flying the American flag.

A story you won't find in your textbook: I'm sure you won't be surprised to learn that I'm a total scary-movie buff, but *The Exorcist* remains my all-time favorite. I've seen it a million times, but I'm always completely creeped out when I watch it. I knew that the movie was adapted from a book, and that the book was based on true events. I figured it was worth a shot to use my blog to try to track down the main character in the book and movie, Regan Teresa MacNeil. Before long, I got this reply from Jake Marriot of Eldersburg, Maryland. Boy, did I feel dumb!

◉◉

Jason, for someone who loves *The Exorcist* and claims to be an expert on the paranormal, you sure didn't do your homework. Yes, the story is true, but it didn't happen to Regan Teresa MacNeil.

The first thing you need to know is that the kid who got possessed by a demonic spirit was actually a boy. In the book and movie, they changed the character to a girl to protect the boy's identity.

A thirteen-year-old boy named Roland lived with his parents in a two-story house in Cottage City, Maryland. One night in January of 1949, the boy was awakened by scratching noises, which seemed to come from behind his bedroom walls and ceiling. Roland's parents called an exterminator to rid the room of mice, but the exterminator didn't find any evidence of rodents, and the noises only became louder and more aggressive as the nights wore on.

Then his bed began to shake violently in the middle of the night. Roland bolted upright in terror. His blankets were yanked from the bed. If he grabbed the blankets to stop them from flying off, he was pulled from the bed and dragged along the floor until he let go.

Objects in his room began moving on their own. Pictures flew off the walls for no reason, the frames shattering as they slammed to the floor. Books tumbled off the shelves and drawers flew open, ejecting clothes into the air.

But these strange incidents took place only when Roland was in the room. During the day, all was quiet.

Roland's parents grew terrified and turned to the minister at their Lutheran church for help. Reverend Luther Schulze told them that he thought Roland was under attack by an evil supernatural force. He took Roland to church and said special prayers to protect him from demons. But the prayers didn't help. The attacks continued.

Reverend Schulze began to wonder whether it was the house that was haunted or the boy himself. He suggested that Roland and his family spend the night in his house so he could see if anything unusual happened to the boy in another location. Roland's parents agreed.

That night, in Reverend Schulze's house, Roland's parents and the reverend watched as the bed in which Roland was sleeping shook and rattled, bouncing across the room. Loud scratching noises were heard, just like the ones in Roland's room at home.

The reverend prayed for the shaking to stop, but that only made it worse. Roland moved to a heavy armchair in the reverend's living room and tried to fall asleep there. The moment he settled into the chair, it started rocking back and forth. The hefty upholstered chair then rammed into the wall, tossing Roland to the hard wood floor.

Returning to the upstairs bedroom, the reverend folded and stacked several blankets on the floor. Roland soon fell asleep on top of the blankets but was startled awake when the pile slid across the room. He sat up quickly, terrified, and struck his head against the side of the bed as the blankets slid under the box spring.

Roland's head hurt from the bump, but a sudden pain in his stomach caused the boy to double over. His mother lifted his pajama shirt and stumbled back in shock. There, scratched across the boy's chest and stomach in bleeding welts, were the words *hell* and *Satan*.

The family was convinced that Roland had been possessed by an evil demon, and they turned to a Catholic priest in the nearby town of Mount Rainier. Father Edward Hughes was skeptical at first, and unwilling to get involved with this unusual case. He did agree to meet with the boy, however, when he saw how upset Roland's parents were. During their meeting, Roland spoke to Father Hughes in Latin, a language the boy had never studied.

This convinced the priest to attempt an exorcism. After receiving permission from his archbishop, Father Hughes attempted the exorcism at Georgetown Hospital in nearby Washington, D.C. During the procedure, Roland fell into a trance, then began struggling against the priest, waving his arms and kicking his legs wildly. He spoke in several languages, a few of which were unidentifiable.

When Father Hughes tried to restrain him, the boy slashed the priest with a piece of the metal bedspring, which he had managed to tear loose. Exhausted, Father Hughes gave up and told the family he couldn't help them.

Relatives of Roland's mother suggested they contact

Reverend Raymond Bishop, a priest in St. Louis with some experience in these matters. Reverend Bishop agreed to meet with the family.

On the night before they left for St. Louis, Roland felt a sharp, burning pain in his back. Removing his pajama top, his mother saw the words *no* and *Louis* carved into the boy's skin in deep, bloody scratches. Apparently, whatever possessed Roland didn't want them to go to St. Louis. Perhaps they were on to something.

In St. Louis, Reverend Bishop referred the family to Father William Bowdern, who decided to stage another exorcism. The ritual was held at the home of Roland's relatives in St. Louis. As Father Bowdern began praying for the evil spirit to leave Roland's body, Roland curled up into a ball and cried out in pain as cuts and welts spread all over him.

He screamed out obscenities in a variety of voices, ranging from a man's deep voice to the high squeal of a little girl. Father Bowdern limited this session to just a few minutes, but he realized that it would be the first of many.

The exorcism went on for weeks, during which time Roland became more violent and abusive. He hurled curses at the priest in many languages. He spat and vomited and urinated on the priest, while screaming about private matters in Father Bowdern's life that he could not possibly have known about.

Each night, Roland's body would contort into impossible, inhuman positions as he hurled abuse at Father Bowdern. Each morning, Roland woke up his old self, exhausted but with no memory of what had occurred the previous night.

Late in the second week, Father Bowdern tried a new strategy. He had Roland wear several religious medals while holding a crucifix in his hands. Though he spoke in other voices, Roland remained calm that night. In a soft voice he identified himself as a fallen angel.

Then suddenly, a deep, booming voice took over. "I am Saint Michael the Archangel," Roland announced. "I order you, demon, to depart!"

Roland's body shook horrifically as spasms shot through him. Then he fell back into bed, limp. A few seconds later, his eyes opened. He smiled and said in his own voice, "He's gone. He's gone."

The exorcism had been successful. The family returned home to Maryland, and Roland has since gone on to a happy and successful life, with only the faintest memories of the terrible, supernatural events of 1949.

So, Jason, now you have the real story behind your favorite scary movie. I've been doing research into demons, possessions, and exorcisms for years, and this is one of my faves. I love your Web site, but like I said before—do your paranormal homework, dude!

MASSACHUSETTS
A Lifetime of Visitations

What I learned in history class: Contrary to popular belief, no women were burned at the stake after the Salem witch trials of 1692. Nineteen were hanged and one was pressed to death by stones.

A story you won't find in your textbook: My blogging buddies send me some pretty weird and freaky stories, and I'm happy to read them in the safety of my bedroom. Sometimes, though, I get a story that I wish I had uncovered—call it paranormal envy. HeavyMettle in Newton, Massachusetts, usually sends me stuff about Revolutionary War ghosts (*zzzzz*) but when I got his e-mail about his meeting with Jean Altman, I was kicking myself. I love alien abductions, especially first-person accounts!

From: HeavyM@massnet.com
To: Jspecter@scarystatesofamerica.com
Subject: abducted (no, really!)

S'up, Specter? I was sorry to see that my run-in with Paul Revere's ghost failed to win a spot on your blog, but I know you won't be able to resist featuring my latest encounter.

I got an e-mail from a friend of a friend asking me to meet with this lady named Jean Altman. It seemed she was having a hard time finding anyone to believe her abduction story. UFO abductions aren't my specialty (sorry, dude, but no matter what you think, Revolutionary War spirits are *way* cooler!) but I thought I'd meet with Ms. Altman just the same. I felt bad for the lady. I knew she could be telling the truth and no one would listen to her. I've met people who've encountered aliens. I even have some evidence. So I figured that the least I could do was let her know she wasn't completely alone.

Our mutual friend made the intros at a local Starbucks and then ducked out. Jean looked pale and tired, her fingers thin and bony.

"You're not going to laugh at me, are you?" she asked anxiously, looking around at a couple of empty seats nearby.

"No way," I replied quickly as we sat down. "I want to hear

your story." I thought of telling her about some folks I've met and others you've featured on your site. But I just pulled out my digital pocket memo recorder and leaned back in my chair. She stared at me for a while, then looked away, glancing down at the floor. Then she told me her story.

◉◉

Jean Altman's first encounter with the alien beings who would visit her a number of times throughout her life took place when she was just six years old. While playing in her backyard one day, she felt dizzy. The world started spinning and then everything suddenly faded to black. As she tumbled to the grass, just before she lost consciousness, Jean heard a soft, thin voice say, "You are progressing well." The next thing she remembered was waking up, thinking she had simply stumbled. She went on playing, quickly forgetting the event.

Five years later, at age eleven, Jean had an identical experience. This time, she was sitting at her desk doing her homework when the dizziness washed over her. Again, she blacked out, her head landing on her schoolbooks. And again she heard the high-pitched voice say, "You are progressing well." Waking up a few minutes later, she assumed that she had just dozed off in the middle of a particularly tough homework assignment.

On a clear, moonless night a year later, the aliens returned. This time, they took twelve-year-old Jean with them. She was out in the yard when she glanced skyward and saw what appeared to be the moon rising over the horizon.

But she knew right away that it wasn't the moon. The glowing white circle in the sky moved too quickly and then expanded, until it had filled her entire field of vision.

Then, without her even being aware of any transition, Jean found herself inside a white room, the glow in the sky replaced by white walls, floor, and ceiling. She panicked, banging her fists against the wall, trying to comprehend what had happened.

"Where am I?" she shouted. "Let me out! I want to go home!"

That's when she spotted three small humanoids with large bulbous heads in the room beside her.

"Yaaa!" Jean screeched in terror. "What's happening? I want to wake up now!"

But Jean didn't wake up, and her living nightmare continued. The beings in the room surrounded her, looking her over, poking and prodding.

"Leave me alone!" she cried, although at no point were they actually hurting her. "I want to go home!" But the ordeal went on. Jean later recalled that the creatures had large almond-shaped eyes, small flat noses, and tiny slits for mouths. During her abduction, the aliens never uttered a sound, yet they seemed to somehow communicate with one another.

After a while, the aliens pushed Jean onto a cushioned seat in a spherical glass container. "Let me out!" she bellowed as the glass container slammed shut, trapping her inside. Her desperate cries for help echoed weakly within her transparent prison, even as she banged her fists on the glass.

The large, clear capsule then dropped through the floor, plunging into a body of water. "I'm gonna die!" Jean screamed. "I'm gonna drown!" She cried hysterically, then realized she could easily breathe as her glass craft drifted quickly through the water, surfacing inside an icy tunnel.

The opaque glistening walls of the tunnel were lined with a series of thick crystalline blocks. Jean was horrified to see that sealed within each block, a human figure stood frozen, embedded in the ice, like a fly trapped in prehistoric amber.

"Oh, no!" she whimpered, pounding again on the glass. "I'm next! I'm their next victim." She swallowed hard as her throat tightened in panic.

The figures were a sampling of people of all races from all over the world, and, as she could tell from their clothing, from various periods in human history. Apparently, these visitors had been coming to Earth for some time and had stopped in all regions of the planet to gather specimens for their museum of human beings.

Terror overtook her, and she was certain that she was about to become the next exhibit in this gruesome display. Her glass capsule plunged into the water once again. She resurfaced inside a large building that looked like an airplane hangar. Floating along an indoor river, Jean peered through the glass of the capsule and saw many planes, which also appeared to be from different periods of human history.

"Maybe it'll be okay?" she said to herself hopefully. "But where am I?"

And then she was no longer encased in the capsule, no longer floating on a river. Not sure how she had gotten free, Jean walked among what she later called a forest of clear glass. Tall, shimmering spokes seemed to sprout from the ground, surrounding her in a maze. A sense of calm and peace overcame her, replacing the panic and terror. A now-familiar voice filled her head.

"Say nothing of this to anyone," the thin, piercing voice commanded. "Forget your travels. We will return for you."

In the blink of an eye, Jean found herself back in her yard. The glowing disc was no longer in the sky, and all memory of the abduction had vanished.

True to their word, the aliens returned for Jean. This time, nineteen years had passed since her last abduction. Now thirty-one, Jean was living outside Newton with her husband and their three children. Her parents had come to stay with her while her husband recuperated in the hospital from a job injury.

One evening, Jean was cleaning up in the kitchen while her parents and children played a board game in the living room. At eight-thirty, all the lights in the house flickered and went out.

Before anyone could grab a flashlight, an eerie orange beam of light poured through the kitchen window, illuminating the house in its pulsating glow.

Jean's father dashed into the kitchen while her mother comforted the frightened children. He peered out the window to find the source of the strange light and spotted five small figures hopping quickly toward the house.

Jean and her father looked on in amazement as the five beings passed right through a solid wood door like ghosts and stepped into the kitchen.

"Dad, what's happening?" Jean cried.

She got no response. Her parents and her children had fallen into a trancelike state of suspended animation, motionless, eyes glazed over.

Jean, on the other hand, was shaking in fear. Then, as if someone had flipped on a light that had been off for years, she suddenly recognized the short, gray-skinned intruders.

"Oh my God!" Jean whispered as the memory of her first abduction came flooding back. "No! Not you! *Not again! I won't go!*"

Jean had been a kid that first time they took her. Now, as she thought about her own children, anger and fear boiled up inside her. She turned to run, hoping to grab a kitchen knife or anything else she could find to use as a weapon, but she was unable to move. Some invisible force was holding her in place.

One of the aliens reached out its three-fingered hand and touched Jean's head. Voices flooded Jean's mind in a confusing, garbled mess of sounds. Then the noises quieted and a single high-pitched voice rang out in her head.

"Your family will not be harmed," the voice said, as if the creature had read her thoughts.

Jean felt a calmness wash over her. Then the alien continued.

"You will not be harmed either."

Unable to resist, and no longer sure that she wanted to, Jean followed the visitors out to her backyard, where she was stunned to see their waiting spacecraft. The metallic, disc-shaped ship glowed orange. A hatch slid open and she followed the aliens inside.

When the door closed behind them, the aliens placed Jean on a circular disc of jellylike material. Wires were inserted into her nose and navel. She cried out in pain, and one of the creatures quickly placed a triangular disc of silvery blue metal on her forehead. The pain vanished instantly.

Following the examination, Jean was put into a clear glass capsule, similar to the one she had traveled in during her previous abduction. This time, a thick gray fluid filled the enclosure, surrounding her and protecting her during the journey from Earth to the aliens' home planet. Somehow, she was still able to breathe.

The ship lifted off, and after what seemed like only a few seconds, they arrived at their destination. Jean emerged from her glass capsule and left the ship along with two of her captors, stepping out into a long stone corridor. Standing on a small platform, they were carried along a moving track that glided through a lifeless landscape of rock.

They approached what appeared to be a large mirror

that loomed like a gleaming wall at the end of the tunnel. Fearing they would crash into its smooth surface, Jean tensed. One of the creatures took her hand, and again a sense of calm passed through her being. Reaching the end of the tunnel, Jean and the aliens passed right through the silvery wall.

They emerged on the other side, into a huge underground landscape bathed in green light. A mist-covered lake and lush, tropical vegetation spread out before them. In the distance Jean could see a city of crystal buildings.

An enormous bird landed in their path. The wondrous creature looked like an eagle but stood more than ten feet tall, with brilliant multicolored feathers covering its body. Intense heat and blinding light radiated from the bird, and a voice again filled Jean's head.

"You have been chosen," the voice said, and Jean knew that the great bird was speaking to her. But it didn't say for *what* Jean had been chosen. It identified itself as the group's leader and introduced itself as Quazgaa. "I will give you formulas to help humanity, but only when humans have learned to look within their spirits."

Jean later recalled the experience as a spiritual awakening, though she had no memory of any specific formulas that could help humankind. Packed once again within her capsule, she was returned to her home.

Stepping from the alien ship into her fog-shrouded backyard, Jean saw that it was still night. She found her family exactly as she had left them. With a blinding red flash, the ship vanished, and her family emerged from their trance, with no memory of what had happened.

Glancing at the clock, Jean saw that a mere four hours had passed since the aliens' arrival. Exhausted, she fell into a deep sleep.

When she awoke the next morning, Jean recalled the entire experience. But when she mentioned it to her father, he thought at first that she was kidding. Then, when she insisted that she was serious, he suggested she see a psychologist.

No one believed her. It caused stress with her family and with the few friends she confided in; some of her friends even stopped calling her. She began hearing whispers of "UFO nut" behind her back.

When her husband came home from the hospital, he said he believed her, but Jean could see in his eyes that he was just trying to be supportive. Like everyone else, he wished Jean could give up her crazy story and get on with her life.

"So," Jean said when she had finished her story. "Do you believe me?"

"Of course," I said, reaching into my backpack. "I want to show you something I brought."

I pulled out a triangular disc of silvery blue metal.

Jean gasped. "That's the disc they used to take my pain away on the ship!" she cried, tears streaming down her face.

"Another abductee I met gave it to me as a thank-you for believing him," I explained. "Here, you take it."

I handed the disc to Jean, hoping that it might, once again, take away her pain.

So, Specter, there's my story. Jealous?

Of course I was jealous! I've got to get out on the road more often.

MICHIGAN
Television Premonition

What I learned in history class: In 1701, Antoine Laumet de La Mothe Cadillac, a French explorer and administrator, founded Fort Pontchartrain-du-Détroit in what is now Detroit, Michigan. The Cadillac automobile is named after him.

A story you won't find in your textbook: Not everyone who sends me stories is a paranormal collector like me and my blogging buddies. A lot of people who send stuff to my Web site are people who didn't go looking for the weird and unexplained—it just came looking for them. One kid, Rachel Miller from Lansing, Michigan, sent me this e-mail.

From: Rmiller@lancom.net
To: Jspecter@scarystatesofamerica.com
Subject: what happened to me

Hi, Jason.

I feel kinda weird writing to you. I don't even know you, and, no offense, but a month ago I probably would have thought someone like you was a paranoid nerd making a big deal out of nothing. But then something happened to me—and either I'm completely insane or some stuff just can't be explained. I started doing some research online—I've had a lot of time since the accident. I found your site, and reading the accounts on there helped me, so I figured sharing my own story might help others. Anyway, do you want to hear my story? This really happened to me a few weeks ago.

RM

Sometimes I still wonder if I'm a paranoid nerd, but stories like Rachel's make me believe I'm on to something real. Here's what she wrote to me.

◉◉

It figures. A month after I get my license, I wreck my brandnew car. Not to mention my leg. Okay, so it's ten years old—the car, not my leg—and it used to be my dad's, but to me it's new. Anyway, the car was back from the shop, but I still had two weeks to sit in the house by myself with my left leg in a cast, hobbling around on crutches.

I was soooo bored! I never thought I'd say this, but I really missed being in school. I mean, all my friends are there. There's no one to IM during a boring weekday afternoon, so I'd just sit around and watch daytime TV. *Lame!*

Then one day the really weird thing happened. I was watching some dumb soap opera on a local channel when it was interrupted by a news bulletin.

"This is a special report," the announcer said urgently. "An explosion has ripped through Lansing High School."

"Oh my God!" I shouted, grabbing the remote and raising the volume.

"Two students and one teacher are confirmed dead, and dozens more are injured. The fire continues to rage out of control as firefighters from four communities battle the blaze. It is believed the explosion took place in the chemistry lab."

I watched in horror as terrible images flashed across the screen. The school was a blazing inferno. Orange flames and thick black clouds of smoke poured from every window of the three-story building.

"The chem lab!" I cried, looking over at the clock. I realized with horror that if I'd been in school that day, I would have been in chemistry class at that exact moment.

Robin! My best friend and lab partner, Robin Richards, was in that classroom!

I snatched up my crutches and hobbled across the living room. *Where did I leave my cell phone? Got to call Robin! Oh my God, how can this happen? Where's the damn phone?*

I looked over at the kitchen table. The phone was right

where I had left it. A couple more crutch hops and I was there. I hit Robin's cell number on speed dial. *Come on, come on, why do they call this stupid thing speed dial!*

It was ringing.

Pick up, pick up, pick—

Click.

"Hey, it's Robin. Tell me something exciting. Call ya back. Bye!"

Beeeeeeep . . .

"Robin, I heard about the explosion," I practically screamed into the phone. "Tell me you're all right. Please tell me you're all right!"

I clicked off and stared down at the phone. Like that was gonna make Robin call me back. I had to do something. I couldn't just sit around here while my school burned down. Looking back, maybe it was a crazy idea. Maybe I should have called the school. But I wasn't thinking straight. All I could think about were those poor kids in my chem class.

All I could think about was Robin.

I grabbed my car keys and hobbled out the front door. I sat behind the wheel of my car with my crutches in the seat beside me and my left leg in its cast extended next to the brake. The doctor told me not to drive until the cast came off, but this was clearly an emergency.

As I turned the key and the car started, a wave of fear rushed through me. This was the first time I had been in the car since the accident. My mind flashed back to that day: the horrible crunching sound, the screeching brakes, my own voice screaming, the searing pain in my leg. It all rushed back to me and mixed with the terror and worry I now felt for Robin and everyone else in my school. I burst into tears. But I had to go. I slipped the car into reverse and backed out onto the street.

I'm only five minutes away, I thought as I put the car into drive and stepped gently on the gas pedal, my right hand shaking on the steering wheel, my left hand holding my left leg off to the side. *I'll make it.*

With one hand on the wheel, I started the trip to my school, a trip I had made hundreds of times before. But somehow it all felt strange, as if I'd never driven on these roads. The houses and stores zipped past. I knew them like I knew my own name. But today they looked different.

My brain began to argue with itself.

She'll be all right. Everyone'll be all right.

How can she be all right? They said the fire was raging out of control!

I forced myself to focus on driving.

As I approached the school, I peered into the sky, expecting to see smoke.

But the sky was clear.

I rolled down my window, listening for sirens.

Everything was quiet.

Is it all over already? Is the whole school gone?

I swung around the final bend to school and held my breath. I bit my lip. *There it is!*

There it is? All of it. Perfectly normal. No smoke. No flames. No nothing.

Was I losing my mind? Had I fallen asleep and dreamed that TV report?

I pulled up to the curb right in front of the school building and parked the car beside the NO PARKING ANYTIME sign. Struggling out of the car, I reached back in for my crutches and made my way slowly into the building.

The rubber tips of my crutches squeaked against the linoleum floor, and the bottom of my cast clunked hollowly as I rushed toward the chem lab.

They're gonna think I'm nuts. They're gonna say I fell asleep and dreamed this, or that I'm bored and this is some stupid prank, or—

I stopped short at the door of the lab and peered through the glass.

Empty!

The lab was fine, but no one was in the class. *What is going on here?*

I spun around on my cast leg and shrieked. I was face to face with Robin.

"Oh my God, you're alive!" I cried, dropping my crutches and throwing my arms around her.

"Yeah, Rache," Robin replied, returning the hug before picking up my crutches. "I didn't die, I still come to school even when you don't. Which brings me to . . . what are you *doing* here?"

"I don't know," I said. "I had this crazy dream, and—I better get home before my mom does. She'll go nuts if she finds out I drove!"

"Come on," Robin said. "I'll help you to your car."

"Weren't you supposed to be in chem lab?" I asked as we reached the front door.

"Hello! Today's Thursday, not Tuesday. Lab's fourth period, not third," Robin said.

She was right. It was Thursday. Since I'd been home, the boring days just blended into each other. Half the time I didn't know what day it was.

"I was just getting to lab a couple of minutes early when I saw you and your four legs," Robin explained.

She helped me down the stairs and opened my car door for me.

Briiiiiing!

The bell sounded.

"And now I'm late," she said.

"Sorry, I—"

Ka-thooom!

A thunderous blast exploded from the school. The ground shook, and I fell against my car as glass, steel, and brick rained down on the parking lot.

I screamed. Flames poured from the far end of the building where Robin and I had stood just five minutes earlier.

"Oh my God!" Robin cried.

The front door burst open and panicked, screaming kids poured from the school, followed by thick black smoke.

Robin and I huddled across the street, watching the terrible chaos. I searched the crowd for the other students in my chemistry class. I spotted a few of them, but some were missing. I knew from the TV report that kids had died. A chill shot through me as I realized that if I hadn't come to school when I did, Robin would have been one of them.

I wish I could have saved everyone. If only I had known that I had been seeing the future rather than something that had already happened.

That's why I wrote to you, Jason. I need to figure out what happened to me. It had never happened before. Maybe it won't ever happen again. But if it does, how will I know that I'm looking at the future?

I have to figure it out, so maybe next time I *can* save everyone.

MINNESOTA
The Traveler

What I learned in history class: In 1990, the Mille Lacs Band of Chippewa Indians sued the State of Minnesota, asserting that an 1837 treaty with the U.S. government gave them the right to hunt and fish free of state regulation on land ceded in that treaty. In 1999, the U.S. Supreme Court ruled in their favor.

A story you won't find in your textbook: There are times I wish I could send myself from one place to another via a high-speed broadband connection, like a giant human e-mail. Can someone out there invent that, please? For one man, however, traveling great distances in the blink of an eye was a snap—although it proved to be a huge problem for his family. His daughter sent me this e-mail.

From: Brenda Possoff (bposs@snoworld.net)
To: Jspecter@scarystatesofamerica.com
Subject: I'm scared

Hi, Jason.

I came across your Web site while I was surfing the Net from my new home. I thought maybe you could help explain what happened to me and my mom. Actually, I mean, how my dad did what he did. I'm sorry, I'm not making any sense. Can I just tell you what happened, and why I'm still scared?

Brenda

Of course I told her she could tell me her story. Naturally, I was curious, and she sounded like she could use a friend. Here's the chilling tale she told.

◉◉

My dad's in jail. He's a really bad man. He killed someone. I used to think he was okay, but even when I was little, I didn't know why he was always yelling at my mom. I'm twelve now, and I still don't really understand what he was so mad about all the time.

Anyway, about a year ago, my parents got divorced. Of course it was tough, but I knew my mom was really unhappy, and I was glad that the yelling and fighting would stop. I didn't see him much for the first few months after that.

Even at his worst, I would never have believed that Dad could commit murder! I was really shocked when we found out that he had gotten into a fight at a bar and things had gotten out of hand. The cops said that he smashed some guy over the head with a bar stool, and then kept beating him. The guy died. I was really upset to hear this. I mean, he was still my dad. And that poor guy. Anyway, my dad got arrested and had a trial and now he's in jail. For a long time.

Then, about a month ago, my mom and I were home one night, watching TV, when we heard a noise coming from the basement.

Thwak! Thwak! Thwak!

It sounded like hammering, like someone was down in my dad's old workshop building something.

Thwak! Thwak! Thwak!

My mom got real scared. "Wait here," she said.

"No way!" I shot back. "I'm going with you."

Mom knew better than to argue with me when I was scared. She opened the door leading down to the basement.

Thwak! Thwak! Thwak!

The hammering continued.

"Who's down there?" my mom yelled.

Thwak! Thwak! Thwak!

Whoever it was didn't care that we heard him. That's when I got a whiff of cigar smoke.

I froze and grabbed Mom's arm. "It's Dad!" I whispered. "Do you smell the cigar? Dad's cigars smelled just like that!"

"It can't be Dad, Brenda," Mom said shakily, sniffing the air. "He's in jail in Indiana. Three states away!"

Thwak! Thwak! Thwak!

I gripped Mom's hand tight. "Maybe we should call the police?" I suggested.

"It can't be him down there," she said, walking back into the kitchen and grabbing a sharp knife. "And I'm tired of being afraid in my own house. I lived with that long enough. That part of my life is over. I'm going down there!"

I nodded. I wasn't sure if Mom was being brave or foolish, but I followed her.

Slowly, she eased down the stairs, pausing on each step to listen. The cigar smoke grew thicker as we headed down.

"Mom, the light," I whispered. "The light in Dad's workshop is on!"

Mom did some projects in there now that Dad was gone, but I knew she hadn't gone downstairs in weeks. And *I* certainly hadn't turned the light on.

We're almost there! I thought when we were just two steps from the bottom. *Please don't let it be Dad!*

One more step. I froze. I couldn't move. I was too scared to take the last step. Mom stepped off the final stair and into the basement. Being apart from her was scarier. I hurried down the last step and grabbed her hand.

We both leaned against the wall outside the doorway of the workshop.

Thwak! Thwak! Thwak!

"One, two, three!" Mom whispered.

On "three" we both stepped through the doorway.

The room was empty. But there on the workbench, sitting in Dad's favorite ashtray, was a cigar. And it was still burning! A hammer rested beside it. Next to that sat several pieces of cut wood nailed together and the plans for a large toolbox Dad had planned to build before he moved out.

"Mom, he was here!" I said.

"That's impossible, honey," Mom replied, obviously freaked out at the burning cigar, but relieved that there was no one in the room. "There are no windows in the workshop, and the door we came through is the only way in or out. And we heard the hammering just before we stepped in."

"But how did this happen, then?" I was the kind of kid who always needed a logical explanation for strange stuff. Otherwise, I wouldn't sleep for a week.

Mom just shook her head. "I really don't know."

And so I didn't sleep too well that night. The next day, I came home from school and let myself in, as usual. Mom always got home a couple of hours after me. As I opened the front door, I heard the TV.

Mom would never forget to turn off the TV, I thought. She's a nut about stuff like that, especially now that we're getting by on just her salary. *Maybe she came home early. Maybe she's sick?*

"Mom!" I called out. "Are you home?"

No answer.

I closed the front door and stepped into the living room. That's when I caught a whiff of something that sent shivers down my back.

It was the musty, sweet smell of a man's cologne—Dad's cologne. The only kind he ever wore. I'd know it anywhere. It was a sense memory that hit me like a ton of bricks. I grabbed the doorknob and flung open the front door. No way was I staying in that house. How could Dad have gotten out of jail? What did he want from us?

Just before I ran back out, I glanced over my shoulder into the living room. There, on the table next to Dad's favorite chair, sat a glass I hadn't seen in over a year—Dad's favorite scotch glass, the one he got the time we visited Toronto. The glass was half filled with a light brown liquid. I didn't bother to smell it. I knew it was scotch. Dad never allowed anybody else to use it, and he never put anything besides scotch in that glass.

I flung the door open and ran outside. I kept running, turning over the facts in my mind again and again. The hammer, the cigar, the TV, the cologne, the glass of scotch. It all added up to just one answer—Dad!

I called Mom at work on my cell phone. I tried to hide just how freaked out I was, but Mom can always tell. She left work early and met me at the park. Then she called the police from her cell phone and they met us at the house.

Mom gasped when she stepped inside and saw the TV on and the glass of scotch.

"Dad's cologne," she said.

I nodded. "I smelled it right away."

The police searched every room in the house, but there was no sign of Dad or anyone else. When Mom and I were satisfied that the house was empty, we thanked the police and tried to settle down as we worked on dinner.

"Could someone be playing a trick on us?" I asked. "Trying to scare us?"

"Who would do that?" she replied. "And how could they get into the house? And how did they get out of the workshop last night?"

Mom called Dad's lawyer, the one who handled his murder case and who was also an old friend of both my parents. She didn't tell him about the weird activity at the house, but she did say she was nervous and wanted to make sure that Dad was still behind bars.

"He's still in jail in Indiana, Betty," the lawyer said. "You know he's got a long time to serve."

"Maybe he escaped?" Mom asked desperately.

The lawyer sighed. "I don't think so, but if it will make you feel better, I'll call the penitentiary to make sure."

A short while later the phone rang. It was the lawyer.

"Betty, I just spoke with him," the lawyer said. "I called the penitentiary and used my lawyer-client privilege. They brought him to the phone and we talked for a few minutes. I didn't mention why I was calling, but he told me he hadn't seen the sun shine in six months."

"Thanks, Jim," Mom said. Then she hung up and shook

her head. "He's locked up in Indiana, honey. I'm glad, but I still don't know what's going on."

We were both exhausted and went to bed shortly after dinner. Of course, that doesn't mean that I slept.

At two o'clock in the morning, I heard something move in the corner of my room. "Mom?" I asked, but got no answer.

I sat up and flipped on my lamp. There, leaning against the dresser, was Dad, smoking a cigar and sipping a scotch.

"*Yiiiii!*" I shrieked as I dashed from the room.

Mom met me in the hall.

"What is it?" she asked. "What happened?"

Before I could speak, we both turned and saw Dad standing in the doorway of my room, smiling.

We tore down the stairs and raced for the front door.

Dad was leaning on the front door, blocking our way.

We ran through the house and out the back door. We dived into the car and Mom sped away.

"It's impossible," she kept saying over and over.

She called the prison herself this time, but they told her that Dad was right there in his cell.

We spent the night at a motel and never went back to the house. We moved into an apartment shortly after that. Then one night the phone rang. I picked it up.

"Hello, sweetheart. Daddy's coming home," said the voice. It was unmistakable. It was my dad! I glanced at the caller ID. It was a pay phone in our area code. Dad was nearby!

We moved again, to a new house, which is where I'm

writing you from. But I'm scared. If Dad can move from place to place like that, if he can get out of a prison three states away and show up here, there's nothing to stop him from finding us anywhere.

He can come and hurt my mom. I don't want to see him ever again.

Can you help us, Jason? Can anybody help us?

MISSISSIPPI
Cemetery Ghost

What I learned in history class: Oxford, Mississippi, was home to one of the twentieth century's greatest writers, William Faulkner. Faulkner, whose most famous works include *The Sound and the Fury, As I Lay Dying*, and *Light in August*, won the Nobel Prize for Literature in 1949.

A story you won't find in your textbook: Occasionally, I get to meet some of my blogging buddies. I was going to be near Greenwood, Mississippi, for my cousin's wedding, so I IM'd one of my online friends, Gothgirl485. She lives in Greenwood, and she's a total vampire and cemetery nut. She collects stories and legends, and even does charcoal rubbings of the gravestones of supposed vampires. When she heard I was going to be near her town, she wanted me to meet her to check out a bizarre statue in a cemetery there.

GG485: JS, s'up, dude? hear u'll be in MS.

ParaGuy: yeah, near greenwood.

GG485: my home sweet home. god, i hate it here! the girls in my school are southern belles. they all think they're scarlett o'hara! all that pink makes me wanna puke.

ParaGuy: what do they think about u?

GG485: they think i'm dracula's girl-friend!

ParaGuy: LOL! it sucks to be differ-ent!

GG485: whatever. it's actually kinda fun to freak them out. anyway, gotta show u something. can we meet when u'r in greenwood?

ParaGuy: whatcha got?

GG485: cemetery ghost, moving statue.

ParaGuy: cool. i am so there!

◉◉

I planned to meet Gothgirl at the entrance to the Hudson Park Cemetery in Greenwood. Like many cemeteries around the country, this one is filled with creepy legends. I was getting psyched about whatever Gothgirl was going to show me. I was also interested in meeting her and finally seeing what she looked like.

The bus from town dropped me in front of the cemetery's main gate. No sign of Gothgirl. It was a clear, sunny day, so the cemetery didn't feel all that scary. It also meant that we weren't going to see what Gothgirl hoped to show me. But I didn't know that at the time.

After a couple of minutes, I spotted a girl on a bicycle pedaling up the bumpy road leading to the cemetery. As she got closer, I knew it had to be Gothgirl. Her T-shirt was black. So was the long skirt she wore. Her jet black hair was right out of a bottle. Her pale white skin looked drained of color, and it set off her bright red lipstick all the more. Oh, yeah. Her bike was completely black too, right down to the painted chrome handlebars.

She skidded to a stop and jumped off the bike, all in one not-so-smooth motion. Her black Doc Martens skidded along the dusty ground.

"Jason?" she asked, raising her thin, arched eyebrows.

She was kinda pretty, although the nose ring and lip stud distracted me. So did the tattoo on her neck of two small round puncture wounds with tiny trickles of blood dripping from them.

I told you she was a vampire freak.

"Hey," I said, waving feebly. "You must be Gothgirl."

"Yeah," she replied, looking up at the clear blue sky. "My real name's Louanne. So you can figure why I use Gothgirl."

"I don't know," I said. "Louanne's kinda pretty."

She looked at me like I had called her a mass murderer, which, now that I think of it, might have been less offensive to her than *Louanne*. She raised those eyebrows again and shook her head.

"Well, I guess it's kinda pretty if you're the type of girl who likes wearing pink," I said, trying to recover. "I'll just call you Gothgirl."

"Whatever," she replied, leading me into the cemetery. "We're not gonna see anything happen today. The weather's too nice. But they're predicting storms for tomorrow. I wanted to show you the statue anyway. You staying for a couple days?"

"I'll be around tomorrow," I replied, though I wasn't sure I wanted to commit to another day of hanging out with Gothgirl. She wasn't exactly warm and friendly.

On the walk through the cemetery, Gothgirl filled me in on the story of six-year-old Jennifer Regan, whose grave we were going to see. Jennifer died about ten years ago and was buried in Hudson Park Cemetery. Her devastated parents commissioned a life-sized statue of Jennifer, swinging happily on a swing. The statue now rests atop her tombstone. Playing on swings was one of Jennifer's favorite activities. Now her happy, smiling face is permanently captured in marble as she kicks her feet toward the sky.

Jennifer, it seems, was always terrified of thunder. She would run into the house and hide under her covers whenever a thunderstorm blew through Greenwood. So now, Gothgirl explained, if you look at the statue during a thunderstorm, you'll see only an empty swing. The carved figure of Jennifer vanishes, hiding from the thunder, only to return when the storm passes.

"There it is," Gothgirl said as we approached Jennifer's grave. Sitting on the grave was an amazingly lifelike statue.

Gleaming sunshine glistened off the flawless white marble. Staring at the smiling little girl, I sensed that Jennifer must really have been a happy child. The statue captured her sense of joy, with no hint that her life would be tragically cut short.

I also got the strong feeling that Jennifer knew I was watching her.

"You okay, Jason?" Gothgirl asked after a minute. I guess she could tell that the statue freaked me out. "You look like you just saw a ghost."

"Maybe I did," I said, but I kept what I'd felt to myself.

"Wait until the storm comes," Gothgirl replied ominously. "I'll meet you back here at the grave tomorrow."

I watched as she rode off on her bike, thinking about how tough it must be to live in a town where everyone thought you were a freak. Then again, I'm not exactly the average boy-next-door back home, either!

When I woke up the next morning, I was thrilled to discover a completely gray sky. It darkened as the morning wore on. I grabbed an umbrella and hopped on the bus back to Hudson Park.

The first drops of rain started to fall as I entered the cemetery. *Cue the scary music!* I thought, opening my umbrella. Looking around, I saw no one else there. *Of course.*

Who in their right mind goes to visit a cemetery during a thunderstorm? That would be me . . . and my friend Gothgirl.

The rain fell harder, pounding the stone slabs and marble mausoleums in torrential curtains of water. The sky grew inky black, and the huge clouds formed a heavy ceiling over my head.

Walking quickly, fighting the wind with my umbrella and beginning to wonder if this was such a great idea after all, I peered through the sheets of tumbling rain and spotted Jennifer's grave. I could just make out the little girl on the swing through the swirling fog, which now joined the downpour in a sloppy soup of nasty weather. Someone tapped me on the shoulder and I jumped two feet into the air. My sneaker landed right in a muddy puddle as I turned and saw Gothgirl.

"What's the matter, ghost hunter, a little jumpy?" she asked, smiling for the first time since I'd met her.

"I'm okay," I said, standing with my foot in eight inches of water. "Forget your umbrella?"

"Don't believe in them," she replied as her mascara ran down her face in streaks of black.

Kaboom!

The first clap of thunder made me drop my umbrella. Not that it was doing me much good. My clothes were soaked and my shoes were completely waterlogged.

"I meant to do that," I said, leaving my umbrella on the ground.

Lightning flashed, splitting the sky in half and illuminating the headstones for a brief second. I flinched.

"Looks like Jennifer's not the only one afraid of thunderstorms," Gothgirl said. "Me, I love 'em!"

"I'm not afraid," I said, squishing closer to the statue.

Kaboom!

The second explosion of thunder was much louder than the first. The rain fell harder, which I didn't think was possible, and the wind picked up. I could no longer see my feet, which were lost in the fog as I sloshed through the muddy grass.

Kaboom!

The next clap of thunder was unbearably loud and felt like it was right above us.

"Look at the statue," Gothgirl yelled loud enough to be heard above the deafening thunder and the pounding splash of rain.

I glanced up at the marble carving. Jennifer was no longer there.

I know I had seen the statue of the girl just a second earlier as I made my way toward her grave. But now, standing in front of it, I saw only an empty swing.

"That's unreal!" I said, forgetting all about the rain and my soaking sneakers.

"Told ya," Gothgirl said, clearly enjoying showing off her local bit of paranormal craziness.

I walked completely around the statue and the grave, but there was no sign of the girl. "No joke, right?" I asked. "You and your buddies didn't rig this up to fool us out-of-towners?"

"My buddies?" Gothgirl said, sounding incredulous. I guess she really didn't have a lot of friends here.

The thunder, lightning, and rain continued relentlessly as I stared up at the empty swing.

I felt a gentle tap on my shoulder.

"Gothgirl, I'm sorry, I—"

Turning around to apologize, I realized that Gothgirl was gone. There was no one there.

"I'm scared," said a sweet little girl's voice from behind me.

I spun around and squinted through the downpour, but saw no one.

Then someone tapped me on the shoulder again. I jumped and spun all in one awkward motion and found myself looking at Gothgirl.

"Nice move there, Baryshnikov," she said. "Trying out for the ballet?"

"Did you tap me on the shoulder before?" I asked, wiping the water off my forehead.

"Nope," she said. "I was walking completely around the statue, like I usually do, but like always, there was no sign of the girl."

"I'm scared," the voice said again, this time from the direction of the grave.

"You heard that, right?" I said quickly, grabbing Gothgirl's arm. She didn't pull away. "Tell me you heard that."

"Heard what?" she said, then snorted. "Yeah, I heard it; it's definitely Jennifer. I've heard her before, but I can never find her."

I walked completely around the gravesite again. The swing remained empty.

I was facing Gothgirl when I felt a tiny hand tap my shoulder from behind. "Do you see anyone behind me?" I shouted. Panic swelled inside me as I spun around, but again no one was there. I was breathing hard. My heart pounded in my chest. I wanted to run away, but Gothgirl already thought I was a dork—or worse, a coward.

"No one," she said. "I'm telling you, it's Jennifer."

"I'm scared!" said the tiny voice again. Then a soft sobbing poured from the grave. It grew quieter and quieter, until I could hardly make it out.

It was then I noticed that the rain had begun to let up and the sky was brightening. It had been several minutes since the last boom of thunder. The sobbing stopped.

"The storm is passing," I said.

"It's gone," Gothgirl replied. "Look."

I turned toward the grave. There was Jennifer back on her swing, smiling and kicking toward the sky. The swing and tombstone were dripping with rainwater. The statue of Jennifer was perfectly dry.

"That was way cool!" I said, smiling through the water still dripping from my hair. "Thanks, Louanne!"

Gothgirl punched me on the shoulder—hard. I could tell we were going to be great friends!

MISSOURI

The Phantom Firefighter

What I learned in history class: The biggest earthquake in American history took place on December 16, 1811, at approximately 2:00 p.m., in New Madrid, Missouri. Scientists estimate that the quake would have measured 8.7 on the Richter scale.

A story you won't find in your textbook: A fellow collector of paranormal tales from St. Louis, Missouri, who goes by the name of GhostShark, sent me this IM:

> **GS:** Dude, gotta tell u about my brother, Justin.
> **ParaGuy:** Lemme guess. He was abducted

by the psychic ghost of an alien with really big feet!

GS: You are like the weirdest dude, dude!

ParaGuy: So what are you gonna tell me? He went to some haunted house?

GS: Close. Actually, it was a haunted firehouse. He just became a firefighter in St. Louis, and all the rookies in the department have to go through a kind of initiation thing. But this one was weird, dude. Right up your alley. Check it out, Jason. This is the story my brother sent me in an e-mail.

◉◉

Hey, little bro. How are things at home? I know I promised to e-mail you, so here it is. Only thing, don't show this to Mom and Dad. They'd just freak out. You'll know why when you finish reading it.

I was so proud that first day when I put on the uniform. Training was hard, but it was worth it. You know this is all I wanted to do since I was a kid and we used to play fire engine. Now here I am, a real-life firefighter.

The first few days were great. I went out on a couple of calls, got to know the guys at the firehouse, and tried my best not to smile all the time. Then, at the end of that week, I ended up alone in the firehouse. Rookies get left behind on calls that don't require the full team.

I put some equipment away and got our other truck into

shape. I had just finished lining up boots and coiling a hose onto the truck when I noticed a strange noise coming from upstairs. I heard a scraping sound, as if someone were dragging heavy equipment across the floor.

"Hey, who's up there?" I shouted. "I thought you guys were all out?"

The only response was the harsh, metallic scuffing noise again. I put down the hose and bounded up the old metal stairs. "Hello!" I shouted again. The noise grew louder the closer I got to the upper floor.

I stepped off the stairs and flipped on the overhead lights. I saw no one, but I spotted half a dozen oxygen tanks scattered across the room. "Cute, guys!" I said, laughing. "Really nice. You know I stacked fifty of those yesterday."

Again no reply.

The lights went off and I found myself in total darkness.

Feeling my way along the railing, trying hard not to fall down the stairs, I reached the light switch and flipped it back on.

"I know you're messing with the rookie!" I shouted to whoever was hiding. "It's okay. I'll pay my dues and restack 'em."

The lights went off again. I was standing right next to the switch. There was nobody else here. This was getting really weird.

Thwip!

I heard the unmistakable sound of someone sliding down the fire pole and hitting the ground on the first floor. Then the downstairs radio blared on. I recognized the song.

It was an old Benny Goodman record from the 1940s that Grandpa used to play for me when I was a little kid.

I flipped the lights back on and dashed for the pole. "Gotcha!" I cried, sliding down.

Thwip!

I hit the ground on the first floor, expecting to see one of my fellow firefighters waiting at the bottom of the pole to laugh at me.

No one was waiting. But what I did see freaked me out. The row of boots I had just neatly lined up were scattered all over the floor. The hose on the fire truck was completely uncoiled, its nozzle dancing in midair like a frenzied snake.

"Okay, guys, this isn't funny anymore!" I cried, feeling the hair on the back of my neck stand up. "How the heck are you doing this?"

The radio station changed suddenly, this time to an episode of an old radio drama from the same period. Spooky music and a witch's cackle echoed through the firehouse as the hose bobbed up and down in front of my eyes.

Suddenly, the hose shot forward, wrapping itself around my arms like an angry python.

"What in the name of—" Completely losing my cool, I struggled to move, but the hose had my arms pinned to my sides.

"Step into *the Inner Sanctum!*" a deep voice boomed from the radio. "And face your own worst fears!"

That's when the ax came flying off the truck, heading right for my head. It felt like time stood still. The image of the ax slicing my head off flashed in front of my eyes as the creepy music from the radio show filled my ears.

I dropped to the floor just as the ax zipped past my head and smashed into the opposite wall, crashing into a row of photos of firefighters who had died in the line of duty. The ax embedded itself in the wall, knocking one of the pictures to the floor.

I hit the cement hard, then rolled along the floor, uncoiling the hose until I was free. Jumping to my feet, I grabbed the ax and yanked it from the wall.

"Show yourself!" I shouted, clutching the ax and preparing for the next assault. I tell you, little bro, I was pissed. But mostly I was scared.

This was no rookie initiation. Something beyond explanation was going on here.

The upstairs lights flickered on and off, on and off, again and again.

"This has gone too far!" I yelled, heading for the stairs.

With the ax gripped firmly in my hands, I inched my way up the stairs, my boots clacking on the textured metal treads, my back pressed against the wall along the staircase. The lights continued to flash on and off, on and off, as a sickening cackle poured from the radio.

Wait! That laugh isn't coming from the radio. It's coming from upstairs!

I tightened my grip on the ax as I approached the top step. Sweat poured from my forehead as I prepared to face my tormentor.

Taking a deep breath, I stepped from the stairs onto the second floor, feet spread apart, the ax raised and ready. The lights went out . . . and stayed out! I felt waves of heat assault my face. Smoke filled my nostrils.

Was the firehouse on fire?

Bwoo! Woo! Woo!

A surge of adrenaline tore through my veins as the siren on the fire truck downstairs blared to life. The engine started and the bell clanged loudly.

Someone's stealing the truck!

The path to the pole—the fastest way down—was cloaked in total darkness. I turned and bolted down the stairs, reaching the bottom in time to see the fire truck begin to pull out of the firehouse.

I ran to the front, leaped on, and threw open the driver's side door.

Nobody was driving the truck!

An unseen force shoved me off the truck, and I tumbled to the floor. The ax skittered across the smooth cement.

Scrambling back to my feet, I raced outside. The fire truck was gone. It had vanished completely. Then a siren screamed behind me. I spun around and there was the truck! I had just seen it leave, but there it was, back in its spot.

The siren and engine shut off. In the eerie quiet, I began to wonder if I was losing my mind. How could the truck drive off by itself? How did it get past me to return to its spot back in the station?

The scream of a siren startled me and I turned to the

street to see our other engine backing into the house. My buddies were back. But what was I going to tell them?

"How'd you do with Frank?" Marty asked as he hopped off the truck and looked around at the scattered boots, the gash in the wall, and the picture lying on the floor. A huge smile spread across his ruddy face.

"Frank?" I asked. "Who's Frank?"

Marty walked over to the wall where the ax had struck. Kneeling down, he picked up the photo that had fallen to the floor. "Frank Knight," Marty said, handing me the picture. It was an old black-and-white shot of a firefighter in uniform. "He was a member of this company. Killed during a real bad blaze back in 1940. Only nobody ever told old Frank to stop coming to work. He likes to give rookies a hard time. Saves us the trouble! We figured that since you were here alone, Frank would welcome you properly!"

Well, little bro, that was my initiation. And you know what? I can't wait for the next rookie to come along!

MONTANA
Harvesting Organs

What I learned in history class: In the Great Sioux War, a coalition of Plains Indians led by Sitting Bull and Crazy Horse fought the U.S. Army. An important early Indian victory was the defeat of General Custer's forces at Little Bighorn. The Little Bighorn Battlefield National Monument can be found south of Billings, Montana.

A story you won't find in your textbook: My e-mail buddy CowboyD's real name is Darren Floyd. He lives on a cattle ranch with his mom and dad in Dupuyer, Montana. When we first became online friends, I thought it was weird that a cowboy was into the paranormal, but when he told me what happened on his ranch, it all made sense.

From: CowboyD@FloydRanch.com
To: Jspecter@scarystatesofamerica.com
Subject: cattle mutilation

Dude,

Love your Web site. Read your blog all the time. Creepy stuff! I never thought about ghosts and UFOs, but now I'm a major fan! It's 'cause of what happened on my dad's ranch. Wanna hear the story?

CowboyD

From: Jspecter@scarystatesofamerica.com
To: CowboyD@FloydRanch.com
Subject: Re: cattle mutilation

CowboyD,

Do I wanna hear the story?
    Do cows . . . uh . . . eat grass?

JS

From: CowboyD@FloydRanch.com
To: Jspecter@scarystatesofamerica.com
Subject: Re: cattle mutilation

• • •

Well, I've seen cows eat just about anything you put in front of them, but I'll take that as a yes.

◉◉

I'm fourteen now, but from the time I was a little kid, my dad, Harvey Floyd, told me the stories he'd heard about cattle mutilations in Montana. He also heard the talk about UFOs and aliens doing it, but he didn't believe any of that. My dad grew up and worked around livestock his whole life. He inherited our ranch, called Floyd Ranch, from my grandfather. Like me, he grew up here.

My dad couldn't figure out why anyone would want to hurt cattle, but he didn't buy the UFO theories. He believed wolves, coyotes, and mountain lions were the more likely killers.

That is, until he saw things with his own eyes.

My mom and dad and I were outside finishing up some chores one evening when we spotted a circle of light shining down from the sky. It lit up the hog pen. Then two pairs of small red and green lights appeared below the larger white light, like flies buzzing around a porch light.

"Wait here," my dad said as he stepped slowly toward the lights. I was real scared as he moved closer to the hog pen. I don't think I ever saw Dad scared before, but I could tell by the look on his face and the way he was moving real quiet that he was spooked.

"There's something wrong," Dad called to Mom. "We shouldn't stay here on the ranch tonight. We have to leave."

Now, I'm not one to disobey my dad, especially with

that look on his face, so I hurried to the car. Mom and Dad got in and we quickly drove away from the ranch. But the weird lights followed us into the darkness. The large white circle hovered just off the road, keeping a few feet behind our car, but the smaller red and green lights flew alongside us, like they were escorting us off the property.

Then, when we were a few miles away, all the lights suddenly spun into a wide U-turn and sped back in the direction of our ranch. My dad kept driving. He told me later that he wanted to turn the car around and drive right back to the ranch. He wanted to find out what was going on and protect his property if those strange lights were some kind of threat, like he suspected they were.

But he couldn't bring himself to do it. He couldn't risk our safety.

"We can go to Wanda's," Mom suggested. That's my aunt Wanda, Mom's sister. She lived in the next town. "Spend the night. Then go back in the morning. I'm sure everything is going to be all right." Weirdly, none of us talked about what we thought those lights might be. I think we just hoped everything would be normal in the morning, that this was all some kind of strange dream.

We drove the ten miles to Aunt Wanda's house and spent the night there. Not wanting to scare my aunt and her family or get them thinking that he was a lunatic, my dad told them that our house was being fumigated and we needed to sleep somewhere else for one night. He said he was sorry for the short notice, and nobody asked any questions.

I didn't sleep so well that night. I was tossing and turning. I couldn't get the picture of those lights out of my mind. My dad, who's usually a good sleeper, told me the next morning that he had a real bad feeling that kept him awake most of the night too.

After what seemed like forever, the sun finally rose. I jumped from my bed and ran downstairs to find Mom and Dad already at the breakfast table, anxious to get back home. After we ate, Mom thanked Aunt Wanda and we headed for the ranch.

At first, when we pulled into the driveway, nothing looked unusual. *Could the whole thing really have been a dream?* I wondered.

But when he stepped into the barn, Dad quickly discovered why the lights, whatever they were, wanted us away for the night.

It was a horrible sight when Dad finally let me see what happened. Three cows were dead. One was torn apart. All its internal organs were missing, but there was no blood around the body.

Another cow stared up at me with empty sockets—no eyes, just holes in the skull. The third cow had had all the blood drained from its body. Its skin hung on its bones like an empty feed sack, squeezed dry. I ran out of the barn, sweating and more nauseous than I've ever been in my life. I was ready to puke. Dad looked like he felt the same way.

"Harvey, Darren, what is it?" Mom cried. She had waited outside.

"Don't go in there, Ruth!" Dad cried. "Just don't go in! I shouldn't have let the boy in!"

Maybe Dad was right. Maybe I shouldn't have gone in. I'll never forget what I saw as long as I live.

Dad hurried to the hog pen, where he had first seen the lights. A nightmarish scene awaited him there, too.

I followed Dad to the pen, where we found a hog standing perfectly still, stiff as a board. Dad pushed the animal and it tipped over, tumbling to the ground like a cut tree. It hit the ground, and the sound of its bones shattering inside its bag of skin pushed me over the edge. I turned and hurled in the nearby bushes.

I wanted to run, but I couldn't look away. I caught my breath as I watched Dad kneeling beside a second hog. This one was lying on its side. Its jaw was missing and its body looked spongy and wet.

Dad looked sick. This was his prize hog. It had weighed in at an enormous 250 pounds. "Help me move it, Darren," Dad said.

I squatted next to him and grabbed the animal's hind legs. We were stunned when we lifted the body easily. It weighed only twenty or thirty pounds now!

"What could have done this?" Dad asked. But I could tell he already knew the answer. The stories he'd never believed were true. Our ranch had been visited by aliens who had conducted bizarre experiments on the livestock. Who else could have mutilated the animals this way?

Mom and Dad decided not to report the incident. They

didn't want to be featured on the front page of the papers as local nutcases. They just wanted to put it all behind us.

Still, I couldn't help wondering if the deadly visitors would ever return for more animals . . . or *human* victims next time!

NEBRASKA
"Watchman, come with me."

What I learned in history class: The name *Nebraska* comes from an Oto Indian tribe word meaning "flat water." That refers to the Platte River, which flows through the state.

A story you won't find in your textbook: I've gotten at least a couple of reports from most states in the country, but for some reason I'd never heard from anyone in Nebraska. Maybe there just aren't that many people living out there, or Nebraskans like to keep their paranormal experiences to themselves. In any case, I finally got this IM from Laura Foland of Ashland, Nebraska.

LF: Hey, Jason, love your blog, but come on, how come you never write about Nebraska? There's more to our state than corn, cattle, and Buffalo Bill, you know!

ParaGuy: It's not my fault! You're the first Nebraskan to get in contact with me. I'm all ears . . . (sorry, bad corn joke!).

LF: How about a cop who wrote in his police log: "2:30 am: Saw a flying saucer at the junction of Highway 6 and 63. Believe it or not!"

ParaGuy: A cop who takes a UFO sighting seriously . . . I gotta hear this.

LF: So you've never heard of our famous Herbert Schirmer? Well, he's famous here in Ashland, anyway.

ParaGuy: Well, here's your chance to put Ashland on the map. Send me the story.

Laura e-mailed me the article patrolman Herbert Schirmer wrote for their local paper.

◉◉

I was out alone on a routine night patrol, covering the same roads I'd driven every night since joining the force. I didn't expect anything different than usual, but the howling dogs were the first sign that something strange was happening. There's a group of strays that hide out in the old Brockway barn, and they can get pretty rowdy, but this night they sounded odd—terrified, maybe. High whimpers mixed in with the usual howls.

I pulled over and sat in the patrol car on the empty road, window down, listening to the dogs and the wind in the trees. It was a damp night, and the smell of winter was in the chilly air.

The raucous chorus of dogs suddenly stopped as a loud, urgent banging cut through the whistling wind. *What is going on here?* I thought as I shut off my engine and stepped slowly from the car.

I unclipped the flashlight from my belt and switched it on. Its beam sliced through the darkness as I tromped across the dried grass, fallen leaves crunching underfoot. The banging grew louder, more insistent.

Who's in that barn? And what the heck are they doing in there?

Approaching a busted window, I pressed my back against the barn and slid toward the jagged glass. A strange, high-pitched whine now joined the banging. I thought about drawing my gun, but decided against it. I figured it was probably just a drifter looking for a dry place to spend the night.

Taking a deep breath, I raised my head and shined my flashlight beam through the filthy glass.

Cows. Just cows. I let out a long breath and squinted

into the barn. The cows seemed disturbed, frantically kicking the walls and bleating loudly. Maybe the dogs had got them spooked with their racket.

I turned around to head back to my car and found myself staring at some kind of strange vehicle. I jumped back, startled. I hadn't heard anyone drive up. In the glow of its red flashing lights, I could just make out a shiny metallic surface, like chrome. But what was it? A big truck?

I stepped closer to the vehicle, trying to get a better look at the thing, but when I pointed my light at it, the beam was swallowed up. It's hard to explain, but it was like the light hit that thing and was absorbed into it instead of bouncing back and showing me what I was looking at.

I slowly stepped forward, trying to make sense of it. My flashlight still revealed nothing. When I was about three feet away, I realized that the thing wasn't making any noise. No engine sound. No nothing.

As I reached out to touch the smooth-looking metal, the red lights flared, growing much brighter. I could see now that those lights were flashing through a series of round windows in the object. The extra light revealed a large, oval metallic disc.

I could see that this vehicle, this disc, didn't have any wheels under it like I assumed. It was hovering eight feet above the road! No legs, no wheels, no wings. It was just hanging in the air, its red lights flashing in sequence around its edge.

Two thoughts crossed my mind:

I gotta call for backup.

And, *Maybe now would be a good time to draw my gun!*

As I reached for my gun, something seemed to seize control of my mind, and I couldn't move my arm.

Frozen in place, I watched in shock as two humanoid creatures emerged from the hovering disc, moving quickly down a ramp to the ground. They wore identical uniforms and each of them had a high forehead, a long nose, gray skin, and round, catlike eyes. One alien held a box-shaped instrument, which flashed and surrounded me with a green glow. The second reached out a bony gray hand and touched my neck.

A sharp, stabbing pain shot through me. But I was still under some kind of paralyzing influence; I couldn't even yell. I could do nothing but watch in total terror.

"Are you the watchman?" the alien who had touched me asked. It spoke without moving its thin, lipless mouth, yet I could hear its high-pitched voice in my head. It peered at me, as if waiting for a response.

Somehow the aliens saw that I was a police officer. Maybe it was my uniform, or the fact that I was patrolling alone, in the dark. I replied, "Yes, one of them."

"Watchman, come with me," the alien commanded, again speaking without opening its mouth.

Compelled to obey, I followed the alien into the spacecraft. The inside of the ship was remarkably featureless. Flat metal consoles lined the blank interior. No buttons, knobs, or computer screens were visible.

"We have come to your planet to get electricity," the alien announced bluntly. "And we will be back again."

An odd purple glow and a high-pitched buzz filled the room. Thin strands of electricity coursed through the air, and I felt my hair stand up. My whole body tingled and itched as if a thousand ants were crawling all over me. I thought my head was going to burst.

And then it stopped—the itching, the sound, and the glow—and I was once again in that dull, featureless room.

"You have seen our purpose. Report to your leader that we mean no harm as long as we can continue to harvest your power. You are the watchman. You will assist us. Now, watchman, come with me," the alien said.

The creature led me slowly down the metal ramp. With each heavy step, I wondered what they were going to do with me, and why they had taken me aboard their ship. Were they going to kill me now that they had revealed their plan? As my foot hit the ground, I instantly felt my will return.

In one swift move, I drew my gun and spun around.

I was totally and utterly alone. The ship was gone. It had vanished silently in an instant, leaving no sign.

I stumbled back to my car, my neck still throbbing. I thought of calling for help, but help with what? There was nothing, just a few upset cows and howling dogs. Struggling to stay focused, I managed to drive myself home. I fell into a restless sleep around six a.m.

When I woke up in the afternoon, I was troubled by the alien's words: "We have come to your planet to get electricity." I placed calls to the three largest power plants in Nebraska. All three reported an unexplainable thirty to thirty-five percent power loss during the early-morning hours. I pulled out a map and discovered that major power lines from all three plants crisscross the area where the aliens had landed.

I now live in fear of their other words: "We will be back!" Those aliens can have all the electricity they want, as long as they don't take me with them!

NEVADA
Psychic Hero

What I learned in history class: Las Vegas is the marriage capital of the world. The city issues more than 110,000 marriage licenses each year. The most popular wedding day is Valentine's Day, followed by New Year's Eve.

A story you won't find in your textbook: A lot of the stories I get are pretty wild, and fun to read. But sometimes I can tell that people are deeply affected by their experiences with the supernatural, and it can take a long time to recover from the trauma of an unexplained event. A man from Nevada sent this story to my Web site, and yes, the psychic element did creep me out. But I also felt bad for the guy; I could tell that his weird experience brought up a lot of painful memories for him. Here's what he wrote.

◐◑

My name is Bruce Edwards, and I'm no hero. You might not agree once you hear my story, but trust me. If anything, I've always felt that I was a coward, even when I was a kid.

When I was eleven, my house caught fire in the middle of the night. I woke up to smoke and flames everywhere. I panicked. My heart froze and terror gripped every part of my being. I wasn't thinking straight. Who would be? I know that now. But there's still no excuse for what I did.

I thought only of getting myself out of the house. I dashed down the burning stairs and raced out the front door. I was standing outside looking up at the burning house. That's when I remembered the rest of my family.

My parents stumbled through the blazing doorway. My father carried the limp body of my eight-year-old sister, Jennie, in his arms.

My parents were in the hospital for a while. They hadn't woken up as soon as I had and were exposed to huge amounts of smoke as they fought their way to my sister's room to get her. Jennie died from smoke inhalation and burns.

I was the only one who didn't suffer. I was a wreck for months, even after my parents were better and moved us to a new house. I blamed myself for not thinking about Jennie. In the thirty years since the fire, not a day has gone by that I haven't thought of her. And then there are the dreams.

All these years I've had a recurring dream about the night Jennie died. It begins the same way. I'm eleven. I wake up to the smell of smoke. I panic and run from the house. I feel relief when I get out. Then I see my father carrying my limp body from the blazing inferno. In the dream Jennie's okay. It's me who died. Sometimes I wish it had really happened that way.

At this point you may be asking yourself what all this has to do with the paranormal. Well, one day not long ago, I had a different dream. It was also about a fire, but this time I was the hero.

I work at a chemical plant, developing rocket engines and highly explosive fuels. Because these experiments involve hazardous materials, we have a lot of safety precautions. All the engineers wear flame-retardant coats.

In my dream, however, I'm sitting at my desk in only a short-sleeved shirt. Suddenly, I hear a thunderous explosion in the next lab, where my friend, Sandra Rhimer, is working.

Rushing from my office, I'm horrified to discover Sandra's lab engulfed in flames. I dash into the inferno and spot her. Her entire body appears to be on fire.

Moving swiftly, I grab her and carry her to the plant's safety shower, where I douse her with water, putting out the flames and saving her life. Only after Sandra is safe do I notice that my own clothes are on fire. I jump into the shower just before the flames reach my skin.

When I woke up from this dream, I was really puzzled.

Why would I, after all these years, suddenly dream about being a hero? It made me feel guilty to imagine being a hero, even if only in a dream, when I had failed my family.

And then I had the dream again, exactly the same as the first in every detail. But the dream made even less sense. It was odd that Sandra was alone. There were almost always three other coworkers in the lab with her. It was also strange that I was only wearing a short-sleeved shirt and not my flame-retardant coat.

And still the dream kept coming back, the way the dream about Jennie had for all those years.

Then one day, a few months later, I was in an office next to my lab doing some paperwork. The air-conditioning wasn't working properly, and since there were no hazardous materials in the office, I pulled off my coat and was working in a short-sleeved shirt. I didn't think anything of it at the time.

Thoom!

Suddenly, a violent explosion shook the building. I leaped from my chair and ran to the door, my heart pounding like it was going to burst from my chest. Sweat immediately began pouring down my face. I smelled the sickly, acrid odor of burning chemicals. Smoke choked my lungs and I gasped for breath.

No! I thought, flashing back to the horrid events of my childhood. *Not again! This can't be happening again!*

Then I thought of Sandra.

Two doors down she was working on an experiment using highly explosive fuels.

The dream. It's impossible. Could the dream be coming true?

I tore from the office, blinded by the smoke, overwhelmed by the sounds of screaming. Panicked people fled the building, rushing past me, running away from the fire.

I headed right into the heart of the inferno. And I wasn't going to leave alone.

I kicked open the door of Sandra's lab. My eyes and throat burned. I waved the smoke away, only to see Sandra's face, arms, and legs engulfed in flames. Her plastic goggles had melted into her hair. She was sprawled across her lab table. And she wasn't moving.

Struggling through the thick black smoke and searing toxic flames, I scooped Sandra into my arms—exactly as I had done in the dream—and turned back toward the door.

A wall of flames towered over my head, blocking the exit. My vision blurred, my skin burned. I lowered my head and charged through the curtain of fire, not thinking, not feeling. Just running.

My legs pumped furiously as I pushed forward blindly, pain ripping across my skin. I stumbled into the safety shower, still holding Sandra's limp body. I cried as the water rained down over us. And then I collapsed.

I woke up slowly, not knowing where I was. *Am I home? Did I have another of my dreams?* I forced my eyes open and saw bandages covering my arms.

This was no dream!

I tried to sit up but fell back in pain. My vision cleared and I realized that I was in a hospital bed. I later learned that I had burns over a large part of my body. But I would live.

"Doctor!" I called out when I saw that I was not alone in the room. The doctor hurried to my bedside. "Sandra Rhimer. She was with me. Is she—" I couldn't finish.

"She's alive," the doctor said, smiling. "She's still in intensive care, but she's going to make it. Thanks to you."

I breathed a deep sigh of relief. This time was different. This time, someone would live because of me.

Sandra and I each spent about six months in the hospital recovering from our burns. It turned out that at the moment of the explosion, two of her coworkers were on a coffee break. The third ran from the lab as soon as the explosion occurred. That's why Sandra was alone.

I still credit the strange dream for giving me the courage to believe that I could save someone. Not long after I got out of the hospital, I had another dream. This one was about me and my sister, Jennie, playing together as young children.

This time, there was no fire.

NEW HAMPSHIRE
Bridge of Sorrow

What I learned in history class: United States Senator and Secretary of State Daniel Webster was born in Salisbury, New Hampshire, in 1782. Webster's reputation as a skilled orator was fictionalized in Stephen Vincent Benet's 1937 story "The Devil and Daniel Webster," in which Webster wins back a man's soul from the devil.

A story you won't find in your textbook: When I hear similar paranormal tales from more than one place, it always makes me suspicious. I assume they must just be urban legends. Some of these stories involve women who, for a variety of reasons ranging from insanity to unrequited love to hateful fathers, murder their children and toss them off a bridge. It is claimed that years later the women's mournful cries can still be heard on the bridges at night. But the story my blogging buddy BizarroBoy603 of Nashua, New Hampshire, sent me made me stop and reconsider what I had once believed were simply tall tales.

◉◎

Hey, Specter. I have a story for you that is *not* an urban legend. It's the real paranormal deal (right up your alley). Before Halloween last year, I thought our town ghost story was just that—a story. But after what happened to me and my girlfriend, I know it's true.

If I recall correctly from my Cub Scout campfire days, a long time ago there lived in my hometown a poor widow with two small children. One day, she met and fell in love with a very wealthy man. She desperately wanted to marry him, but he wouldn't have her because he hated children.

Devastated, the woman took her kids to a bridge over a river just outside the city. Crazy with grief, she stabbed her own children to death and then tossed their dead bodies into the river. It just happened to be October 31.

She then went back to the man's house to ask if they could be together now. When he saw the woman standing there in her blood-soaked yellow dress, he was disgusted. The man told her to leave and never return.

She shrieked in horror at the realization of what she had done. Driven to madness, she raced back to the river, wailing and tearing clumps of hair from her head. She dived into the water again and again but could find no trace of her children.

Finally, she climbed the bridge, stabbed herself in the stomach, and jumped into the river at its deepest point. Now it is said that when you cross the bridge at night, you can hear the wailing of the mother—sometimes mournful, sometimes hysterical, but always terrifying.

Tiffany and I joked about the over-the-top story as we drove onto the bridge last Halloween on our way to our friend Dan's party. His parents were away, and the whole school was going. I was dressed as a superhero, complete with cape, tights, boots, and an equipment belt loaded with gadgets and tools (yes, I am an unapologetic comic book geek). Tiffany dressed up like a giant red crayon, wearing a red dress, red tights, red boots, and a cone made out of construction paper on her head.

I stopped the car in the middle of the bridge and turned off the headlights.

"What are you doing?" Tiffany asked as I shut off the engine and rolled down our windows.

"It is Halloween, you know," I replied in a spooky voice. "The anniversary of the night that woman killed her kids and threw them off this bridge. *Ooooohhhhh!*"

"Could you try to not be a total geek for five minutes, Kevin?" Tiffany asked. (By the way, Specter, Kevin is my real name, and yes, Tiffany totally digs me.)

"I don't want to be late to Dan's—"

She was cut off by an unearthly howl that made the hair on the back of my neck stand up.

"Gimme a break," Tiffany moaned. "It's Halloween. You know Mike and Booger or whoever are down there trying to scare people. They know everyone's going to Dan's party, and you can't get there without passing over this bridge."

"Then let's go see if we can scare them back!" I said excitedly, jumping out of the car before Tiffany could protest.

I wasn't quite sure how the sight of a superhero and a red crayon was going to scare the guys, but Tiffany followed me and we made our way down the embankment.

I pulled a flashlight from my costume's equipment belt and aimed the beam at the area under the bridge. I couldn't see anyone, but we heard the painful, gut-wrenching howl again. This time it was obviously coming from the river. I focused the flashlight on the water's surface, which began to bubble furiously.

As the water churned, it turned bright red, like someone was pumping blood from beneath the surface. Then a woman's head appeared, rising from the center of the roiling crimson circle.

When the woman's body was completely out of the water, the bubbling stopped. The woman floated, hovering just above the river's surface. Her yellow dress was covered in blood, which poured from her midsection and dripped into the river.

"Bravo, Booger! You have outdone yourself this year, my man! This blows away the hangman stunt you pulled on Wayne's lawn last year," I shouted, looking around for the guys.

"I just want to know how one of you guys squeezed into that dress," Tiffany added, giggling.

"*Yiiiiii!*" shrieked the hovering figure, tearing at her hair as blood flowed freely down the front of her dress.

"Okay, now this is just freaky," Tiffany whispered as she grasped my arm. We watched a second longer. The woman sure didn't look like any of the guys. "Let's go, Kev. I'm not laughing anymore."

The figure shrieked again, and that was it for Tiffany. My giant red crayon dashed back up the embankment. I followed her, training my flashlight ahead of us.

"What about the rest of the show?" I yelled as I chased her back up to the bridge. "We have to congratulate Boog—"

I stopped short and grabbed Tiffany close to me. Standing in the middle of the bridge was the bleeding woman. She leaned over the railing, screeching in pain while tearing out clumps of her hair and tossing them into the water below.

"How could she have gotten up here so fast?" Tiffany asked, trembling. "She's right near our car!"

I approached the crying woman slowly. "Hey, lady? Um, is this a joke? Did Mike put you up to this?" She didn't seem to notice me.

As I drew nearer, she suddenly turned toward me. As she raised her hand over her head, I saw a bloody knife clutched in her bony fingers.

This was no joke.

"*Yiiiiii!*" she shrieked, unleashing a sound that literally knocked me off me feet. I fell hard onto the bridge's roadway. I take a lot of beatings in wrestling practice, but that shriek felt like a total body slam.

"Kevin!" Tiffany yelled in terror, racing to my side.

"Let's get out of here!" I shouted, scrambling to my feet.

I grabbed Tiffany's hand and started sprinting down the road, but when I glanced over my shoulder, I saw that the woman was gone.

"Where did she go?" I asked nervously as we stopped running.

"I don't know," Tiffany panted, clutching my arm.

I stumbled to the railing and shined my light down into the river. There was no sign of the woman. No blood in the water. I looked down at the road where she had been standing. No blood. No puddle. No evidence that the wailing woman had ever existed.

"Let's just go!" Tiffany said, helping me back to the car. "I'll drive."

My whole right side was in wicked pain, so I didn't argue. After helping me settle into the passenger seat, Tiffany slipped behind the wheel and turned the key in the ignition.

Nothing happened.

"Why won't the car start?" Tiffany cried, turning the key again and again. The car coughed and sputtered but refused to start up.

I glanced into the rearview mirror. The blood-soaked apparition had returned and now strode menacingly toward the car, her scarlet knife raised high.

"She's back!" I yelled. "Babe, we gotta get out of here!"

Tiffany frantically tried again to start the car.

Thump!

Tiffany and I spun around to discover that the woman had thrown her body against the back window of my car, her arms spread wide, her twisted face pressed against the glass. She lifted herself and moved to the back door on the passenger side.

"She's coming in!" Tiffany cried, pounding the gas pedal with her foot. The engine grumbled, sputtered—then finally started.

The bloody woman shoved her knife through the open back window, its red blade passing just inches from my head.

"Go *now!*" I shouted.

Tiffany floored it and the car sped off with a piercing squeal. She looked terrified as we raced off the bridge.

"Baby, are you okay?" she asked shakily. "That . . . thing . . . almost drove her blade into your skull. Should we call the police or something?"

I sat there bathed in cold sweat. I could only concentrate on slowing my heartbeat. It was going a mile a minute.

"Let's just get to the party so we can forget it. If we called the police, they'd ask us where we were going in our costumes. I don't want to get Dan in trouble."

We arrived at Dan's party about ten minutes later. The place was packed, and people spilled out onto the front lawn.

"Hey, sweet costumes!" Dan said as we staggered through the front door, trying to look normal. He was dressed like a pirate, complete with a hat, a puffy shirt, and a fake parrot on his shoulder. "What are you, Tiff, a crayon?"

"Yeah," Tiffany replied, forcing a smile and adjusting her paper cone.

We'd begun to head to the kitchen when Tiffany stopped. "It's her!" she gasped, grabbing my arm.

Standing in line for the bathroom was a girl wearing a bloody yellow dress. Her face was covered in white makeup, her hair teased into random clumps.

"Thank God somebody gets my costume," said the girl, smiling at us. "I thought I was being so original going as the ghost of the bridge lady! Ooooooohh!"

"You stupid idiot!" Tiffany yelled. "You almost drove a knife into my boyfriend's head!"

"What are you talking about?" the girl replied. "Is this a joke? I've never seen you in my life!"

"You were just at the bridge and you know it! Did Booger and Mike put you up to this?" Tiffany shouted.

"I've been here for over an hour!" the girl shouted back. "And I don't hang out with people named *Booger*!"

The girl stormed off into the living room.

Dan walked over. "Hey, what just happened there?"

I filled Dan in on our terrifying ride over, but he looked a little skeptical.

"Dude, that was my friend, Andrea," Dan explained. "She was one of the first people to get here tonight. If this happened to you like ten minutes ago, it wasn't her. She was most definitely here. Also, Mitch, Zach, Booger, and Mike got nailed by the cops earlier for egging people's cars. Rich told me they've been at the police station all night. Their parents won't bail them out this time."

I believed Dan. When Tiffany was screaming bloody murder at Andrea, I noticed her dress. It was yellow, but the fake blood was crusty, and the dress itself was dry. I apologized to Dan, and Tiffany and I went outside.

"I just did a good job making a fool of myself," Tiffany said as we leaned against my car.

"Hey, it's okay. And we still don't know who the freak on the bridge was. I mean, what kind of lunatic thinks it's funny to—" I stopped short. My heart began racing as goose bumps slowly crept over my body. I pointed at the backseat of my car. There, plunged in the center of a spreading crimson pool, was the bloody knife of the woman on the bridge.

NEW JERSEY
Devil in the Dark

What I learned in history class: Elysian Fields, a private park in Hoboken, New Jersey, was the site of the first officially recorded baseball game. On June 19, 1846, the New York Nine beat the Knickerbockers by a score of 23 to 1.

A story you won't find in your textbook: New Jersey is famous for a lot of things: Princeton University, *The Sopranos,* and Bruce Springsteen (my dad's hero). But for a collector of the paranormal like me, it's all about the Jersey Devil. No, I'm not talking about the hockey team. The Jersey Devil is one of the oldest and most dangerous paranormal creatures ever reported. I put out a call on my blog for people to send me their stories about the loathsome monster, hoping I could compare them and get to the truth behind the legend. Lauren Buxbaum from Leeds Point, New Jersey, sent me this IM:

> **Sparklegrrrl:** Hi. I have a cool story about the Jersey Devil. I got a B+ on my paper about it, and I would have done better if my teacher weren't a total supernatural skeptic. We had to do a historical report and include a first-person account in it. My history teacher totally embarrassed me in front of the whole class when he was like, "Miss Buxbaum, I loved your paper. I would have given you an A+ if the first-person account you claim is true wasn't a tall tale. Your research was solid so you get a B+ but next time, save the stories for your creative writing teacher." I was soooooooooo mad because I did NOT make this up AND I totally deserved an A+. And I worked for weeks on it and . . .

I cut short the rest of Lauren's rambling IM—she sure was bitter about her grade. Some of my teachers would probably give me an F and call my parents if I wrote a story about some of my experiences and claimed they were true, so I didn't think she got off that badly. Anyway, I did ask Lauren to send me her history paper. And she's right—she did deserve an A+.

◉◉

Is it a pterodactyl left over from the Jurassic Age? Or is it a sandhill crane seeking revenge for the loss of its habitat due to humans building on and developing the land? Maybe it's a hideously deformed human child, or even the incarnation of pure evil itself.

New Jersey historians disagree on what exactly the Jersey Devil is, but most agree that the creature's storied existence began in the small town of Leeds Point in the 1700s.

A number of the tales refer to a Mrs. Leeds, whose thirteenth child was born with horns, a tail, wings, and a horselike head. She hid the child in the basement, but it managed to escape and wreak havoc for generations.

Other stories tell of a witch named Miranda Leeds, who gave birth to a seemingly normal baby who only minutes later transformed into a hideous creature with hooves, a forked tail, bat wings, and a horse's head. When the transformation was complete, the beast proceeded to kill everyone in the room (including its mother), then fly up the chimney. After circling the village several times, striking fear into the hearts of the townspeople, it flapped its huge, powerful wings and headed off to begin its centuries-long reign of terror.

The legend grew through the years as the Jersey Devil appeared all over the Garden State, from Burlington to

Haddonfield, Woodbury to Bristol. Descriptions of the creature varied, but an overall picture began to form: a six-foot-tall flying creature with a three-foot tail, leathery, batlike wings, and the face of a dog, horse, disfigured child, or the devil himself, depending on who you ask.

The creature is reported to emit a blood-chilling screech as it attacks its victims, often stopping them in their tracks.

As I researched the creature's exploits further, I came upon some astounding tales. Strange footprints have appeared on New Jersey farms around the bodies of dead chickens and cows. Police have spotted the flying beast and shot at it, describing its cry as a cross between a piercing scream and a growling bark.

People have seen the devil circling above their homes, later finding hoofprints on their roofs. Others reported hearing a beating of wings and an unearthly screech, only to sadly discover in the backyard the body of a beloved pet with its throat torn out. In Vineland, a German shepherd was found twenty-five feet away from the collar and chain to which it had been attached. The body was torn to pieces. The hoofed tracks surrounding the body could not be identified as those of any known animal.

The Jersey Devil has also attacked motorists. A Salem, New Jersey, cabdriver told of stopping on the side of the road to fix a flat tire. Suddenly, a flying beast appeared, landing on the roof of his cab. The creature—which he described as tall, like a man but completely covered with hair, and with a long tail that came to a point, wide wings, and an eerily childlike face—shook the car violently. The terrified cabbie fled, abandoning his vehicle. Police received at least a dozen calls within minutes of the attack from people in the area who reported a large screeching bird with a long tail circling above their homes.

Two couples parked in the Pine Barrens reported hearing a loud screeching sound seconds before something landed on the roof, smashing it inward. As they ran from the car, they turned back to see a monstrous birdlike creature destroying the car. It tore the roof off with its huge claws, then shredded the seats with its razor-sharp beak. The couples fled, but returned later to the damaged car. Again they heard the shrieks and this time saw the beast perched in a tree, tearing away the bark as it beat its mighty wings.

Not one to go along with legend lightly, I sought out an elderly woman named Margaret who had actually seen the creature herself right here in Leeds Point. Margaret said she would be happy to share her story with me when I called her. I rode my bike to her small farm and she welcomed me into her home.

"Why did you choose the Jersey Devil for your history report?" she asked, handing me a glass of iced tea.

"Everybody in class was doing something boring like a paper on Walt Whitman or Thomas Edison, and I wanted a unique topic. Something cool about Jersey. I studied up on the Jersey Devil. Did you know that lots of people believe it was born right here in Leeds Point?"

Margaret smiled. "Yes, I have heard that."

I switched on the tape recorder I'd borrowed from my grandma, and Margaret began her story.

Margaret had always lived on a farm in this part of New Jersey. From the time she was a little girl, she recalled mysterious livestock attacks. Every so often, her family's farm would be invaded during the night. The next morning brought horrible scenes of mutilated animals and damaged property.

Others in her town were occasionally troubled by these attacks, but it seemed that no farm was hit as frequently as Margaret's. Then, one winter evening, when she was about sixteen, Margaret was finishing up her evening chores by the light of a full moon when she caught a glimpse of a shadow in the snow. She looked up and spotted what appeared to be an enormous bird silhouetted against the moon. Then she saw the tail.

"I'd never seen a bird anything like that," she told me. "And that's when it let out a scream. No ordinary bird could make that sound!"

As the flying beast swooped down toward her, Margaret froze in fear, unable to run. She stared up at the creature and caught sight of its head. "It had a wolfish snout, and its screech changed to a snarling growl as it revealed a mouth full of sharp canine teeth."

The creature was closing fast. "I couldn't move my legs. I could barely breathe, much less scream," she recalled. "I was certain I was going to die right there in the snow. I looked down at the pitchfork in my hands. Hurling it like a javelin, I tossed the tool up, hoping to scare off the devil.

But it swerved easily out of the way and kept coming toward me. I was doomed."

Blam! Blam!

Suddenly, two gunshots rang out. "I turned my head and saw my father. His shotgun was still smoking. He had heard the beast's cries, and burst from the farmhouse with his gun."

The two shotgun blasts seemed to scare the creature away. It howled, and flew off into the night.

"I hate to think what might have happened to me if my father hadn't come out," Margaret said as I finished my interview with her. "That was the most scared I've ever been in my life. And I don't scare easily."

"Wow!" I said. "That's a great story. Did you ever see the creature again?"

"Fortunately, no," she replied. "Though that doesn't mean that it will never return."

"Thanks!" I said. "This is really going to help me with my paper." As I got up to leave, I realized that I had never gotten Margaret's last name.

"Leeds," Margaret told me. "My family has lived here for a very long time."

It was then that I looked up at her bookcase and took in the long rows of ancient books with titles referring to sorcery and spells.

"If you don't mind me asking, are you into witchcraft?" I asked nervously.

Margaret smiled. "A bit. It's mostly just a historical interest of mine. These books were handed down to me by generations of Leeds women, starting with my great-great-great-great-grandmother, Miranda Leeds."

She kept smiling, while I nearly dropped my iced tea. Miranda Leeds was the witch who gave birth to the Jersey Devil!

Maybe the creature wasn't violently attacking the Leeds farm at all—maybe it just wanted to come home.

NEW MEXICO
The Roswell Incident

What I learned in history class: Santa Fe, New Mexico, is both the oldest state capital and, at 7,000 feet above sea level, the highest capital city in the nation. It's also the oldest community settled by Europeans west of the Mississippi.

A story you won't find in your textbook: Sometimes I just get lucky! For months, the online paranormal community had been buzzing about the huge convention of UFO enthusiasts (maybe they thought they'd offend someone by calling us UFO freaks?) that was going to take place in Roswell, New Mexico. Yup, Roswell, the mecca of UFO lore, the site of a crashed UFO in 1947 from which alien bodies were recovered. Sure, the government did its best to convince the public that there was no spaceship or aliens. But those who were actually there know better. Anyway, like I said, sometimes I'm lucky. I got to go to the convention. And, as it turned out, so did a bunch of my blogging buddies.

◉◉

I couldn't believe it. Just being in Roswell was amazing, and the UFO convention was turning into a reunion for me and my online pals. I had never met most of them face to face, though we'd been communicating for a long time.

There was FreakBoy from Arkansas, who had told me about shadow people.

"Dude, cool to meet you!" FreakBoy said when we met, as planned, under the giant replica of the crashed Roswell ship. "You're shorter than I pictured."

"Thanks," I said, rolling my eyes. These were, after all, my friends. Not the most socially gifted crowd you'll ever meet.

I felt a hand tap me on the shoulder and jumped in surprise.

"Just like old times, huh, ghost hunter?" said a familiar voice from behind me. "Still jumpy."

"Gothgirl!" I shouted, unable to keep from smiling. "Or should I call you Louanne?"

She punched me in the arm. Just like old times, indeed. Gothgirl and I had shared a bizarre afternoon in a cemetery in her Mississippi hometown.

I watched as a strange-looking figure made his way

through the noisy crowd. The Cubs baseball cap and "Don't Trust the Government!" T-shirt gave him away.

"CubManiac!" I cried, herding the new arrival into our ever-expanding group. "Been to any games lately?"

"Did the government cover up the Roswell incident?" my friend from Illinois replied. "Of course!"

"I think baseball is stupid," Gothgirl said under her breath.

I could tell we were all going to get along famously.

"Check out this weirdo!" FreakBoy said, pointing to a kid wearing a silver spacesuit and mask.

Look who's talking, I thought.

The kid pulled off the mask. "Jason, it's me, BizarroBoy from New Hampshire!" he said, extending a foil-wrapped hand. "Cool costume, huh?"

"Yeah, for a dork," FreakBoy muttered. "I think the *Star Trek* convention is next door. This place is for serious paranormal enthusiasts only."

Maybe this "reunion" wasn't such a great idea after all.

Fortunately, I was saved by the sudden appearance of a tall, skinny kid wearing a cowboy hat.

"You gotta be CowboyD, right?" I asked, bringing him into the group. "Nice to meet you." Introductions were made all around. "CowboyD sent me a creepy story about cattle mutilation on his dad's farm in Montana."

"Yeah, I read that on Jason's blog," CubManiac said. "Scared the crap out of me!"

"Nice to meet you guys," Cowboy D said. "Y'all paranormal bloggers?"

"No, we're the U.S. Olympic hockey team," snapped Gothgirl. "We're here for the Ice Capades."

When is the presentation going to start? I wondered anxiously.

"Any more of your geek squad coming, ghost hunter?" Gothgirl asked, rolling her dark eyes.

"Your attention, please!" came an announcement over the convention hall's PA system. "Please find your seats. The presentation is about to begin!"

Thank God! I thought. My little fan club and I made our way into a large tent. We took our seats and listened as some old guy told the story of the 1947 UFO crash in Roswell. The first thing the speaker said was "These are the facts as we have generally come to accept them. They are now a matter of public record." Guess he's trying not to get sued. Anyway, here's what I learned.

The summer of 1947 was a particularly active one for UFO sightings throughout the United States. During the first few days of July of that year, Army Intelligence had been tracking an unidentified flying object on radar in southern New Mexico. Then, on the night of July 4, 1947, the radar indicated that whatever they were tracking had crashed to earth thirty to forty miles northwest of Roswell.

On July fifth, a local rancher named W. W. "Mack" Brazel rode out onto his property on horseback to check on his sheep after a violent thunderstorm. Brazel came upon strange-looking pieces of metal debris, which were scattered over a large area. He then found a long but shallow trench carved into the ground that extended for a few hundred feet.

Brazel had never seen any metal quite like these pieces. He dragged them to a nearby storage shed on his land and shared his discovery with some neighbors, who thought the wreckage might be from a UFO or a government project. They suggested that Brazel report the incident to the local sheriff.

A couple of days later, Brazel drove into Roswell and reported the incident to Sheriff George Wilcox. Wilcox passed the report along to intelligence officer Major Jesse Marcel of the 509 Bomb Group, who was stationed at a nearby army base. Major Marcel left the base to investigate Brazel's story.

On July sixth, Major Marcel and senior Counterintelligence Corps (CIC) agent Captain Sheridan Cavitt visited Brazel. The rancher showed them a large piece of the debris that he had dragged from the pasture. The officers spent the night on Brazel's ranch.

The following morning, Major Marcel visited the debris field that Brazel had discovered. Marcel reported that "something must have exploded above the ground and fell." As Brazel, Cavitt, and Marcel surveyed the field, Marcel tried to determine from which direction the object had come.

Marcel also reported that the debris was "strewn over a wide area, I guess maybe three-quarters of a mile long and a few hundred feet wide." He held a flame from a cigarette lighter up to small bits of metal he found among the debris to see if it would burn or blacken. It did neither. Along with the metal pieces, Marcel also found what he described as weightless I-beam–like structures that were three-eighths by a quarter-inch long. He could not bend or break these mysterious rods. Some of these I-beams had unfamiliar characters written on them in two colors. Marcel also described metal debris that was only the thickness of tinfoil. This material also seemed indestructible.

Marcel filled his staff car with the debris, then left, stopping by his house on the way back to the base to show his family what he had discovered. "I didn't know what we were picking up," he told them. "I still don't know what it was. It could not have been part of an aircraft or any kind of weather balloon. I've seen rockets sent up at the White Sands testing grounds. It definitely was not part of an aircraft or missile or rocket."

His son, Jesse Jr., described the foil and I-beams as "purple. Strange. Never saw anything like it. Different geometric shapes and circles." His father told Jesse that he thought he had found the wreckage of a crashed flying saucer.

Marcel immediately ordered the crash site closed to the public while the wreckage was cleared by the military. On July eighth, a press release was issued by Lieutenant Walter G. Haut, Public Information Officer at the Roswell Army Air Base under orders from the commander of the 509 Bomb Group at Roswell, Colonel William Blanchard.

At eleven that morning, the press release was sent to

two local radio stations and the local newspaper, the Roswell *Daily Record*. By two-thirty that afternoon, the story was out on the AP wire service and spread all around the country. The press release read:

> The Army Air Forces here today announced a flying disc had been found.

The headline in the late edition of the July 8, 1947, issue of the Roswell *Daily Record* read:

RAAF (Roswell Army Air Field) Captures Flying Saucer on Ranch in Roswell Region

The story went on to say:

> The intelligence office of the 509 Bomb Group at Roswell Army Air Field announced at noon today that the field has come into possession of a flying saucer. According to information released by the department, over authority of Major J. A. Marcel, intelligence officer, the disc was recovered on a ranch in the Roswell vicinity, after an unidentified rancher had notified Sheriff George Wilcox that he had found the instrument on his premises.

But the following day, July 9, the first press release was canceled and called a mistake. A second press release was sent out stating that the 509 Bomb Group had mistakenly identified a weather balloon as the wreckage of a flying saucer.

While all this was happening, Glenn Dennis, a mortician working at the Ballard Funeral Home in Roswell, received a curious phone call from the morgue at the airfield. The mortuary officer there asked Dennis if he knew where he could find some small hermetically sealed coffins. He also requested information about how to preserve bodies that had been exposed to the elements for a few days, without contaminating the tissue. Someone must have found and removed bodies there, though to this day nobody knows who picked them up. It wasn't Major Marcel.

Glenn Dennis drove out to the base hospital that evening. When he arrived, he saw large pieces of metal wreckage sticking out of the back of a military ambulance. One thin piece had strange engraved markings on it.

When Dennis tried to enter the hospital to keep an appointment he had made with a nurse to discuss the coffins, he was forced to leave by military police. The next day, he met with the nurse off the base. She told Dennis about the unusual bodies being held in the hospital and drew pictures of them for him. Within a few days of this meeting, the nurse was transferred to England. Her whereabouts remain unknown.

Colonel Blanchard, Major Marcel's commanding officer,

sent Marcel to see General Ramey, commanding officer of the Eighth Air Force at Carswell Fort Worth Army Air Field. Marcel brought some pieces of the wreckage—which Colonel Blanchard admitted were unlike anything he had ever seen—to show to General Ramey. Marcel placed the wreckage in the general's office before the general showed up for their meeting.

When General Ramey arrived, he told Major Marcel that he wanted to be shown on a map the exact location where the wreckage was found. The two officers left the general's office and went to the base's map room.

When they returned, the wreckage Marcel had brought was gone. In its place were pieces of a weather balloon. General Ramey said that he recognized the remains as part of a weather balloon. The true evidence had vanished.

Brigadier General Thomas DuBose, the chief of staff of the Eighth Air Force, later said, "The whole balloon part was a cover story. That was the part of the story we were told to give to the public and the news."

From that day on, the military tried to convince the news media that the objects found near Roswell in July of 1947 were nothing more than the wreckage of an ordinary weather balloon.

The remainder of the wreckage in Roswell was crated and stored in a hangar. The army sent out another press release, which read: "Reports of flying saucers whizzing through the sky fell off sharply today as the army and the navy began a concentrated campaign to stop the rumors." The release also explained that Army Air Force

Headquarters in Washington had "delivered a blistering rebuke to the officers at Roswell."

The presentation ended. I rose to my feet, along with everyone else in the hall, and applauded loudly. Of course, I'd love to get into the base at Roswell and see what the army is hiding in those crates and coffins. Who wouldn't? It's obvious to me that General Ramey switched the real UFO wreckage with some weather balloon pieces and was covering up the truth. While most people connected to the case are long gone, I'm sure the evidence of a large cover-up is locked up in Roswell.

I only hope that someday the truth is revealed.

"That was so cool," said CubManiac, proudly pointing to his "Don't Trust the Government!" T-shirt. "Thanks for telling me about this, dude. I gotta go. My mom's waiting for me back at the hotel. I'll see ya online, Jason."

I said goodbye to my friends and got another punch in the arm from Gothgirl.

"Maybe we could do a little investigating of our own while we're here," she said mischievously. "We could get to the bottom of this Roswell thing once and for all. What do you say?"

"I thought you'd never ask," I replied.

NEW YORK
Impressions of a Missing Boy

What I learned in history class: On May 24, 1626, Peter Minuit, the director general of the Dutch West India Company, traded goods such as beads and cloth with the Manhattoe tribe. The goods were valued at sixty guilders, roughly the equivalent of twenty-four dollars. In exchange, the Dutch West India Company received Manhattan Island.

A story you won't find in your textbook: One of my IM buddies, who uses the name PsychicFreak (PF), contacted me about a woman in upstate New York.

PF: Yo, J. Got a great psychic story for you.

ParaGuy: I already knew that.

PF: What? Are you messing with me?

ParaGuy: Nope. Yesterday I had a vision that you would IM me today with a story.

PF: Serious?

ParaGuy: Yeah.

PF: Whoa. How come no psychic powers are rubbing off on me? I know just as many psychics as you do.

ParaGuy: Guess I'm just lucky. By the way, I'm totally messing with you.

PF: C'mon, man! Don't do that to me. I should have known—you're already too weird to have psychic powers, too.

ParaGuy: Uh, thanks, I guess. So what's the story?

PF: This really happened to some lady my mom knows upstate named Mary Barber. Her kid got lost in the woods. Here's what she told me.

◉◉

It started as one of the best days I can remember. My husband, Philip, my six-year-old son, Timmy, and I were at a community picnic at beautiful Seneca Lake. The sun was shining brightly that warm Sunday morning in

August, giving no hint of the panic and terror that was to come.

As the afternoon slowly slid toward evening, families began packing up their coolers and picnic blankets. It was then that Philip and I noticed that Timmy wasn't with the group of kids with whom he'd been playing soccer.

"Tim!" Philip called, raising his voice enough to be heard over the din of happy picnickers. He got no response.

"Timmy!" I shouted, running this way and that and desperately looking in all directions as the sun started to set.

As panic set in, I rushed through the crowd, frantically asking if anyone had seen Timmy. A few of the kids said they had been playing soccer with him, but that the game had ended about half an hour earlier.

"Tim!" Philip shouted again.

"Timmy!" I called out, the hopeless feeling in my gut growing more intense by the second. Others joined in, calling out for our son.

Everyone stopped what they were doing and fanned out around the picnic grounds. Philip called the local sheriff, Marty Sampson, on his cell phone, and within a few minutes more than a hundred people, including the sheriff, his deputies, and members of the fire department rescue squad were combing the dense woods surrounding the lake's picnic area.

As darkness crept in, Philip and I were frantic. Well, no, not frantic. That's too feeble a word to describe what I was feeling. I was hysterical at that point.

The police and rescue squad distributed as many flash-lights as they could gather and the search continued. Everyone yelled Timmy's name as loudly as they could.

It was now pitch-black outside, and thick fog started rolling in off the lake. I felt completely helpless, but I was not going home without my son.

That's when Clark Kasem, a firefighter from the rescue squad, suggested that we call his tenant, a man named John McMahon, who was known in the area for his psychic powers.

I didn't believe in psychics, and neither did Sheriff Sampson. But I was desperate and ready to take help from anyone.

"I don't go in for all that stuff, Clark," Sheriff Sampson said. "You know that. This guy could send us off on a wild-goose chase for all we know."

"Sheriff, I don't see the harm in talking to this man," I said, fighting back tears. "We've got to do *something*!"

"He's got a good reputation, Marty," Clark said to the sheriff. "We've got nothing to lose."

Sheriff Sampson nodded. Then Clark called up John McMahon, who agreed to come down to the lake.

"I'll need an item of Timmy's clothing," John said, hurrying from his car a few minutes later.

I fumbled through Timmy's backpack, barely able to open the zipper, my hands were shaking so much. I fished out his jacket and handed it to John.

Closing his eyes, John McMahon grasped the jacket tightly.

We all turned off our flashlights. A tense silence descended.

Minute after excruciating minute slipped by in the total darkness. *What's this guy doing?* I thought. *We're wasting our time!*

Then the psychic spoke softly. "I see a stone house with a row of overturned boats."

"That's the old boathouse on the far side of the lake," Philip said. "Is he in there? That's awfully far from the picnic area."

"Maybe," John replied. "That's the clearest image I received."

"Let's go!" I said.

"Mary, this fog is impossible," the sheriff said. "I think we have to wait—"

"I'm not waiting!" I screamed, switching my flashlight back on. "My boy is out there. Someone may have taken him. Or he could be hurt. I'm going."

I hurried toward the edge of the lake, unable to see much more than my own flashlight beam slicing through the thick fog. Philip ran along beside me. The sheriff and John McMahon followed.

The fog was too thick to risk taking a boat across the lake. We were going to have to walk around the edge. The evening chill turned my fingers numb, but I gripped the cold metal flashlight as if it were a lifeline leading directly to Timmy.

As we traveled around the lake, the open shore gave way to a dense area of woods. The first fallen leaves crunched under my feet as I wended my way between the trees.

Hoo-hoo-hoo!

The piercing cry startled me and I dropped the light. Everything went dark. The fog closed in on me like an evil spirit, and I felt my heart pounding in my chest.

An icy hand grabbed my arm, and I screamed.

"Mary, it's me," Philip said, shining his light on the ground so I could retrieve my own. "You got so far ahead of us, I thought we'd lost you, too."

"Let's keep going," I said, flipping my light back on and plunging ahead.

The wind picked up, rattling leaves in the barely visible trees. But I plowed forward, keeping the shoreline to my left as best I could.

I spotted a building in the distance. "The boathouse!" I cried. "Tim!" I ran toward the stone structure. Rowboats were lined up along the near side of the building. I swung around to the front and stopped at a small wooden door.

"I get a very strong impression of Tim inside this building," said John as he ran up beside me. He clasped Tim's jacket firmly in his hands.

"Tim!" I shouted.

Silence from within.

I grabbed the rusty doorknob. I wanted to open the door more than I've ever wanted anything in my life. But I couldn't bear to find out what I feared was on the other side.

I shook the wobbly knob, bit my lower lip, then flung the door open.

"Tim!" I choked out a strained cry as I swept my beam over the cobweb-covered interior.

Among the broken boats and oars I saw—nothing! No Tim! I don't know if I was more relieved that he wasn't lying in there, hurt or worse, or more panicked that we were no closer to finding him than we had been an hour ago.

I turned to John McMahon, furious. "Why did you bring us here? Why are you doing—"

"Wait, Mary!" Philip cut me off. "I found something." Kneeling down beside an overturned boat, Philip picked up Timmy's baseball cap, which peeked out from the edge of the boat.

"Oh, no!" I cried, stepping back, nearly fainting. *Was Timmy under there? Was he . . .*

Philip grabbed the edge of the boat and flipped it over. I gasped as I trained my light on the spot.

Nothing. No sign of Tim.

"Tim was obviously here," Philip said, gripping the cap close to his chest. "But he moved on."

"If I may," John said gently, reaching out his hand.

Philip handed him the cap.

Again, John closed his eyes and held the cap for what felt like an eternity.

"I get a very strong sense of a small log cabin next to a large rock," John said.

"Is he alive? *Tell me!*" I screamed.

"I can't tell," John replied calmly. "But I think we should go this way."

He pointed to a trail leading away from the boathouse and into the woods.

Philip led the way now. I followed. What else could I do? I had pinned my hopes on the powers of this man. So far he had found Tim's cap. That was no coincidence, right? But what would we find at this cabin? A shirt? A sneaker?

I pushed the horrible thoughts away and stumbled blindly through the fog, caught up in the vague hope that we'd find Tim alive.

We moved deeper into the woods, following a path that was harder and harder to make out. *This all looks the same,* I thought. *Where is this log cabin? There are no buildings here. We're in the middle of the woods for no reason!*

And then the trail ended. Dense trees closed in all around us. The loud rustle of leaves in the high branches seemed to mock our efforts. We had come to a dead end.

"Where did you take us?" I screamed at McMahon. "Where is my son?"

An eerie howl split the night.

"Coyotes!" the sheriff said.

The howling grew louder as more and more animals joined in the bloodcurdling chorus. Tim was still out there among them.

McMahon remained silent. He gripped the cap once more and closed his eyes. "There!" he said softly, pointing to his right along the thick tree line.

I whipped my flashlight beam to the right and it fell upon a large boulder.

"There's the rock!" I cried, running toward it, tripping over tree roots as I struggled to keep my balance. "But where's the cabin? This is wrong!"

"Tim!" Philip shouted.

Again, no answer.

I reached the rock. There was no sign of Tim. Taking a deep breath, I stepped around the rock and trained my light on the ground.

No Tim. But my beam caught something familiar. I knelt down and picked up a plastic toy log cabin. It was Tim's, part of a frontier play set we had bought him for his birthday.

He had been here. But how long ago? And where was he now?

John took the toy in his hands. "That way!" he said confidently, pointing behind us.

Would we finally find Tim, or just another of his possessions?

I rushed in the direction John indicated, ignoring the branches scratching my arms and face. Then I tripped over something buried in the leaves and found myself sprawled out under a tree.

Crawling back through the leaves, I discovered that I had tripped over the body of my son!

"Tim!" I screamed, shining my light into his face. His eyes were closed. I felt his ruby-colored cheek. It was cold. "No!" I screamed.

Then I heard him breathe. I shook him gently and he opened his eyes.

"Mommy?" he cried, then burst into tears. "I got lost. I was so cold. I called for you over and over but couldn't find you or Daddy. I tried to walk home but couldn't find you!"

"Thank you, John McMahon," I said, weeping with joy. "Thank you for finding my son!"

NORTH CAROLINA
The Headless Conductor

What I learned in history class: On December 17, 1903, Wilbur and Orville Wright made the first successful sustained flight in a heavier-than-air craft in Kitty Hawk, North Carolina. They chose Kitty Hawk—specifically, a sand dune called Kill Devil Hill—because of its remote location and strong, steady winds.

A story you won't find in your textbook: My relatives are spread out all over the country, and every year we have a reunion in a different town. This year it was Charlotte, North Carolina. My parents got it in their heads to take a train, which was cool. I love looking out the window at the world rushing by.

We arrived at night, and a few minutes before we pulled into the station, I peered out the window at the track ahead of us, which curved sharply to the right. A bright light appeared on the track directly in front of us. The light swung back and forth in an arc, as if someone were standing right on the tracks with a flashlight or a lantern. I yelled out, terrified that we were going to hit someone. But when we passed the spot, nothing was there. As the tracks curved to the left, I ran to a window on the other side of the train and looked back. There, behind the train, was the light, still swinging back and forth, as if we had passed right through whoever or whatever was holding it. Then suddenly, the light vanished. Needless to say, this threw my paranormal meter into overdrive. So when we arrived, I decided to ask around about the strange light on the tracks. What I discovered shocked and spooked me. Here's what happened.

◉◉

The evening after we arrived in Charlotte, I took a break from the family festivities and walked back to the train station. I spoke with a man working in an office there, explaining to him exactly what I had seen. The man appeared nervous and uncomfortable as I spoke.

"Can't help you, son," he said, turning back to his paperwork.

I got the strong impression that he was hiding something. Undaunted, I strolled over to a group of teenagers who were hanging out on the steps in front of the station.

"What are you looking for, kid?" asked a tall boy with curly black hair, who looked to be about fifteen.

I recounted my tale for the group.

"Oooh!" moaned a short girl with bright red hair and a silver stud in her nose. She was trying her best to sound creepy. "You saw the Headless Conductor!"

"Headless Conductor?"

"Yeah," answered the boy. "I guess you're not from around here, huh?"

I smiled and shrugged. "Nope. Is that a crime?"

"Yeah, it's a crime," the girl said. "I'll call the cops."

"Give him a break, Janine, will ya?" The boy turned to me and continued. "Some railroad guy carrying a lantern was hit by a train years ago. Knocked his head clean off his body. Now, every night, his ghost comes back to that spot to look for his head."

"Weird, huh?" the girl said, curling her hands into the shape of claws and making a creepy face at me.

"I've heard weirder," I replied. *If they only knew.*

"Come on," whined Janine. "This is boring, and I'm hungry. Let's go get something to eat."

With that, the group got up from the steps and shuffled down the road.

"Good luck with your ghost, kid," Janine called back as they disappeared around a corner.

Slightly confused and more than a little discouraged, I strolled along the platform, staring down at the tracks, trying to decide if I should go back to the spot where I had seen the light, to see if it would appear again that night.

"Looking for something, young man?" asked a voice from behind me.

I spun around and saw an older man sitting on a bench on the platform. He was wearing a train engineer's uniform, complete with striped suspenders and a striped cap. "I didn't notice you there," I said, regaining my composure.

"Didn't mean to scare you," the man said. "The name's McCarthy. Leon McCarthy. You look like you're lost."

I introduced myself. "You work for the railroad, right?" I asked. I guess it was a dumb question. Why else would he be at a train station, dressed in that uniform?

Mr. McCarthy just nodded.

"I think I saw the ghost of the Headless Conductor," I said.

"What did those kids tell you about him?" Mr. McCarthy asked.

I repeated the brief tale they had told me.

"Wanna hear the full story?" he asked.

"Sure," I replied. "I collect stories about weird stuff like that."

"Is that so?" Mr. McCarthy said. "Well, come with me and I'll show you something you can add to your collection."

He stood up slowly and walked to the far end of the platform. Intrigued, I followed him. At the end of the platform, he jumped down to the track and switched on a flashlight. I leaped down beside him, pulling out my own flashlight, and we strolled away from the station, following the tracks in the direction from which I had arrived the previous night.

As we walked, guided by the bright beams, Mr. McCarthy filled me in on the tale of the Headless Conductor.

"Years ago, trains signaled each other using lanterns," he began. "A fella named Joe Baldwin here in Charlotte worked as a conductor along this line. One night, Joe was riding in the last car of his train, as he usually did. Suddenly, he realized that the train was slowing down. He ran to the front of the car, only to see that it had separated from the rest of the train, which sped away from him as the car he was in slowed to a crawl.

"Just then, Joe heard the whistle of another train—a train that had been following his! Running to the back of the car, which had almost rolled to a complete stop, Joe looked out in horror at the headlight of the train speeding right toward him. Grabbing his lantern, he stepped out onto the rear platform and waved his lantern back and forth, trying desperately to signal the engineer in the train behind him to stop.

"Nobody knows if his lantern went out or if the other train's brakes malfunctioned, but whatever it was, the second train barreled right into poor old Joe. The next morning, the cops found Joe's body lying right on the tracks. But they never did find his head. Since then, people say you can see Joe's headless ghost out with his lantern, searching for his missing head."

"Have you ever seen him?" I asked as we stopped walking.

"Sure," Mr. McCarthy replied. "Just about every night. Right here."

Whooo-whooo! Whooo-whooo!

The piercing cry of a train whistle split the quiet night.

Far in the distance, I could make out the single headlight of a train heading our way. As we stepped a few feet back, to get a safe distance from the tracks, a second light appeared. This one was much closer and fainter. It arced back and forth across the tracks.

My own flashlight beam revealed a flickering lantern being swung back and forth by a man—a man with no head! "It's Joe!" I whispered, excitement and terror coursing through my body.

"Yup," Mr. McCarthy replied. "Right on time."

Sweeping its lantern to and fro, the headless body squatted down, groping on the ground at either side of the tracks.

"He's looking for his head!" I cried.

"Yup," Mr. McCarthy repeated.

The train tore down the tracks, zipping closer and closer to Joe.

"It's going to hit him again!" I shouted, just as the train reached the spot where the lantern swung.

The flickering light vanished as the train rumbled past us, car after car clattering by, just a few yards from our faces. When the last car had rattled past, the swinging light reappeared, in exactly the same spot it had been before the train's arrival.

"Mr. McCarthy! He's back!" I shouted, turning toward him.

But Mr. McCarthy was gone.

"Mr. McCarthy?" I yelled again, frantically sweeping the area with my flashlight. There was no sign of the man who had been crouched beside me just seconds earlier. Glancing back, I saw that Joe and his lantern had vanished as well.

Standing up, I hurried back toward the station, frightened and alone. When I reached the platform, I scrambled up, then dashed to the office.

"I saw him!" I shouted breathlessly.

"Saw who?" the man in the office asked, clearly annoyed at my return.

"Joe Baldwin," I replied. "I saw Joe Baldwin holding his lantern, looking for his head."

"Who told you about Joe Baldwin?" the man asked, showing interest for the first time.

"Mr. McCarthy," I explained. "Leon McCarthy."

His eyes opened wide as he leaned his face in close to mine.

"Leon McCarthy has been dead for years," he said.

"That's impossible!" I cried. "I just saw him. I just spoke with him."

"Leon McCarthy died the same night as Joe Baldwin," the man explained.

"What?" I cried. "But how?"

"Leon McCarthy was the engineer driving the train that hit Joe Baldwin!"

NORTH DAKOTA
Wake Up, You're Dead!

What I learned in history class: What is known today as Fargo, North Dakota, used to be called Centralia. In the 1870s, Northern Pacific Railroad chose to honor William Fargo, the railroad's director and financial backer, as well as a partner in the Wells-Fargo Express Company, by naming the town after him.

A story you won't find in your textbook: Out-of-body experiences are amazing. The thought that you can travel around the block or around the world while never leaving your bedroom intrigues me, and I posted that thought one week on my blog. Richard Johns of Fargo, North Dakota, wrote me with his story. His journey was the type that usually features a one-way ticket!

◉◉

It was supposed to be the best day of my life.

I had been accepted into medical school and was getting ready to begin my journey toward realizing my lifelong dream of becoming a doctor. Then, about a week before I was to head off to school, I got what I initially thought was a really bad chest cold.

"Just my luck," I said to my mom as I stopped my packing to try to get some rest.

"Have some soup," she said, placing a tray next to my bed. "You'll be just fine by the time you have to leave."

She was wrong.

As the days passed, I got progressively worse. The chest cold developed into pneumonia, and just three days before I was supposed to leave, I ended up in the hospital. I felt horrible and could barely breathe, but I insisted on leaving. Ever since I was a child, I had dreamed of becoming a doctor. Here was my chance, and I had to get to school. Nothing, not even pneumonia, was going to stop me.

I tried to get out of the hospital bed but crashed to the floor, too weak to stand. The nurses lifted me back into bed, and this time I stayed there. I couldn't even lift my hand to wipe the sweat from my brow, let alone try getting up again.

Later that night, I could hear my mom speaking gently to me. I couldn't make out what she was saying, but it sounded like she was crying and praying. I tried to tell her that I was burning up with fever and for her to get someone to help me, but I was too weak to speak. My doctor came in as one of the nurses was checking my temperature. I heard the nurse say, "Doctor, his temperature has soared to 106.5!"

My mother's crying grew louder.

I felt trapped in a dizzying haze. The room took on a strange appearance as my vision blurred. Everything started melting away. I heard the familiar clicking and banging sounds of an MRI machine but had no sense of being inside its confining tube.

And then, much to my surprise, I woke up. I felt alert. My symptoms were gone. My head was clear and my vision was normal. Sitting up in my hospital bed, I realized I was alone in the room. I thought my mother might be at the cafeteria getting some coffee. I stepped out of the bed and easily kept my balance. "Whatever they did, it worked," I said, stretching my arms over my head. "I feel great!"

Then I glanced at a calendar on the wall. *Oh, no,* I thought. *I've got to leave for medical school tomorrow morning.* Then I looked over at the clock. 6:55 p.m. "I better get out of here now!"

I rushed for the door and then realized that I was wearing a hospital gown. *I'm not going to get far in this getup,* I thought. *Better find my clothes.* I looked around the room for my things, but the closet was empty, as were all the drawers in the dresser, which had held my personal belongings.

Where did all my stuff go? I wondered. *And where are my clothes?*

I searched every corner of the room, then finally thought to look under the bed. I turned to crouch but froze in fear as I noticed a man lying there. "How can someone be there?" I said aloud. "I just got out of that bed!"

The figure in the bed was lying perfectly still with his eyes closed. While he looked familiar, I didn't bother to investigate. School began the next day, and I had a lot to do if I was going to get started on my dream.

Ignoring the fact that I was wearing a hospital gown, I dashed into the hallway. Frustration swept through me as I searched for anyone who could help me.

"Excuse me!" I shouted at a nurse. "Where are my clothes? I need my clothes. I have to get out of here."

The nurse ignored me and kept walking.

An orderly arrived with fresh sheets for the bed.

"Hey!" I shouted desperately, my anger growing. "I need some clothes."

But the orderly also ignored me. He actually brushed right past me.

"Forget this. Maybe Mom has my things," I said. I hurried down the stairs and out onto the street, with my open hospital gown flapping behind me. This was no time for modesty. I wanted to get the heck out of there. Stepping into traffic, I tried to wave down a car or a cab—anything that could get me home.

No one stopped.

Frustrated to the point of rage, I tore back into the hospital. I would *make* them tell me where my clothes were, and then have them call me a cab. I felt fine now. The illness had passed and I was not going to miss the start of medical school.

Reaching my room, I peered in and saw that the man in my bed was gone. In fact, the entire bed was gone. Glancing to my right, I saw the orderly pushing the bed down the hall. I hurried after it.

I slipped into the elevator beside the orderly and the bed.

"Who is he?" I asked, recalling the feeling that I somehow knew the man. "Is he okay?"

"Man, what a shame," the orderly muttered, shaking his head. "This one was so young."

"So he's *not* okay?" I asked. "What's wrong with him?"

The elevator doors slid open and I followed as the orderly wheeled the bed through a set of double doors. Walking slowly down the empty, featureless hallway, I reached the doors just as they closed, revealing a sign on the front.

"Morgue?" I muttered to myself. "Why are they taking that guy to the morgue?"

I burst through the doors and found myself in a cold, dimly lit room. Rows of dead bodies filled the space. There was no sign of the orderly—or any other living person. Just me and a roomful of corpses, lying on dull metal tables covered in white sheets.

Terrified, I ran down the row of tables, tearing off the sheets, revealing diseased, injured, mutilated bodies. I saw children and old people, all beyond any hope of recovery.

At the end of the first row, I tore the sheet off a body

and recognized the face. It was the man who had been in my room. The man who looked so familiar. As I stared down at the dead man's face, the corpse opened its eyes, and I knew why the man looked so familiar to me.

I was looking at my *own face*, peering into my *own eyes*. "How is this possible?" I screamed as the dead man continued to stare up at me.

The light in the room grew brighter and I squeezed my eyes shut against the glare. When I opened them, I was lying on a cold metal table in the morgue, looking up at a doctor. In one hand the doctor held a syringe. In the other he grasped a piece of paper.

"What happened?" I asked. I could feel my heart pounding as if it was going to explode from my chest.

"Young man, you were dead," the doctor reported, his own face pale and covered with sweat. "I—I signed your death certificate." He showed me the piece of paper he held in his hands. I then read the details of my own death. Cause of death: heart failure. Time of death: 6:57 p.m. The date was today's date.

"The orderly who brought you down saw your eyes open," the doctor continued. "He called me and I injected adrenaline directly into your heart. I can't explain what happened."

I tried to comprehend what I had just experienced. How could I have watched my own dead body being wheeled down the hall? Had I left my body when it died? And what had brought me back?

I remained in the hospital for a few more days before fully recovering from my fever. Although I arrived at medical school a bit late, I was happy to have gotten there at all. And believe me, I swore that when I became a doctor, I would wait a good long time before signing anyone's death certificate!

OHIO
How to Solve Your Own Murder

What I learned in history class: Ohio is the home state of seven presidents, more than any other state. Ulysses S. Grant, Rutherford B. Hayes, James Garfield, Benjamin Harrison, William McKinley, William H. Taft, and Warren G. Harding were all born in Ohio.

A story you won't find in your textbook: Sometimes a person who is about to be murdered will try to leave a clue behind to help the police find the killer. But Maria Carrillo, a Filipina immigrant living in Cleveland, Ohio, didn't leave behind any clues. She simply told police who had killed her—in her own voice! Well, her ghost did, anyway. Dr. Arnold McMaster e-mailed me this bizarre story of how

Maria's ghost, speaking through Arnold's wife, Kate, fingered her own killer!

◉◉

My wife, Kate, and I were friendly with Maria Carrillo. Maria was a nurse at the hospital where I'm a doctor and Kate works as a physical therapist. I know that Maria came to the United States from the Philippines, like so many immigrants before her, looking for a better life. She thought she had found it here in Cleveland. But her life was cut tragically short.

One day not long ago, Maria failed to show up for work. She didn't call to explain, which was not like her. Repeated calls to her apartment went unanswered. After two days, her worried supervisor at the hospital called the police, who broke down the door to Maria's apartment. Inside they discovered her lifeless body sprawled out on the bedroom floor. She had been stabbed repeatedly. Police searched the apartment but didn't find many clues. They began an investigation, which quickly led to nothing but dead ends.

That's when my wife and I entered the picture. Kate and I were home one evening a few weeks after Maria's death.

"Some coffee?" Kate asked as we finished cleaning up the dinner dishes.

"Sure," I said, turning to reach for the coffeepot.

Suddenly, Kate fell back against the counter, dropping the dish she was holding. It shattered into a million pieces on the tile floor.

"Kate!" I shouted. "What's the matter?" I could see she was shaking.

Kate dropped to her knees and stared straight ahead. Then her eyes rolled up into her head.

"Kate!" I cried, dropping to the floor beside her. Her head snapped back as she fell forward.

I caught her before she hit the floor and laid her down gently, cradling her head in my hands. "Kate, can you hear me?"

Kate remained limp in my arms, completely unresponsive. Her eyes were open, showing only white.

I grabbed my bag and pulled out the small light I use to examine patients' eyes. Shining the light into Kate's eyes, I watched as her pupils rolled back down. But she stared up blankly, still not acknowledging me.

Could she have had a stroke? I thought. *Some other kind of attack?* But the symptoms didn't match any condition I knew.

I grasped her wrist and quickly took her pulse. Kate's heart was racing! *This doesn't make any sense. If anything, her heart rate would slow upon her losing consciousness.*

I grabbed my cell phone and dialed 911. I knew I had to get her into the ER as quickly as I could. Mere seconds could make the difference between life and . . . I couldn't even think it.

Then, before the 911 operator picked up, Kate bolted upright and a second later climbed to her feet as if nothing had happened.

"What was that?" I asked, ending the call with a deep sigh of relief. But my relief was premature.

Kate walked out of the kitchen, acting as if she hadn't even heard me. She headed to the bedroom, her hands pinned to her sides. Her strides were steady but stiff and robotic.

"Kate, can you hear me?" I yelled, hurrying along behind her.

Reaching the bedroom, Kate stretched out on the bed and rolled onto her back. Suddenly, her entire body began shaking violently. Her arms whipped around wildly, her legs kicking at the air as if she were trying to push something away.

The convulsions grew more intense. I was terrified. I rushed back to my bag and quickly prepared a syringe with a mild sedative, hoping to reduce the convulsions. Then I hurried back into the bedroom.

As I stepped toward Kate, a powerful, invisible force shoved me away from the bed. I rushed back toward Kate but was again shoved halfway across the room. As I reached for my phone to try 911 again, Kate stopped shaking. Her jaw dropped open, and a low, guttural sound emerged from her mouth.

The sound gradually morphed into actual words. But the voice coming from Kate's mouth was not her own. It was as if another person were transmitting her voice through Kate.

Kate repeated the same phrase over and over. A chill shot down my spine as I listened.

"I am Maria Carrillo."

"Is this a weird joke, Katy?" I asked, though I knew my wife would never play a prank like this.

"I am Maria Carrillo," she repeated.

I felt the blood drain from my face. I recognized the voice. I had worked with Maria long enough to know her voice, her accent. No doubt about it, Maria's voice was coming from my wife's mouth.

"I am Maria Carrillo."

Now I was able to approach the bed. I peered deeply into Kate's eyes. They remained vacant and hollow. Her arms hung limply at her sides. Nothing moved but her mouth.

"I am Maria Carrillo," she said again. Then she continued. "I have returned, and I am using this body to tell you that I was brutally murdered by Felix Allen."

I fell back in shock, grabbing the dresser to steady myself. Felix Allen was an orderly in the hospital where we worked with Maria.

Kate, or rather, Maria went on. "Felix Allen followed me home, then forced his way into my apartment. He said he was going to take all my jewelry. I grabbed him and tried to stop him, but he was too strong. He knocked me to the floor, then stabbed me. As I lay there dying, he taunted me, telling me he was taking my jade bracelet, my marcasite earrings, and my gold necklace. He said that he was going to give my pearl cocktail ring, my most treasured possession, to his girlfriend. That ring was given to me by my mother. It is inscribed with the words 'Love, Mother.'

"I cursed at him, and that's when he went berserk, stabbing me over and over until I finally saw no more. Please catch him, and send the ring back to my mother. No one else should have it now."

Then Kate's eyes closed, and she seemed to fall into a deep sleep. I rushed to her side and took her pulse. Normal.

A few minutes later, Kate woke up with a terrible headache and absolutely no memory of what had taken place.

"Welcome back to the land of the living," I said, smiling. "You had me worried for a minute there."

"What happened?" Kate asked. "I was in the kitchen, and then . . . How did I get in here?"

I tried my best to explain what had happened. Needless to say, Kate was skeptical. After all, she's not the one who stood here listening to a dead woman talk!

I felt compelled to go to the police, even though I suspected they'd think I was crazy. I know I would have diagnosed psychosis if a patient of mine in the hospital had told me this story. But, starved as they were for leads, two veteran detectives agreed to pay a visit to Felix Allen.

After obtaining a search warrant, the two detectives showed up at Allen's apartment one evening. Armed with a detailed list of what had been stolen—conveniently provided by the victim—the detectives searched the apartment while Allen looked on.

One by one, they found the jade bracelet, the marcasite earrings, and the gold necklace. Then Allen's girlfriend happened to stop by—and she was wearing a pearl cocktail ring.

One of the detectives, threatening to arrest the girl-friend as an accessory to murder if she didn't cooperate, convinced her to take off the ring. There, engraved on the inside of the band, were the words "Love, Mother," exactly as Maria's ghost had said.

Confronted by the overwhelming evidence, Felix Allen confessed and was later convicted of murder. I asked the cops if I could take the ring and make sure it was returned to Maria's mother in the Philippines. The police agreed.

And so the case was officially closed—*un*officially solved by the ghost of Maria Carrillo.

OKLAHOMA
Helping Hand

What I learned in history class: On April 19, 1995, an explosion ripped through the Alfred P. Murrah Federal Building in Oklahoma City, Oklahoma, killing 168 people. Until the September 11 attacks in 2001, it was the largest terrorist attack of any kind in the nation's history. The bomber, Timothy McVeigh, was tried, convicted, and later executed.

A story you won't find in your textbook: Most of the stories I've uncovered about encounters with UFOs and aliens tell of mysterious vanishings, horrific abductions, and terrible torture. The sight of unexplained lights or flying saucers in the sky fills people with fear and apprehension. But Robin Marley of Clayton, Oklahoma, had a different sort of story. Her visitors had no hostile intentions. In fact, without her visitors' help, she might have lost her mother.

◉◉

Mom was working the late shift and called to ask me to pick up my eleven-year-old brother, Jeff. Christmas was coming and Mom was trying to put in as much overtime as she could. I didn't mind being Jeff's chauffeur if it helped Mom.

"I should be home by the time you and Jeff are getting ready for school tomorrow, okay?" she said.

"Sure, Mom," I said. "See you tomorrow."

I'd made plenty of trips to shuttle Jeff to and from movies or soccer practice. This cold evening, Jeff and a bunch of his friends had gone bowling.

As I drove the forty-five minutes from home to the bowling alley (why does everything have to be so far apart in Oklahoma?), I couldn't help thinking of the prom, so many months away. I needed a lot more babysitting jobs if I was going to save up enough money for the dress I wanted, not to mention the jewelry, tanning sessions, and shoes. I started to make a mental budget and got discouraged. As I drove along narrow two-lane roads lined on either side by high banks of snow, the strapless pink dress I hoped to wear come springtime felt a million dollars away.

When I arrived at the bowling alley, Jeff and his friends were in the final frame of their last game. I hung out with a couple of my friends who worked at the snack bar. We gossiped a little and talked about the huge winter storm that was supposed to hit the next morning.

The kids soon finished bowling. My friends' manager was hovering around the cash register, which meant they were going to get in trouble soon if we didn't stop talking. Jeff and I each said our goodbyes and headed for home.

"How'd you do?" I asked once we were in the car.

Jeff shrugged. "I bowled a hundred and ten," he said. "Pretty good. Two guys were ahead of me, though."

Normally, I don't try to engage in conversation with Jeff. Since he's six years my junior, we don't have a whole lot to talk about. But I knew he liked bowling a lot.

"So you had fun, right?" I asked.

"Yeah," Jeff replied. "Especially when Matt Peters threw three gutter balls in a row. You know, he's Mr. Perfect Form."

"Well, that's cool," I said, finishing my sisterly duty for the night.

I turned on the radio and Jeff pulled out his PSP. Because everything is so far apart in Oklahoma, you learn to entertain yourself in the car. When we were about halfway home, I glanced in my rearview mirror and spotted a red light, which appeared to be trailing us. "Oh, man," I said, thinking it was the cops. Following driver's-ed procedure, I started slowing down and began to pull over to the side of the road. That's when I looked into the mirror again.

The red light was rising into the air.

"What the heck? That's no police car," I said, looking back over my shoulder.

The red light pulled up alongside our car. This is going to sound crazy, but the light was attached to a cigar-shaped metal craft that hovered beside us, keeping pace with the car.

"What is that?" Jeff shouted, the panic obvious in his voice. "Is that a UFO?"

"I don't know! I don't know!" I shouted back, desperately trying to find another—any other—explanation for what we were seeing.

The craft rose above my sightline. Based on the eerie red glow bathing the road around us, it now seemed to be directly above our car.

Suddenly, a brilliant crimson light, many times brighter than the soft glow, flooded the car. Total panic overtook me as I realized I could no longer see the road. I kept my foot on the gas, though. Maybe that was stupid, but I didn't want to stop and be at the mercy of whoever was driving that ship.

"What's happen—" Jeff started yelling, before his voice was cut off suddenly.

"Jeff!" I shouted, stories of UFO abductions flashing through my mind. "Jeff, are you all right?"

Jeff only stared straight ahead into the blinding red light coming through the windshield. His mouth hung open and his body appeared frozen in some kind of a trance.

Just as I realized that there was something very wrong with my brother, I discovered that I couldn't move. My limbs felt locked, my head forced by some outside power to turn and stare straight into the radiant scarlet light. Then a terrifying thought seized me.

If I can't move, I can't control the car! We're going to crash!
I felt the car drift over toward the shoulder of the road. I
mentally braced for impact, certain we were about to smash
into a tree or a road sign, wishing I could at least lean over
to protect my little brother.

And then the car slowed, coming to a gentle stop on
the shoulder. The bright red light faded and was replaced
by a spinning circle of white light. As the white light
flashed through the car, I became aware of a low humming
sound that grew in intensity.

This is it! I thought. *This is when they beam us up to their
ship and we're never heard from again. Or worse, they cut us
open and experiment on us, then send us back, and we spend the
rest of our lives completely traumatized and deformed!*

But I was wrong.

Through the dull humming sound, I began to hear a
voice, faint at first, then growing louder. The voice was
jerky and uneven, as if a foreign language were being trans-
lated into English by somebody who didn't quite understand what he was saying.

Holding my breath, I listened as the words became
clearer. "Mother . . . in trouble," the mechanical-sounding
voice said. "Mother . . . accident . . . Hiline Road . . ." Then
it continued. "Mother . . . needs . . . your . . . help. . . . Branson's barn."

The voice concluded with a single word: "Hurry."

The humming stopped. The bright white light disappeared, and I watched through the windshield as the

spacecraft drifted slowly upward, its red lights fading into the star-strewn sky.

I could move again, and I turned to Jeff, who was breathing hard. I was grateful to see he could also move and speak again.

"Did you hear that, Robin?" Jeff asked excitedly. "Do you think something's wrong with Mom?"

Putting aside the fact that Jeff and I had just lived through what I could only call a UFO encounter, I thought of Mom working the late shift. She always drove on Hiline Road, a back road, on her way home from work. But she wasn't due home until the next morning. She wouldn't be on Hiline Road now.

"I don't know," I told Jeff, pulling back out onto the road. "Call Mom's cell and find out."

Jeff tried calling but there was no signal. "We're in a dead zone, but I'll keep trying," he said.

As I drove, I tried to sort through the details of what had happened. Jeff was asking me a million questions, but I ignored him. I needed to think. If someone had told me that morning that I was going to come that close to a UFO, I would have thought they were crazy. I'd also have expected to be more upset by the experience. Now it actually seemed sort of cool. For a moment I pictured myself becoming one of those wackos who hang out by the side of the road waiting for their alien friends to return.

But then I thought about the message. Was it true? Was

Mom in some kind of danger? It made no sense—she was at work.

"You okay?" I asked, looking over at Jeff, who had finally fallen silent.

He nodded. "A little freaked out," he said. "Now I'm really worried about Mom."

"Me too," I replied.

Driving quickly, I turned onto Hiline Road and sped toward Branson's barn. "We're getting close to the barn," I said. "Roll down the window and look out your side."

Jeff rolled down his window and stuck his head out into the darkness. Just past the barn, he spotted something.

"Robin!" he cried. "Stop!"

I slammed on the brakes and pulled over. Jeff and I scrambled out of the car. I tried not to scream as I spotted a car that had slid into a ditch at the side of the road. "It's Mom!" I shouted, climbing down into the ditch.

The front end of the car was embedded in the far wall of the ditch. I flung open the front door and saw my mother slumped against the inflated airbag. Blood trickled down the side of her face. Groceries were scattered all over the car.

"*Mom!*" I screamed, hoping against hope that she was still alive.

I gently took her hand in mine. She stirred and moaned.

"She's alive!" I called back to Jeff. "Try the cell phone again! Call 911!"

Jeff ran back to the car. "We've got a signal!" he yelled as he called for help.

I knew I shouldn't move her, so Jeff and I just stayed by her side, holding her hand, whispering softly that everything was going to be all right. She moaned and managed to speak just a little. I pieced together the fact that her manager had let everyone go home early because of the approaching storm.

A few minutes later the ambulance arrived. The paramedics carefully removed Mom from the car.

"It looks like cuts and bruises, and maybe a mild concussion, but no major injuries," one of them said. "We'll take her to the hospital for tests, but she should be fine."

I nodded, tears of relief running down my face. I actually gave my brother a hug.

"Good thing you found her," one of the paramedics said as they loaded Mom into the ambulance. "This is a pretty quiet road, and she could have been lying there for hours, even days. With this cold and the storm coming in, she would have frozen to death. You kids saved her life."

We had a little help, I thought as Jeff and I got back into the car to follow the ambulance to the hospital.

OREGON
The Lonely Lighthouse

What I learned in history class: From 1843 through the 1870s, the Oregon Trail was the route used by most people traveling to Oregon. The trail ran from Missouri to Oregon and stretched for two thousand miles.

A story you won't find in your textbook: My parents have dragged me to plenty of boring lighthouses on our family road trips, and I'd never seen one that contained more than some historical placards, outdated technology, and a bunch of tourists. Well, I made the mistake of knocking lighthouses on my blog one day after a particularly tedious trip with my parents. By the next day, I was being bombarded with haunted lighthouse stories. The one that creeped me out the most was the tale of the Yaquina Bay lighthouse in Newport, Oregon, sent in by Jeremy Bradon. This lighthouse collects souls.

◉◉

Listen, Specter, I know you're the self-proclaimed paranormal guru, but that doesn't mean you've seen it all. Lighthouses can be seriously freaky places, and I know firsthand about one of them. Two of my friends and I went to explore the Yaquina Bay lighthouse in my hometown of Newport, Oregon. It's been deserted for decades now, but that doesn't mean it's unoccupied!

Local legend tells the story of a group of teenagers a long time ago who decided to sneak into the lighthouse late one night. A girl named Muriel, the mastermind of the plan, led the way in and discovered a secret panel. Behind the panel began a series of hidden passageways that ran all over the lighthouse, including a path that led right out to sea.

Muriel's friends—a lot less brave than her (or a lot smarter, depending on how you look at it)—worried that they would all get caught by the police for trespassing. They wanted to leave, but Muriel wouldn't hear of it. She pressed on, crawling through the opening behind the secret panel and disappearing down a passageway. Her friends called to her, too afraid to follow.

"I'll be right out," Muriel shouted back. These were the last words anyone ever heard her speak.

After a few minutes Muriel's friends got nervous and began shouting for her. They received no reply. Their concerned voices echoed along the hollow passageways.

They never found Muriel's body. When she failed to return after an hour, her friends called the police. They searched every inch of the winding, hidden passageways. All they found was Muriel's bloodstained handkerchief on the landing at the top of the spiral stairs that led to the light.

From that time on, it is said that late-night visitors to the abandoned lighthouse have been able to hear Muriel's ghost crying mournfully. It is also said that although the lighthouse hasn't operated for years, when Muriel's cry is heard, the light on the top of the structure briefly glows, as if Muriel herself has lit the old lantern.

Now, you would think this story would be enough to scare kids away from the lighthouse. But teenagers in Newport are probably just as dumb as kids in your hometown. My friends Trent Finn and Dana Billings and I got it into our heads to check out the haunted lighthouse for ourselves. It was the stupidest mistake of our lives.

One summer night we rode out to the lighthouse on our bikes. A starless sky greeted us, along with the crashing waves of a restless ocean. As we dropped our bikes and looked up, Dana pointed and gasped.

"The beacon!" she cried. "It's lit. Muriel must be home tonight!"

A low, sorrowful wail sounded, barely audible above the noise of the churning sea.

"You guys hear that?" I asked, panic rising in my gut. I was ready to jump back onto my bike and pedal for home. "What is that?" I looked from Dana to Trent, and they were both smiling daringly. "Come on, you guys. Let's come back another time. Like when the light's not on."

"And miss finding Muriel's ghost?" Trent said, grinning at Dana. "Come on, Jeremy, it's like she put a welcome mat out for us. You don't want to be rude, do you? Not to a ghost?"

I didn't want to look like a total wimp, so I reluctantly followed my two friends into the lighthouse.

"I'm going right to the top!" Dana declared as we pulled out flashlights and started up the spiral stone staircase. "I gotta check out the beacon. Say hello to Muriel!"

Around and around we climbed. Dana seemed to have limitless energy. Trent and I followed, huffing and puffing.

Dana stopped suddenly when she reached the landing at the top of the stairs.

"Look!" she whispered, the horror clear in her soft voice.

All three of our flashlight beams converged on a pool of fresh blood spreading on the old stone floor of the landing.

"This is where the police found Muriel's bloody handkerchief," Dana said. "She was here tonight, lighting the beacon!"

"But it's off now," Trent observed. "See?"

Sure enough, the large lantern that had been visible from outside was dark.

"I think we should go," I said. "This is too creepy. How did that blood get there?"

"But we haven't found the passage yet!" Dana cried.

"They boarded that up years ago," Trent said.

"That's why I came prepared," Dana replied, slipping off her backpack and pulling out a hammer.

The three of us made our way down the stairs, back to the first floor. Searching the wall near the base of the stairway, Dana and Trent discovered a piece of rotted plywood nailed to the cracked plaster.

"Give me a hand!" Dana cried, shoving the claw of the hammer behind the top edge of the board. She yanked hard, tugging the decomposing plywood away from the wall. It creaked, then moved out a few inches. Trent grabbed the top edge and prepared to pull.

"Dude, lend a hand here," he said.

"I don't want to do this," I moaned.

"One, two, three!" Dana counted. The three of us yanked hard on the board. It sprang free with a sickening crack, revealing a square opening in the wall.

Without a word, Dana crawled into the hole. Trent followed. I remained behind. "I'll wait here," I said. "I'm allergic to secret passageways."

I paced back and forth, glancing at my watch, then peering into the opening. I could clearly hear the sound of the waves crashing on the shore below. I recalled the legend that said that one branch of the passageway led down to the ocean.

"I hope they didn't fall in," I muttered as I paced. Sweat dripped from my forehead now. My heart pounded in my chest.

"Dana!" came a faint cry from the passageway a minute later.

Oh my God! It's Muriel's ghost, calling to Dana! I thought, my hand shaking as I once again fought the urge to run.

"Dana!" repeated the voice, louder this time.

I peered once again into the opening and screamed as a flickering light appeared. Then I realized it must be Trent and Dana returning. I felt like such a baby.

A few seconds later, Trent's head popped through the opening. His face was red and dripping with sweat. "Did she come back this way?" he asked, panting, the fear obvious in his voice.

"Dana?" I asked. "She was with you."

"It's so dark and cramped in there, I could hardly see where I was going," Trent explained. "Dana moved so fast I couldn't keep up with her. I saw her flashlight beam disappear around a bend and that was it. I lost her. I called out for her, but she didn't answer. She was heading up at the time. Come on. Let's go back up the stairs!"

Around and around we ran, back up the stone stairs. Reaching the top landing, Trent stopped short, and I almost fell back down the stairs as I crashed into him. There on the landing beside the pool of blood sat Dana's backpack.

"Dana!" we both shouted, again and again, but the only

answer was our own terrified voices echoing off the stone walls. Trent picked up the backpack, and blood dripped onto the floor.

"Ahh!" he shrieked, dropping the bag, which tumbled down a few stairs before coming to a stop. Trent looked at me in shock.

"What happened to her?" I shouted, as if either one of us had the answer.

"We've got to go tell someone!" Trent cried. "Come on!"

We raced down the stairs and out of the lighthouse. As we picked up our bikes, Trent glanced back and sucked in a deep breath.

"Jeremy, look!" he gasped.

The beacon was lit.

As we pedaled away furiously, the same low wail we'd heard when we arrived reached my ears on the wind. But now it was clearly accompanied by a second cry, the two despondent voices mingling in horrifying harmony.

The police investigated, searching every inch of the lighthouse, but found nothing more of Dana than her blood-soaked backpack. As with Muriel, no body was ever found. Could Dana's body have plunged into the sea? Is that what happened to Muriel all those years ago? If so, why were the bloodstained items found at the very top of the lighthouse? These questions will remain unanswered.

Once a month, Trent and I visit the lighthouse. We don't dare go inside. We simply toss a bouquet of lilies, Dana's favorite flower, into the ocean.

And so the legend of the ghost of the Yaquina Bay

lighthouse has gained a new chapter. The story now goes that Muriel grew lonely after wailing in isolation for all those years and sought company, waiting for someone else to enter the secret passageway.

Now when the sky is dark and the lighthouse beacon is lit, the voices of Muriel and Dana join together, crying out for the lighthouse's next victim.

PENNSYLVANIA
"Leave us alone!"

What I learned in history class: On November 19, 1863, President Abraham Lincoln delivered a short speech at the close of ceremonies dedicating the Civil War battlefield cemetery at Gettysburg, Pennsylvania. About five thousand people were present that day to hear Lincoln's now famous Gettysburg Address.

A story you won't find in your textbook: We've all heard about houses haunted by the spirits of the dead who once lived there and who remain to annoy or frighten the current occupants. But for one family in the town of Indiana, Pennsylvania, the ghostly infestation went way past creaky floorboards, glimpses of spectral figures, and toilets flushing on their own. The Beacon family bought an eighty-year-old house on a quiet street in Indiana in the early 1970s. Strange stuff began happening almost immediately. By the mid eighties, what had once seemed to be harmless pranks had escalated into dangerous assaults. Soon the Beacons feared for their lives. I learned more about the story from the Beacon family's close friend and neighbor, Doris Lightner, who saw many of these events firsthand, and even took part in an exorcism attempting to rid the house of evil. Here is the e-mail she sent me.

◉◉

Hello, Jason. When I'm allowed the time, I do like to browse through your site. I noticed you posted a query on your message boards for more information on the famous Beacon family haunting. My name is Doris Lightner and I was a very close friend and neighbor of the Beacon family in the 1970s and 1980s. I can tell you that what at first were just bizarre events that spooked the family soon turned into a horrifying nightmare.

In the first few years after the Beacons moved into their house, they experienced a series of unexplained phenomena. One cold winter evening in 1974, Jerry Beacon had just completed work on some renovations on the house. He had put down new carpeting in the living room and replaced the fixtures in the bathroom.

As Jerry stretched out on the couch to watch some television, he glanced down and saw a large red stain on the brand-new carpet. Just as he was about to go ask his wife, Jane, if she knew who had spilled something, the television burst into flames. Grabbing a fire extinguisher, Jerry put out the blaze. No one knew where the stain had come from or how the television had caught fire.

Heading up to bed, Jerry went into the bathroom he had finished renovating that morning and was horrified to see deep gouges carved into the new sink, bathtub, and wooden cabinets. In each case, four long, parallel gashes had been cut, as if a wild, sharp-clawed beast had gone berserk in the room.

Over the next three years, the unexplained events continued. Toilets flushed by themselves. Unplugged radios blared on in the middle of the night. Drawers opened and closed, untouched by human hands. Footsteps were heard on the stairs after all the family members had gone to bed. Jerry's favorite rocking chair rocked back and forth on its own. Pipes burst, flooding the basement. When Jerry soldered them, they would burst again and again. Now, Jerry was a pretty handy guy who helped me out with chores from time to time, so I know he knew how to fix things right.

But all this was only the beginning. Great evil was to follow.

By the late 1980s, the family—Jerry, Jane, and their children, Hillary, Rita, Samantha, and Kate—had grown frustrated by the unexplained occurrences but refused to sell their house. They loved the neighborhood and believed they deserved to enjoy the home they had worked so hard to buy. They would not be driven away by ghosts. For what other explanation was there at that point? Then, in 1989, things got really ugly.

On a hot July evening, the Beacons' living room suddenly turned icy cold. The temperature plunged below freezing as ice caked the walls, and the Beacons could see their breath curling in mists.

A few days later, Jane was home alone doing laundry when a low, gravelly voice called out her name.

"Who's there?" she asked loudly. She received no reply.

Hurrying up the stairs, Jane searched every room in the house but saw no one. As she approached the basement stairs, a voice from down in the laundry room bellowed up at her. "You filthy beast," it snarled. "Get out of this house!" The voice was accompanied by a foul smell wafting up from the basement.

Terrified and enraged, Jane grabbed a kitchen knife and charged downstairs. When she reached the basement, she saw no one, but the horrid odor remained. And the laundry room had been trashed. The clean clothes, which moments earlier had been neatly stacked, were now strewn everywhere. Shirts and towels were shredded and lay in pieces on the floor.

That same night, Jane saw a tall, faceless figure floating through the kitchen. The dark form resembled a human, but its shape kept changing, as if it were made of liquid or smoke. Too stunned to scream, Jane watched in terror as the shadowy apparition passed right through the wall and into the living room.

"Jane!" Jerry cried from his club chair in the living room. "Come in here!"

Jane dashed into the living room to see the same faceless specter floating past Jerry and heading upstairs to where the children were asleep. It quickly disappeared from view. Jane and Jerry ran after it, determined to protect their children.

Crash!

A terrible crash shook the house before they got upstairs.

"Mommy!" came the heart-rending shriek from the bedroom Samantha shared with Kate. Bursting into the room, Jane and Jerry saw the ceiling fan lying in pieces on the floor. They hugged Samantha and Kate, who were unharmed but quite shaken up.

"Help!" came the cry from Hillary and Rita's room down the hall.

Racing to the room, Jerry saw the dark figure grab Hillary and yank her from her bed. She tumbled to the floor.

"Daddy! What's happening?" Hillary shrieked as she buried her head in her hands.

Jerry reached out for the specter, but his hands passed right through it. Then the apparition vanished like smoke.

"That's it!" Jerry announced as he helped Hillary to her feet. She was uninjured but completely terrified. "We are getting out of here!"

Jerry herded his family out of the house and into the car. Taking nothing but the clothes they were wearing, they drove to a nearby motel and settled in for the night. They would talk about their next step in the morning.

At 2 a.m., Jane suddenly felt a cold, clammy hand grab her ankle. She woke up to see the same dark, faceless figure that had been in the house. Its shape continued to shift as its hands pulled Jane from the motel bed. She landed hard on the floor, and screamed.

Jerry leaped at the creature, which spat putrid fumes at him, sending him reeling backward, choking and gasping for breath. Then the figure once again evaporated into the air.

Desperate, the Beacons contacted Herman and Elizabeth Cutler, psychic researchers and demonologists. The family returned to the house with the Cutlers, who began their psychic investigation immediately.

Seeing the family reenter the house, I hurried over and comforted them as Herman and Elizabeth Cutler went from room to room, touching every wall, opening every closet door, exploring the whole house inch by inch. The Beacons had told me about many of the strange events in their home, and how much they had suffered. From the moment I entered their house, I felt that something was horribly wrong. I waited anxiously to hear the Cutlers' findings.

When they had completed their tour, the Cutlers announced that they felt the house was indeed haunted.

I could have told them that, for Pete's sake!

The Cutlers explained that they sensed the presence of two evil spirits. One was a minor spirit, probably responsible for the early annoyances and damage to the house. But the other spirit was a true demon who would readily attack and harm members of the family.

I was asked to join hands with the Cutlers and all the members of the Beacon family in the living room. Then our entire group began to pray. This usually was enough to drive the demons away, Herman explained optimistically. And so I prayed quite loudly, along with everyone else. Fear coursed through my veins, but I fought back the terror with all my strength.

Suddenly, a mirror hanging on the wall began to glow a sickly green hue. It shook violently, then flew off the wall, sailing right at our group. We scattered just in time, and as the mirror struck the opposite wall, it shattered into a million glittering fragments.

"You filthy beast, get out of this house!" cried a hideous voice—the same one that had earlier commanded Jane to leave.

"They're too powerful!" Herman Cutler said as the chaos subsided. "We've got to call in Father McDermott."

We left the house, and I insisted the family stay with me for the time being.

A few days later a priest named Father Richard McDermott arrived at my home and we all went warily together to the Beacon house. Experienced in performing exorcisms, Father McDermott lit candles and incense, sprinkled holy water at various points around the house, and began praying.

I watched in complete amazement as the entire house

began to shake. Father McDermott remained perfectly calm as panic overtook the rest of us. Then a dark figure emerged from the floorboards.

A horrid stench assaulted my nose. Then, before I could run, the shadowy figure engulfed me, possessing my body with its malevolent presence. Horrific images flashed through my mind—burning buildings, rotting corpses, and other scenes of death and destruction. I felt a tangible evil invade every fiber of my being. I vaguely remembered hearing the voices of Father McDermott and Jane as the terrible images filled my head.

Then I blacked out.

When I finally came to days later, I learned that the exorcism had been unsuccessful and that the Beacons had given up, leaving their house forever. The evil that had invaded my body remained. It's still here, Jason. Waiting.

Alas, this is where my story must end. The hospital only allows us to be on the computer for half an hour each day, and I have just received my signal. Please come and visit me—I could tell you so much more.

Signed,
Doris Lightner

The e-mail had a signature line that read: *This communication has been sent from a patient at the Pennsylvania Psychiatric Hospital in Scranton.*

RHODE ISLAND
Death of a Vampire

What I learned in history class: Rhode Island is the smallest state in the United States, but it has the longest official name: State of Rhode Island and Providence Plantations. From east to west, the state measures thirty-seven miles, and from north to south forty-eight miles.

A story you won't find in your textbook: I told you about my pal Gothgirl and what a total vampire freak she is. I thought our little adventure in that Mississippi cemetery was frightening enough, but then I got this IM from her. Seems she's been spending a little too much time in cemeteries for her own good!

GG485: JS, s'up, dude?

ParaGuy: Hey, GG! Long time no IM. I haven't talked to you since Roswell.

GG485: Yeah, well, I've worked hard to forget that group of losers you call friends.

ParaGuy: You're my friend. Does that make you a loser?

GG485: Bite me, okay?

ParaGuy: Do I sense a vampire story coming?

GG485: Good guess, psychic boy. This one goes way back, but we're not talking capes and bats and all that "Good Evening, Velcome to Transylvania" stuff. I uncovered this legend on a family road trip—don't ask.

ParaGuy: I hear ya. Those can be a serious drag.

GG485: My folks are all "We're going to explore America!" and I'm all "Whatever! Can I just stay home?" But, of course, I couldn't. So we ended up in Rhode Island. That's where I heard this local story. And you know I just had to get a rubbing of that gravestone. That's when the seriously creepy stuff happened.

ParaGuy: Tell, tell, tell!

GG485: Chill, dude. I'm telling, I'm telling. But I have to start with the local legend that brought me to the cemetery. The story begins on a farm in rural Exeter, Rhode Island, in the 1880s. George T. Brown was a successful farmer and was happily married to Mary Eliza Brown. They had two daughters, Mary Olive and Mercy Lena, and a son, Edwin. You know, like a perfect family.

◉◉

But then George's luck ran out.

In the fall of 1883, his wife, Mary, got sick with tuberculosis. No vaccine or cure existed at the time, and the disease was, like, everywhere. By December of that year Mary was dead, and George was a grieving widower with three children to raise by himself.

Then, a few months later, more bad luck. George's twenty-year-old daughter, Mary Olive, gradually lost her strength, healthy color, and appetite, the first signs of the dreaded disease. By June of 1884, Mary Olive was dead too.

For the next seven years, George, Mercy, and Edwin struggled along, trying to move forward after so much death. But then the horrible disease returned.

Nineteen-year-old Mercy got tuberculosis and deteriorated very quickly. She died in January of 1892. Soon twenty-four-year-old Edwin began showing signs of the illness as well.

Poor George Brown couldn't do anything but wait for his son to die. He wondered how he would ever get on with his life. He also worried that the disease might come for him next. Part of him hoped it would.

Local superstition was that when one family was hit hard by tuberculosis, the cause might be a dead family member rising from the grave to devour the living. In other words, a member of the family had become a vampire and was slowly picking off the others, infecting them with the disease.

Hello! That got my attention!

George was a very down-to-earth guy who didn't believe this legend for a second. But many of his neighbors did (I did, too, when I heard it!), and they soon began insisting that he do something to protect himself—and them—from the possibility that his wife or one of his daughters might be a vampire.

People back then believed that you could cure tuberculosis by digging up the dead body of a relative who had died from the disease and burning the corpse's heart. The ashes of the burnt heart would then be mixed with water and consumed by those suffering from the disease (yuck!), hoping for a cure, or by healthy people to protect them from getting sick.

George wanted no part of this, but his neighbors wouldn't let it go. Finally, George agreed to have the bodies of his family dug up.

On March 17, 1892, Mary Eliza, Mary Olive, and Mercy were dug up from their graves. The bodies of the two

Marys were totally decayed. Their flesh was gone, their bones rotted.

But when the body of Mercy was unearthed, George was shocked to discover that it was still fresh, even warm to the touch. Also, Mercy's body had shifted from the position it had been in on the day she was buried. A doctor cut open her chest, revealing a red heart still filled with blood. When the heart was sliced open, fresh, warm blood dripped out.

George Brown's neighbors were horrified.

"Mercy Brown is a vampire!" they screamed.

George didn't know what to do.

All the blood was drained from Mercy's heart; then the organ was burned. The ashes of Mercy's heart were dissolved in water and given to Edwin in a desperate attempt to save his life.

It failed. Edwin died less than two months later, in May of 1892. However, no one else in Exeter contracted tuberculosis after that day. George himself lived to be eighty years old, and the townspeople firmly believed that on that fateful day in March of 1892, they had killed a vampire named Mercy Lena Brown.

> **GG485:** Sick stuff, huh, JS!?!
>
> **ParaGuy:** So, naturally, the minute you heard this story you rushed right out to the grave with your paper and charcoal to do a rubbing!
>
> **GG485:** Wouldn't you?

ParaGuy: Any sane person would. So what happened? I know you didn't get in touch just to tell me this dusty old legend.

GG485: Correct-o-mundo, dude! Check this out!

⊙⊙

I snuck out of another boring tourist thing—the world's oldest schoolhouse or whatever—and headed right for the cemetery where Mercy Brown was buried. I had my pad and charcoal with me—I never travel without them.

For all the fuss about the legend, it was kinda hard to find the grave. No big markers, no line of tourists, no plastic gravestone replicas for sale. Just a normal stone slab with her name and birth and death dates carved into it.

I knelt down on the grave and placed my rice paper over the stone. As soon as my charcoal touched the paper, I felt like something had grabbed my throat. My chest grew tight and I started coughing uncontrollably.

No way! I thought at first. I'm rubbing the grave of someone who died of TB and I start coughing? You and I both know that weird stuff happens, but this seemed too obvious. Maybe a bug just flew down my throat or something. I tried again, and this time, no coughing. As I finished transferring the image of the gravestone onto my paper, I heard what sounded like a woman crying.

I looked around. This was, after all, a cemetery, so mourners would be expected. But I was completely alone. A second voice joined in the chorus of sobs, then another and another. Some of the voices were female, some were male.

I stood and slowly backed away from the grave. The sounds of crying slowly morphed into coughing. One by one the voices barked out horrid, raspy, gut-churning coughs.

Then my throat seized up again and I had my own hacking fit.

I turned and ran from the cemetery, gasping for breath. As soon as I stumbled back out through the front gate, my coughing stopped and my breath returned to normal. I rolled up my new rubbing and headed back to meet my folks. I decided to keep this little adventure—like so much of my life—to myself. My parents wouldn't believe a word of it anyway.

Our happy little family trip finally ended. Back home in my room in Mississippi, I unrolled my new prize and tacked it up on my wall. But that night I woke up covered in sweat, feeling sicker than I've ever felt in my life.

I'm getting TB! I thought. *I caught TB from a woman who's been dead for over a hundred years!*

Through my fevered haze I flipped on my lamp and looked over at the gravestone rubbing. Was I hallucinating? Blood oozed from the paper, running down in thin red streams that began to form letters.

M-E-R-C—

The blood was spelling "Mercy Brown"!

I turned away from the wall. That's when I caught my first glimpse of her. Standing silently in the dark corner was a ghastly pale, dark-haired woman, dressed in clothes from the 1800s.

She stepped toward me now, raising her arm to reveal long, bony fingers. I backed up against my headboard, clutching my blanket around me—like that would help! Was I delirious with fever, or had the vampire risen and come to claim my soul?

As she stepped into the small pool of light cast by my bedside lamp, I caught sight of her throat—or what used to be her throat. The flesh of her neck was rotted away, exposing her bloody, diseased windpipe, ravaged by the TB.

This isn't real! This isn't real! I kept repeating to myself.

That's when she lunged for me. Her mouth opened wide, revealing long fangs that were brown and rotted with age and decay. A sickening hiss escaped from her lips, filling the room with the stench of death.

She yanked the covers from my bed and grabbed my ankle.

I tried to scream but my own throat felt parched, damaged, silenced by her overwhelming presence. Then it struck me—the rubbing!

I spun off the bed, crashing hard to the floor—but at least I had broken free of her grasp. Crawling along the floor, I scrambled toward my desk and pulled myself up to a standing position.

The vampire advanced toward me. I knew I had only one chance. Grabbing the matches I kept on my desk for lighting candles, I scrambled to the wall, feeling the creature's hot breath on my neck.

I tore the rubbing from its pushpin and yanked a match free of the matchbook. The vampire paused, her eyes open wide with fear. Could she have known my plan?

Then she lunged for me again, grabbing hold of my arms. Letting out a foul breath, she bared her fangs and dug her gnarled fingers into my wrists.

I can't light the match! She's too strong. My head throbbed. My eyes burned. *I'll only get one shot at this!*

I kicked out with my right leg, catching the vampire in her midsection. She stumbled back just one step, but it was enough. She had released my arms.

I struck the match, its tip exploding into flame. I touched the match to the edge of the rubbing and tossed the paper into my metal trash can.

As the fire consumed the paper, the vampire collapsed to her knees, shrieking in pain. Her whole body appeared to be enveloped in flames, though thankfully nothing in my room caught fire. The paper finished burning with a black wisp of smoke spiraling toward the ceiling.

A second line of smoke curled upward from the spot on the floor where Mercy Brown had fallen. She was gone, returned to the grave—for now.

My fever broke instantly. My cough disappeared.

I was bummed. I hated losing a gravestone rubbing for my collection, but you do what you gotta do, right, Jason?

SOUTH CAROLINA
Lizard Man

What I learned in history class: The seventh president of the United States, Andrew Jackson, was born in Waxhaw, South Carolina, on March 15, 1767. A major general in the War of 1812, Jackson became a national hero when he defeated the British at New Orleans.

A story you won't find in your textbook: As you can see from the stories in this book, I'm into all kinds of paranormal events. I like stories about ghosts, creatures, UFOs, psychics . . . you name it. But some of my fellow paranormal collectors specialize. Like my IM buddy MonsterMavin. His Web site is devoted only to stories about, well, monsters.

He recently IM'd me about a guy from South Carolina who contacted him.

> **MonsterM:** We have a winner!
> **ParaGuy:** What are we talking about this week, pal?
> **MonsterM:** Are you sitting down, Jason?
> **ParaGuy:** Dude, I'm not IM'ing you while I'm running a marathon. Of course I'm sitting down. Now what are you talking about?
> **MonsterM:** A lizard who walks upright like a man.
> **ParaGuy:** Okay, and what do you call this creature?
> **MonsterM:** Are you ready?? Lizard Man.
> **ParaGuy:** Did it take you all night to come up with that?
> **MonsterM:** Genius works in funny ways. Anyway, a seventeen-year-old kid named Dave Stomer from South Carolina sent me his story. Check it out, Jason. Lizard Man . . . I love it!

◉◉

One night I had just finished working the late shift at a local restaurant. Driving the familiar winding road through the swampland that surrounded my hometown of Bishopville, South Carolina, I fought to keep my eyes open, battling the sleepiness I always faced after an eight-hour shift.

I didn't know that in a few minutes I would be more awake than I had ever been in my life.

After six months on the job, I felt as if my car could drive the route back home itself. Then suddenly—*blam!*—my right front tire blew. My car skidded out of control on the damp road beside Scape Ore Swamp. My eyes opened wide as I tapped the brakes and eventually got the car under control. Bouncing over to the side of the road, I was thankful there were no other cars out or I surely would have caused an accident.

Still riding the adrenaline rush, I pulled out my flashlight, jack, and spare tire and began to change the flat. When the car was jacked up and I was struggling to loosen the lug nuts, I heard a low squishing sound coming from the swamp just off the road.

Thwish, thwish, thwish.

It sounded as if large flippers were slapping through the soupy mud. But who would be out here in the middle of the night, tromping around this mosquito-infested marsh? I aimed my flashlight in the direction of the sound but saw nothing. Turning back to the tire, I had managed to loosen a nut when I heard the sound again—only louder this time.

Thwish, thwish, thwish.

Peering into the darkness, I caught a glimpse of two glowing red dots. *I've got to be imagining this,* I reassured myself. I was just remembering all the scary swamp stories my older brother had told me when I was a little kid.

I pulled the flat tire off the car and slipped the spare on, relieved that I had remembered to fill it with air the last time I'd checked the tires. As I spun the final lug nut back into place, I heard the squishing sound again, accompanied now by a thin hiss.

Again I swept the beam toward the swamp, and that's when I saw it. At first it appeared to be a tall man in a long green coat. But as my eyes adjusted, I saw a seven-and-a-half-foot-tall lizard, walking upright on two powerful legs. Its skin was green and brown. Every inch of its body was covered by thick scales. I looked down at the creature's three-toed webbed feet twitching in the mud.

The monster hissed again and stared directly at me. The lizard man's head was huge, and its bulging, froglike red eyes glowed like coals in the flashlight's beam. But this was no frog. Its broad mouth opened to reveal two rows of razor-sharp teeth. The three thick fingers of its hand were also webbed and ended in long, sharp black claws. Brown, putrid liquid oozed from the side of its mouth, as if the creature had been formed from the muck of the very swamp itself.

Okay, focus. Get the car down and get the heck out of here . . . now!

I fumbled with the lug wrench. The monster continued toward me, hissing as it increased its pace.

Yanking hard on the wrench, tightening the last nut, I chucked the wrench into the trunk, then frantically pumped the jack to lower the car.

Come on! Hit the ground! Hit the ground!
Done!
I turned and found myself staring at the lizard man's legs!

I yanked the jack from beneath my car, holding it out in front of me, trying to figure out some way to use the tool to defend myself.

An overpowering stench of rotten swamp poured forth from the creature, stinging my nostrils and bringing tears to my eyes. The beast hissed and lunged toward me, swiping at me with its scaly clawed hand.

I instinctively raised the jack, smacking the lizard's hand away. The creature howled in pain, then stepped back. *It's like somebody crossed a frog with a huge bear,* I thought. *Now* that sounds funny, but it wasn't then. I realized that my defensive maneuver with the jack had bought me only a few precious seconds.

I jerked open the car door, threw the jack in the backseat, and jumped inside. Reaching out to close the door, I felt a sharp sting in my wrist. I looked down and saw the lizard man's slimy but powerful hand wrapped around my left wrist, its claws digging into my skin. The creature stood outside my door, hissing and drooling. Its disgusting stench made me nauseous, and I felt my stomach tighten.

I gripped the steering wheel tightly with my right hand as the beast began pulling me from the car. I didn't want to die on a lonely road, dragged to a watery grave in the stinking quagmire of Scape Ore Swamp.

My eyes scanned the dashboard frantically for any kind of weapon. I spotted a pen in the change holder between the seats. With no time to think, I released the steering wheel and grabbed for the pen.

Got it! I felt myself being pulled out of the car. Whipping my right hand across my body, I drove the point of the pen into the creature's arm. The beast snarled in pain, then let go. Tugging my door shut, I turned the key in the ignition and the engine roared to life—just as the lizard man grabbed my door handle.

Punching the button to lock all the doors, I stepped hard on the gas and pulled away. In my sideview mirror, I was shocked to see the lizard man running after me.

I knew it could never catch me. I took a deep breath, looking down at my throbbing, bleeding left wrist.

But I was wrong about the lizard man.

I glanced at my mirror. The monster was catching up. Even as I accelerated, the creature gained on me, moving closer and closer, its face now filling the mirror. The creature's arms and legs blended into a green blur, lit by the moonlight. And then the lizard man vanished from the mirror.

Thump!

It was on the roof! Black claws edged over the windshield, digging into the roof, trying to peel it open like a can of sardines. I swerved hard to the left, then back to the right, trying to shake the creature off. Its foot slipped from the roof at one point and slammed down on the sideview mirror, snapping it off the car.

I spotted a diner just up ahead.

People! I thought. Maybe someone here can help me!

It was early morning but about a dozen cars filled the parking lot. I wasn't sure what anyone else could do against this beast, but at least I wouldn't die alone.

Slamming on my brakes, I turned into the lot, barely missing a large group of people who had just gotten off a bus. As I skidded to a stop, the lizard man tumbled off my car, hitting the blacktop hard, then rolling back onto its feet.

It released the sickening hiss I had heard back at the swamp and charged toward the crowd.

Panicked screeches filled the parking lot as people scattered in all directions.

A man dropped his cell phone, which began ringing as it bounced across the blacktop. He started chasing it, then thought better of it and turned and dashed toward the diner.

A woman shrieked in fear, threw her backpack to the ground, and started running.

Several people bolted into the woods behind the parking lot. A few turned back to the bus.

Big mistake.

The lizard man grabbed the back end of the bus and began shaking it violently. The people who were heading for it stopped and turned in the opposite direction.

The beast hissed again, then headed at full speed for the front door of the diner. The customers inside stared in terror at the huge creature racing toward them. They began scrambling toward the back of the building.

There must be a back exit, I thought, thankful that the creature seemed to have forgotten about me but now desperately hoping everyone else would escape its wrath. After all, I was the one who had brought it here. I had put so many others in danger. What had I been thinking?

By the time the lizard man crashed through the locked front door, the diner had emptied completely. In a rage, the beast ripped up tables that were bolted to the floor and flung dishes in every direction. As I grabbed my cell phone to dial 911, I watched as it smashed a full carafe of coffee with its fist.

The lizard man howled in anguish as the scalding liquid seared the scaly skin of its arm, which bubbled and oozed. The monster exploded through a window on the side of the building and vanished into the darkness. Its horrible hissing faded from the morning air, and people crept out from their hiding places.

They surveyed the damage and tended to those in shock, but I was too exhausted even to talk to anyone. I headed for home.

When I finally arrived home, I was shaken up and bleeding, but at least I was alive. After cleaning my cuts and scrapes, I went back outside to check my car. The side-view mirror was gone and the roof was carved with long, deep grooves. To think it had all started with a simple flat tire.

My wrist would heal in a few days, but one thing was for certain. As long as that thing was still out there, I was going to find a new route home!

SOUTH DAKOTA

"My father has disappeared. . . ."

What I learned in history class: Located in the Black Hills of South Dakota, Mount Rushmore National Memorial depicts the faces of four former presidents of the United States. It took four hundred men working more than fourteen years to carve out the faces of George Washington, Thomas Jefferson, Theodore Roosevelt, and Abraham Lincoln.

A story you won't find in your textbook: Sometimes I listen to a radio show out of South Dakota that streams live over the Internet. The host is a psychic named Margery Brigham. One night I decided to put her psychic powers to the test—and have a little fun with her too. I worked up the courage to call the show. It took a while, but I finally got through.

"Hi, Margery. My name's Jason, and, um, I'm a psychic, too."

"Really," Margery replied. I couldn't tell if she believed me or not. "Well, what do you do with your psychic powers, Jason?"

"I help the police solve crimes," I answered.

"That's a very noble use of your powers," Margery said. "Tell me about some of your cases."

"Well, I helped police in New York find a boy named Timmy Barber, who was missing in the woods. And I helped the police in Colorado solve the murder of a woman named Marilyn Tilbett, and I—"

"Jason?"

"Yeah."

"You're not telling me the truth, are you?"

"Well, I—"

"You know about those stories, but you weren't the psychic responsible for solving them, were you?"

"How did you know?" I blurted out. I knew it was dumb the moment I said it. "Right. You're a real psychic. Actually, I'm a collector of stories about psychics and other paranormal stuff. Got any good ones?"

"Of course."

"What's your best story?"

"All right, I'll tell you, even though you lied to me."

◉◉

"Hello, you are on the air."

"Yeah, hi. Um, my dad's gone missing. I want to know if you can help me find him."

That's how the phone call to my radio call-in show began. Most of the calls I get involve missing pets or valuables, or predictions for the future. A few times I've even helped out the police. This obviously distressed teenager called and identified himself as Justin Livermore.

"Tell me what happened, Justin," I said.

"Two nights ago, my dad went for a walk and just never came back. I was staying overnight at my friend's, and when I got home the next morning, my mom was frantic as she told me the story. She had called Dad's friends, the store where he worked, and a few of the local bars where he liked to hang out, but no one had seen him. We called the police, but so far they haven't been able to find him. That's why I'm calling you."

I told Justin to send me a photo of his father, along with a few of his personal belongings. The next day a package arrived at the radio station. The framed photo showed Justin with his mom and dad standing in their living room. Justin had also sent me a watch and a ring that belonged to his father.

That night at home I set the ring, the watch, and the photo of the Livermore family on my kitchen table. Closing my eyes, I placed one hand on the watch and the other on the ring. I breathed deeply, opening my mind to the psychic energy I believe to be inherent in all objects.

Suddenly, a flood of intense, haunting images rushed

into my mind's eye, like a slide show zipping by at lightning speed.

Flash!

A chain-link fence.

Flash!

A bloodstained bedsheet.

Flash!

A wrench, a shovel, a pickup truck, and finally, a rifle.

I opened my eyes, let go of the objects, and fell back in my chair, breathing hard. I felt passionate emotion and horrific violence connected to the watch and the ring. I sensed that this was more than a simple missing persons case.

I stared at the photo, preparing myself to receive the psychic impressions it had to offer. I placed the palms of my hands on either side of the frame.

Enormous waves of rage radiated from the image. But were they coming from the mother, the father, or the boy? I experienced a sensation I've never had before. The random images and emotions radiating from the objects before me gelled into an incredibly realistic vision. I was looking through someone else's eyes! I instantly knew where I was. I recognized the furniture from the photo—I was standing in Justin's living room.

I passed by a mirror and paused. The face staring back at me was that of Justin's father! I was viewing events through his eyes.

I caught a glimpse of quick movement in the mirror. I

spun around, but not in time to stop the shadowy figure from slamming me in the head with a blunt metal object.

Searing pain shot through my skull as I hit the floor. Blood poured down my face and into my eyes, impairing my sight. The distorted figure moved swiftly, clutching a bloody wrench in its tightly clenched fist.

Wiping the blood from my eyes and fighting off waves of dizziness, I looked up into the barrel of a rifle. In that instant I knew that Justin's father wasn't missing. He had been murdered.

This was by far the strongest psychic connection I'd ever made. So strong, in fact, that I had no idea what would happen if I were to be shot while inhabiting this vision.

Would I die too?

I fought to regain my feet, but the loss of blood was too great.

Slumped in agony on the floor, I heard the click of the trigger.

The world spiraled into slow motion. I could actually see the bullet leaving the barrel of the rifle, roaring toward my head. But I couldn't move.

Blam!

I felt the life drain out of me. I knew that Justin's father was dead, but was I?

Somehow, I continued to watch in horror through the dead man's eyes as the murderer wrapped my disfigured body in a bedsheet. I felt myself being dragged along a gravel driveway, then dumped into the back of a pickup truck.

My vision was obscured by the cotton sheet as I bounced along in the cold metal truckbed. The truck screeched to a stop and I tumbled to the ground. I could just make out the shadowy image of a figure digging furiously beside an old chain-link fence in the woods. The world spun as the killer rolled my body into the shallow grave and tore away the sheet. Shovelful after shovelful of dirt rained down on me.

Peering up from my own grave, I watched as the clouds broke and pale moonlight shined down on the face of my killer—Justin's mother! She was instantly recognizable from the photo. The dirt continued to cover me. I was being buried alive.

Was I still alive?

Everything became silent and dark.

My eyes snapped wide open. Cold sweat drenched my body, and my heart raced as I took great gasps of air. I was back—back in my own body, looking down at the photo of the Livermore family.

I called the police and told them what I had seen. Of course, they were skeptical, but my clues gave their investigation a new direction. Justin's mother was soon arrested. The police later learned that she had discovered that Justin's dad was cheating on her, and in her rage she had killed him. She called the police to file a missing persons report to throw them off the trail, and to keep the truth from her son.

But she could not keep the truth from me!

TENNESSEE
The Bell Witch

What I learned in history class: Memphis, the largest city in Tennessee, is home to Graceland, the mansion where Elvis Presley lived and died. Graceland is the second most visited house in the country, after the White House.

A story you won't find in your textbook: The only thing dangerous about most homework assignments is getting a bad grade. But thirteen-year-old Alan Marcus of Tennessee sent me this story about what happened to him and his buddy Sam Turpin when Alan decided to investigate an old legend for his history project. Here's what he wrote.

◉◉

I stared down at my homework assignment and groaned. "Write about an important event or person in Tennessee history," it read. I said it aloud, but it didn't sound any more exciting. I groaned again. Everyone was going to write about the Civil War, Davy Crockett, or Al Gore. I had to think of something different if I was going to pull my grade up. It was already Sunday afternoon and my paper was due first thing Monday morning.

I picked up the phone and called my best friend, Sam Turpin, who wasn't in my history class. He didn't have to do the assignment, but maybe he'd have an idea anyway. Sam had lived in Adams, Tennessee, for all of his thirteen years, while my family had moved here just a few years ago.

I explained my problem to him.

He thought for a second and said, "Why don't you write about the Bell Witch?"

"You mean that old spook story?"

"It's more than that," Sam explained. "It's part of Tennessee history."

At least it sounded more interesting than some Civil War battle, so I listened as Sam recounted the tale of the Bell Witch.

Some woman named Kate Batts accused this guy John Bell of cheating her in a business deal in the early 1800s. It all blew over, but then, in 1817, shortly after Kate Batts died, the strange stuff began in the Bell household. It started with unexplained knocking and scratching noises and was soon followed by actual attacks.

Bell's twelve-year-old daughter, Betsy, was the main

target. Her blankets were yanked off her bed at night. She was kicked, scratched, pinched, and stuck with pins. Her face was slapped and her hair pulled. These assaults resulted in cuts, bruises, welts, and claw marks on her body. During each attack, Betsy recalled seeing the vague form of a woman and hearing a raspy, manic voice cursing her and her father.

John Bell was the next target, and it was during his encounters that the spirit identified itself as the ghost of Kate Batts. Bell's tongue swelled in his mouth, leaving him unable to talk or eat and barely able to breathe. During one of these episodes, the attacking spirit announced, "I am Kate Batts's witch, here to torment John Bell to his grave and straight into hell!"

Several friends of John Bell's spent the night in his house, but each one was driven off, nursing bruises on his face and head.

Kate Batts got her final revenge late in 1820. John Bell's strange mouth illness returned. His throat and tongue swelled as his face contorted in pain. Lying in bed, unable to move, he was brutally beaten by the witch, who cursed at him as she struck his swollen face again and again. On December 20, 1820, John Bell died. The witch shouted triumphantly at Bell's death and even disrupted his funeral, laughing, cursing, and singing in the rafters of the church. She disappeared only when the final shovelful of dirt covered John Bell's coffin.

Kate Batts left the Bells' home after that. It is believed that she fled to a cave on the Bell property and that her evil spirit remains there to this day. A man named Bill Eden, who owned the property for many years, opened the cave up to visitors. Those who ventured into the cave reported seeing apparitions and hearing strange scraping and growling sounds.

Sam finished his story. "So, what do you think?" he asked me.

"I think we should go check out that cave," I replied, totally caught up in the tale. "My history teacher is always telling us we should use primary sources, so let's go talk to the Bell Witch!"

Sam agreed. He'd been curious about the cave for years but could never get anybody to go with him to check it out. I grabbed my bike and met up with him, and we rode to the foot of the rocky ridge that contained the Bell Witch Cave. There was a house in the distance, but nobody around, so we made our way down the ridge and into the cave.

We inched through the narrow passageways, guided by the faint electric lights that Bill Eden had installed years earlier. Many of them were blown, but a few still shined dimly.

"Hold on a second," I whispered to Sam, stopping and standing perfectly still. I had heard something strange. And there it was again—the unmistakable sound of scuffling footsteps on stone. As the scraping noises continued, they were joined by the sound of labored breathing.

"Come on!" I whispered excitedly. "There's someone in here. Let's go check it out."

"All right," Sam replied nervously.

As we ventured further into the cave, we soon came to what appeared to be a dead end. Then I noticed a curved opening where the back wall met the floor. It looked as if we might just be able to squeeze through. The sounds of the footsteps and the breathing drifted through the opening from the other side of the wall.

"Me first," I said, kneeling down, then stretching flat out on my belly.

"Be my guest," Sam said. I could tell from his voice that he was starting to wonder why he had suggested I research the witch in the first place.

Wiggling my body like a snake, I managed to squeeze through the narrow opening. "Okay," I called back. "Your turn."

Sam followed, cramming himself through the narrow gap between the wall and the floor.

On the other side, I led the way along a narrow path. As we passed a small chamber to the right, a sudden growling sound froze us in our tracks. Something dark moved among the shadows in the chamber. The raspy growling grew louder and the shifting shape began to take form.

"It's a big black dog!" I shouted. "I saw a dog moving."

Foolishly stepping into the chamber, I was over-whelmed by the stink of rotting flesh. My knees buckled as the horrid smell invaded my nose. I heard a deep growl and saw by the glow of the soft electric lights a black dog charging toward me out of the darkness.

"Al!" Sam shouted, rushing to my side. He yanked me to my feet. We turned to run, but the snarling dog had vanished.

"I bet that dog was the spirit of the Bell Witch," I whispered, stepping from the chamber into a large open room.

"No, I don't think so," Sam replied in a terrified whisper. "But *that* is!" He pointed across the dimly lit cavern to where the wispy form of a woman floated above the floor.

"Leave my home!" she snarled. An unearthly cackle filled the cave.

"I just want to ask you a few questions," I asked boldly. "It's for a school paper."

"Are you kidding me?" Sam yelled, grabbing my arm. "Let's just do what she says."

The ghostly figure vanished as he spoke, dissipating into swirls of white mist.

I felt a hand grab my hair and yank my head back. "Yow!" I cried, falling onto my back. "Get her off of me!"

"There's no one there, Al!" Sam shouted, watching helplessly.

I felt needlelike claws scratch my cheek. Blood trickled from the wound—real blood. I managed to struggle up into a sitting position, but she held me down.

"I can't get up," I gasped, wiping away the blood with my sleeve. "I feel like there's a four-hundred-pound weight pressing down on my shoulders."

Sam grabbed me under the arms and tried to lift. "I can't budge you!"

I struggled to move, sweat pouring down my face and

stinging the cuts on my cheek. Now, in addition to the weight on my shoulders, I felt a pair of powerful arms clamp around my chest. "C-can't breathe," I gasped.

"What should I do?" Sam screamed. "Al?"

A hideous image flashed in front of my face as I fought to take a breath. An ancient gnarled woman, her hands dripping with blood, reaching for my throat. I could barely hear Sam screaming my name as all sound was eclipsed by her terrible voice.

"Leave my home!" she cried.

Then suddenly, the pressure on my chest and the weight on my shoulders stopped. The old woman was gone, and I was staring up at a wide-eyed Sam.

"Are—are you okay?" he stammered, helping me to my feet.

"I don't know," I replied, still trying to catch my breath. "Let's get out of here now!"

Sam led the way back through the cavern, the small chamber, and the passageway until we arrived at the narrow opening at the bottom of the wall. He wriggled through first.

I jammed myself into the opening, worming my way through. When I was halfway through the opening, with my head in one room and my feet still back on the other side of the wall, I felt a pair of hands grab my ankles.

"I'll get you!" snarled a voice. It was the Bell Witch! Why had she let me go only to grab me again here? It was like she was playing a game of cat and mouse.

And I was the mouse!

"She's got me!" I screamed, struggling to squirm the rest of the way through but unable to overpower the clawlike hands clutching my ankles.

Sam dropped to his knees near my head and grabbed my wrists, pulling hard. Sam and the witch were playing tug-of-war with my body! I began to slip back. My waist disappeared behind the wall. In another few seconds she would have all of me!

Sam counted to three and tugged hard, launching his own body backward in one enormous thrust. I thought he'd pull my hands right off my arms as he struggled against the power of this ancient evil force.

But it worked. I popped through the hole, collapsing next to Sam. The next second we were running to the entrance of the cave. We jumped on our bikes and pedaled madly for home.

I wasn't hurt badly, just pretty freaked out. The scratches on my face were only minor. I cleaned myself up and went to work writing my history paper—on Davy Crockett!

TEXAS
Tiny Helping Hands

What I learned in history class: Texas is the only U.S. state that is home to three cities with populations greater than 1 million. They are Houston, Dallas, and San Antonio.

A story you won't find in your textbook: It's not often in the time since I've become the official collector of all things weird and scary that members of my family have actually gotten in on the act to help me out. But shortly before I left on a family trip to Texas (I told you I have a lot of relatives all over the country), I e-mailed my sixteen-year-old cousin, Janet, to ask her about a local legend in her area.

From: Jspecter@scarystatesofamerica.com
To: Jtw@txnet.com
Subject: Spooky legend

Hey, Jan.

Looking forward to seeing you next week.
    Ever hear of the legend of the Shane Road train tracks?

Jason

    My sweet, loving cousin wrote back:

From: Jtw@txnet.com
To: Jspecter@scarystatesofamerica.com
Subject: Re: Spooky legend

Hey, squirt.

Yeah, it'll be good to see you, too.
    So what's with this legend? Another one of your creepy investigations? How old are you, anyway? Are you gonna keep doing this stuff forever? You know, soon girls are gonna think you're really weird.
    Anyway, no, I never heard about the Shane railroad tracks. But I have a feeling I'm about to!
    Love ya, squirt.

Jan

◉◉

I hate it when she calls me squirt. She's been doing that since she was twelve and I was eight. And I hate it when she tells me what girls like and what they don't. I'm not looking for dating advice. Anyway, I wrote her back and told her about the legend, since I was going to need a ride to check it out. I was hoping I could talk her into driving me.

From: Jspecter@scarystatesofamerica.com
To: Jtw@txnet.com
Subject: Re: Spooky legend

Hey, Jan.

It's a really scary story, and it happened right there in San Antonio. Here's the tale:

On a stormy morning a few years back, a train rumbled swiftly along the tracks. The engineer peered through the pouring rain, keeping up his speed and trying to stay on schedule in spite of the poor visibility.

As he approached Shane Road in San Antonio, he thought he spotted something just ahead on the tracks. Squinting through the downpour, he hoped that the object was just a trick of the light filtering through the curtain of water falling from the sky.

But as he got closer he realized that this was no illusion. Whatever was up ahead was very real—and sitting right on the tracks!

As panic swept through him, he yanked hard on the

brake line and sounded the train's whistle. The whistle's piercing screech combined with the horrible squeal of the train's steel wheels, locked in place and scraping against the tracks. Only the friction of metal against metal stood between safety for whatever was on the tracks and a potential disaster.

But the tracks were slick, soaked by the pouring rain, and the train was moving too fast to stop in time. The horror of the situation came sharply into focus. The engineer realized that the object stuck on the tracks was a school bus filled with terrified children. They pressed their faces against the rain-streaked windows, staring in horror as a thousand tons of unstoppable steel raced toward them.

Apparently, the bus had stalled on the tracks, and before the children could get out, the train appeared. No one survived the crash, and the community was stunned by the tragedy. Each year the parents of those lost in the tragedy meet at the tracks for a memorial service, and streets in the town have been renamed for some of the children.

Only a few months after the horrible accident, reports of strange activity at the Shane Road tracks began. People walking in the area reported hearing the voices and carefree laughter of children.

But the strangest part of the story, the part that really caught my interest, were the tales of cars being pushed away from the tracks, even when they weren't actually in danger of being hit. In some cases the cars were pushed uphill. Folks in the area came to believe that the children who had died that terrible day had returned to make sure that no one else suffered their fate. They became guardians of the tracks and protectors of those who might venture too close.

So, Jan, what do you think? Want to check it out?

Jason

Of course she didn't. But when I got to Texas, I was able to talk her into driving me out to the tracks.

◉◉

"So, let me get this straight, squirt," Janet said as we pulled away from her house. "You want us to drive up to these railroad tracks, turn the car off, and wait to see if a bus full of ghost children pushes us to safety. Is that the idea?"

I admit, hearing it laid out by my extremely skeptical cousin did make the plan sound a bit crazy. But I was prepared for this reaction.

"It's perfectly safe," I explained, watching as Janet rolled her eyes. "I picked up a train schedule, and there are no trains coming through here for two more hours. This is the perfect time to try it!"

"No, squirt," Janet snapped back. "Never is the perfect time to try it!"

We discussed—all right, argued—about this for a little while longer, but she gave in. After all, I let her get away with calling me squirt.

A few minutes later we approached the tracks on Shane Road.

"Move closer," I said.

"Closer?" she repeated, shaking her head.

"We have to be close enough to look like we might be in danger," I explained calmly. "That's when the children have been known to come and help."

Jan eased the car forward until the front bumper was hanging over the tracks.

"Now turn the car off, put it in neutral, and take your foot off the brake," I said.

"Jason, are you sure there are no haunted houses or alien landing sights in San Antonio we could explore instead?" she asked. "You know, something a bit safer than driving on railroad tracks."

I could tell she was nervous. She called me Jason.

"Jan, it's okay," I said, smiling. "Trust me!"

"Great," she said, reluctantly shutting off the engine, slipping the transmission into neutral, and easing her foot off the brake. "Remind me again how I let you talk me into this?"

"My natural charm?" I suggested.

Janet laughed a little more loudly than I would have liked.

We waited for a few minutes, but nothing happened. The car stayed put.

Then I heard it. A train whistle.

We both turned quickly to the right and spotted a train coming down the track. It was still a fair distance away, but we both freaked.

"Jason!" Janet shouted. "Not funny! Is this some kind of sick joke?"

"I checked the times!" I yelled back, pulling the schedule

from my pocket and realizing with horror that I had been looking at the weekend schedule. This was Tuesday!

As Janet reached for the ignition, we felt the car begin to roll backward.

"Keep your foot off the brake!" I shouted. "Let them take care of us."

The car continued to roll back, away from the tracks. And it wasn't gravity. We had been sitting there in neutral with no brake and the car hadn't moved at all until now.

When we were about twenty feet clear of the tracks, the train zoomed past. I got a really creepy feeling watching it pound past the spot where our car had hung over the tracks just a moment ago. As the last car rumbled from sight, Janet let out a huge sigh.

"That's the last time I let you talk me into something dumb like this," she shrieked, obviously still shaken. "We could have been killed!"

"No, not really," I said softly. "Look."

There on the edges of the front windshield were a bunch of tiny handprints. More small handprints covered the side windows as well.

"I told you they would take care of us," I said.

"Oh my God," Janet whispered, smiling incredulously.

That's when we heard the faint sound of a child's laughter.

UTAH
Rest in Peace

What I learned in history class: The name *Utah* comes from the Native American Ute tribe and means "people of the mountains." Today Utes inhabit only a small part of their former territories. The Northern Ute live on the Uintah-Ouray Indian Reservation in northeastern Utah.

A story you won't find in your textbook: One of the strangest tales I've ever heard was the story of Justin Rayburne, who lived near Altamont, Utah. What grabbed my attention was the fact that Justin's experience involved both a UFO abduction *and* a ghost. Now, that's something you don't hear every day! Justin's best friend, Jim Bolton, e-mailed me the story.

Justin and I had been best friends since kindergarten. We went on adventures together and always seemed to escape trouble at the last second. It was a lot of fun, and I knew Justin would always be there for me. Every year we went camping in the Unita Mountains as a beginning-of-summer ritual. This year we were both fifteen and about to begin our summer jobs in a few days, so we wanted to have fun while we could.

After the sun went down one warm evening, we stretched out beside our tent and gazed at the stars. Neither of us said much. We were content in our silence . . . until the unexpected disturbance occurred.

I saw it first—a blue glow that seemed to skim along the mountain peaks.

"What's that?" I asked, pointing as the shapeless blue orb drew closer.

"I don't know, a plane?" Justin said.

"I never saw a plane like that."

We scrambled to our feet. "Maybe we should get into the tent," I suggested.

"And miss whatever this is?" Justin replied. "No way."

Always the cautious one, I stayed close to the tent. Justin climbed up to a rock ledge to get a better view. It was a move he would soon regret.

The glowing object picked up speed, almost as if it had spotted Justin. Shading his eyes and squinting against the light, Justin was soon just a small silhouette from where I stood. The edges of the glowing object kept moving and changing shape. In a few seconds the glow from the orb had completely filled the sky before us. And then it surrounded Jason's body.

I looked on in horror, watching as my best friend was swallowed up by the glow. "Justin!" I shouted. "Get down here!"

Then the glow vanished as quickly as it had appeared, like someone had turned off a light switch. And Justin was gone.

"Justin!" I screamed, looking around desperately. I scrambled up to the rock ledge, but there was nothing to see or do. There was nowhere Justin could be hiding. Whatever that thing was had just abducted my best friend.

Fear overtook me. "Justin!" I shouted again and again, all the time knowing it would do no good. My desperate voice weakly echoed in the star-filled night. Then all was silent again.

I ran back to our tent and rummaged through my bag for my cell phone. Just as I was about to call for help, the blue glow returned, appearing suddenly over my head. It moved closer, filling up the sky. Then, just as suddenly, it vanished—but not before spitting Justin onto the ground at my feet.

"Justin! What happened?" I asked, kneeling. "Are you okay?" A thousand other questions raced through my mind.

"I don't know," Justin said, blinking as his eyes adjusted to the darkness. "I was floating in the blue light for a minute, then I felt a sharp pain on the left side of my head, and then I was back here." He touched the left side of his head. When he removed his hand, it was covered in blood.

346

I pulled out a flashlight and saw a large round wound on his head. "We have to get you out of here."

"Wait!" Justin yelped. "Don't tell anyone about this, okay? It'll be our secret."

"Why?"

"I can't explain what just happened to me," Justin said. "But I don't want to spend the rest of my life with everyone looking at me like I'm weird. Like I'm some kind of UFO freak or something. Let's just tell everyone that I slipped and hit my head on a jagged rock. Okay?"

He seemed weirdly desperate about it, so I agreed. "Yeah, fine, whatever," I said as I dialed 911.

"Promise me, Jim!" Justin yelled. "Promise me!"

"Okay! Okay! I promise! Take it easy."

I gave our information to the operator and was told that a medivac helicopter was on its way. I grabbed a T-shirt and pressed it against Justin's head to try to stop the bleeding. The blood kept coming.

An hour later, Justin was admitted to a nearby hospital. I paced the waiting room, wondering what had happened to my friend. I figured the doctors should know the truth so they could help him, but at the same time I had vowed to stay silent. I said that Justin had tripped and hit his head on a rock, and I repeated the same story to Justin's parents when I called them from the hospital. A short while later, a doctor found me pacing.

"We've got your friend stable," the doctor reported. "And the bleeding has stopped, but he's having trouble remaining conscious. We're going to keep him overnight just to observe him. Why don't you go home and get some rest?" After he assured me again that Justin would be fine in the morning, I called my parents to pick me up.

I tossed and turned in bed, worrying about Justin. In the middle of the night, I heard a scuffling sound in the corner of my room. "Who's there?" I whispered, sitting up in bed. I glanced at my clock. It read 3:23 a.m.

"Jim, it's me," said a familiar voice.

"Justin! What are you doing here?" I whispered loudly, flipping on the light. "Why aren't you in the hospital?" There was something odd about Justin's appearance. He appeared pale, like a faded photo. And there was no sign of his head wound.

"I came to say goodbye," he said.

"What do you mean, 'goodbye'? Where are you going?"

"I'm going with them, Jim," he said calmly. "I understand now. They've selected me. Don't worry. I'll be fine. Goodbye, Jim."

"What are you talking about? This is crazy." I watched in amazement as Justin faded from view. A second later, he was gone.

"Justin?" I felt like I was losing my mind. I didn't sleep for the rest of the night.

Early the next morning, I had my parents drive me to the hospital. When I arrived, my heart sank. Justin's mom and dad were sitting in the waiting area, and they looked devastated.

"Mr. Rayburne, Mrs. Rayburne, what happened?" I asked, fearing the worst.

"Oh, Jimmy," Mrs. Rayburne cried. "Justin died last night."

I dropped to one knee and hugged her. Then I began to cry too.

I didn't know if I should tell them what I'd seen.

The doctor I had met the previous night came over to the group. "I'm terribly sorry, Mr. and Mrs. Rayburne, I just need you to sign some papers."

I stood as the doctor handed the papers to Mr. Rayburne. I glanced at the form as Mr. Rayburne took it, and my eye caught two things. First, the cause of death was listed as unknown. Second, the time of death was listed as 3:23 a.m.

"Justin died at three-twenty-three in the morning?" I asked.

"That's right," the doctor said. "I'm sorry. He just never woke up."

"So he didn't leave the hospital last night?" I asked, wondering how Justin could have been in my room.

"Of course not," the doctor said, a bit annoyed. "I told you he never regained consciousness. Now, Mr. and Mrs. Rayburne, I'm going to need you to ID the body."

"I want to come too," I said, growing frightened and more confused.

"If it's okay with the parents," the doctor replied.

"Of course," Mr. Rayburne said, reaching over and squeezing my hand.

I followed the others into the morgue. The room was cold and silent. I hated thinking about Justin in this horrible place. We crossed the large room to a far wall lined with large drawers.

"If you're ready," the doctor said.

"Yes," Mr. Rayburne replied quietly.

The doctor slid open a drawer labeled "Rayburne, J."

I held my breath and closed my eyes. I heard Mrs. Rayburne gasp. Steeling myself, I opened my eyes.

The drawer was empty!

"I don't understand," the doctor said, clearly shaken. "I saw the body placed in here myself."

Mrs. Rayburne fainted into her husband's arms. A thorough search of the morgue turned up nothing. Over the next two days every inch of the hospital was searched, but Justin's body was never found.

A few nights later, I sat alone in my room and started to cry again. I heard a soft voice in the dark.

"Don't be sad, Jim." It was Justin's voice.

"Where are you?" I insisted. "You're not dead? Your folks are a mess."

"Tell them not to cry, Jim," Justin said. Again he had the appearance of an old faded photo. "I'm with the ones who came for me. I can rest in peace."

Then Justin was gone.

I've been back a number of times to the mountains where he and I encountered the blue glow, but I never saw the strange light, and I never heard from Justin again.

VERMONT
The Endless Suicide

What I learned in history class: Montpelier, Vermont, is the smallest state capital in the United States, with a population of about eighty-five hundred people. It's also the only state capital without a McDonald's.

A story you won't find in your textbook: Many of the hauntings I've encountered involve ghosts that are somehow tied to a particular house or place. Sometimes the location and the haunting have to do with events in the ghost's mortal life. More often they have to do with how that mortal life ended. Caroline Carlson of South Burlington, Vermont, sent me this account of her own haunted house.

◉◉

Hi, Jason. I've been on the psychic boards of your site a lot in the past, but now I have something to write in about myself.

My husband, Randy, and I had finally bought our dream house in South Burlington, Vermont. Little did we know at the time that our dream would turn into a total nightmare. Our first few weeks were filled with unpacking, painting, and making plans to decorate the place with new furniture. Everything seemed perfect. That is, until Randy headed out to the hardware store one Saturday afternoon about a month after we moved in, leaving me alone in the house.

Now, I have to add that I lurk around your psychic boards because I have always believed that I had some psychic abilities. I swear that my dead grandmother has communicated with me at times of stress in my life. I have had premonitions about future events, both good and bad, that have come to pass.

My husband liked to tease me about it, until the time I dreamed that his brother was flying on wings high above Earth, when suddenly the wings burst into flame. I woke up in a cold sweat and told Randy about my dream. He shrugged it off, but the next morning the phone rang with the news that Randy's brother had been killed in a plane crash.

On that Saturday afternoon, I was painting an upstairs bedroom when I heard footsteps.

"Randy, is that you?" I called out. "Are you back already?"

The footsteps grew louder. They were pounding up the

stairs. I put down my paintbrush and looked over at the door to the bedroom. A tall man with gray hair, dressed in a bathrobe, ran into the room with a wild expression in his eyes.

"Who are you?" I screamed. "What do you want?"

The man did not respond as he raced right in front of me, heading for a wide-open window on the far side of the room. Without hesitation, the man dove out the third-story window.

"Oh my God!" I cried, racing to the window. I stuck my head out, fully expecting to see the strange man splattered all over the sidewalk below.

I saw nothing. No sign of the man. It was as if he had leaped out the window and vanished.

When Randy returned home, I filled him in on my strange experience.

"I locked the door when I left, and just unlocked it when I came home," Randy explained. "I don't know how someone could have gotten in."

"And where did his body go?" I asked, more than a little spooked. I stuck my head out the window again, but there was absolutely no sign of a body.

Was our house haunted? I pushed the possibility out of my mind and did my best to forget the bizarre incident.

Until it happened again.

The following weekend, I once again found myself alone in the bedroom, touching up the walls. Randy had to run out to pick up some more paint.

"You okay here alone?" he asked me before he left.

"Hey, if this is going to start to feel like home, I've got to be able to be here by myself," I replied. "But thanks, sweetheart. Just be sure to lock up on your way out."

As I painted, my thoughts drifted to what the bedroom would look like when it was done. I was just picturing different placements for the bed when I heard it again.

The pounding of footsteps running up the stairs froze me in terror. *Not again!* I thought. But yes—the sound was unmistakable!

The gray-haired man in the bathrobe dashed into the room, just as he had done before. "Wait!" I shouted, before I even registered what I was doing. I stepped directly into the man's path. "I can help you!"

Maybe it was because I was right in his way, or perhaps it was my own psychic abilities, but it seemed as if the running man had heard my words. As he reached me, I felt the man's spirit blend with my own.

I shrieked as his tortured mind melded with mine. I felt the excruciating pain of a mind intent on death. Trapped. No way out. A lifetime of hurt, abuse, disappointment, and rage flooded my brain, overwhelming my consciousness.

And then I felt my body move. Caught up in the running man's spirit, I fought helplessly as he dragged me along with him to the open window, to the suicidal plunge that was certain to follow, to death on the pavement below.

"No!" I bellowed. "Let me go!" But I was powerless. In my mind I was watching the man leap out the window as he had done the previous week. Only this time I felt myself carried along in his mad leap.

As my body cleared the window frame, my hands shot out, grabbing for something, anything to stop my fall. I caught the edge of the windowsill and gripped its wooden frame with all my strength.

I stopped falling. My legs slammed against the side of the house, just below the window. And then the man was gone. I felt his anguish and despair leave me, only to be replaced by my own panic as I dangled helplessly three stories above the ground.

"Help!" I cried. "Somebody help me!"

A few passersby gathered below. "Hang on!" one of them shouted. "Don't let go!" yelled another as he dialed 911 on his cell phone.

I knew that the door was locked. No one could get into the house to help pull me back in. No one except Randy.

Randy told me later that he saw the crowd gathering in front of our house from two blocks away. Everyone was pointing up. When he got close enough to see what was happening, he dropped the paint cans he was carrying and broke into an all-out sprint.

My fingers ached as I maintained my grip on the windowsill. Then they began to cramp and grow weaker. *I'm gonna fall!* I thought as my left hand slipped free. "Randy!" I cried, dangling by one hand. "Randy," I repeated weakly as my right hand cramped and I slipped from the sill.

"Gotcha!" Randy cried out, grabbing my wrist just as I slid free. "Give me your other hand!" I reached up and Randy took me by both wrists, pulling me back into the room. We collapsed together onto the floor.

"Are you okay?" he asked, panting, trying to catch his breath. "What happened?"

I filled Randy in on the details of my second encounter with the suicidal spirit, just as the wail of police sirens filled the air. I reassured the police that everything was all right, telling them that I had slipped while cleaning the window.

Then I called the real-estate broker who had sold us the house. His records indicated that the man who had first owned the house, fifty years ago, had indeed committed suicide by jumping out the third-floor window after his wife had left him. Not surprisingly, our agent had neglected to volunteer this lovely fact when showing the house.

I have to say that we were never troubled by the desperate spirit again. I believe that my psychic close encounter with the man and his pain may have freed his soul from its misery, and from the house that Randy and I now call home.

VIRGINIA
The Hotel Down the Road

What I learned in history class: Jamestown was the first permanent English settlement in North America. It was also the first seat of English government in Virginia, from 1607 to 1699.

A story you won't find in your textbook: If you could travel back anywhere in time, where would you go? Ancient Rome? The Old West? Back to the time of the dinosaurs? I know I'd love to pop back to Roswell, New Mexico, in 1947, and see what really crashed there. I thought about all the possibilities of time travel when I heard the tale of the Devries family, who spent one very unusual night in a hotel

357

just outside Harrisonburg, Virginia. The Devries daughter, Abby, e-mailed me the story.

◉◉

I live in Virginia, and normally my parents like to go some-place cool on vacation, like Disney World or New York. Lately money's been tight, so my mom decided we'd stay home this year and "explore Virginia" together like one big happy family.

Please!

My dad packed the car and told me and my brother that we were just going to "take off with no planned route! We're the kings of the road!"

Thanks, Dad, but I'd rather be queen of Madison Avenue.

After a long day of driving with nothing to do and nothing to look at besides trees and fields, my parents finally decided to find a place to stay for the night.

"There's a motel," my dad said, pointing to a neon sign up ahead.

"Oh, honey, I know we're trying to save money on this trip, but I was really hoping for something a little nicer than some roadside motel," my mom said. "You know, like a bed-and-breakfast or a fancy old inn."

"No fussy froufrou places, *please!*" my brother, Seth, moaned.

"I'm beat," said Dad, who had been doing most of the driving. "Let's just stay here tonight, and then we can try to find a fancier place tomorrow. Agreed?"

I just wanted to go to sleep and so did my brother, so

everyone agreed and Dad pulled into the motel parking lot. When we got into the lobby we were faced with a NO VACANCY SIGN.

"Is there another place to stay nearby?" Mom asked the guy behind the counter.

I was checking out the clerk (no, not in that way). He was a weird-looking short guy with thin graying hair slicked back over his head. He had this crazy handlebar mustache twirled into a curl at each end. He also wore a formal uniform, dark blue with brass buttons, closed all the way up to his chin.

"There's the hotel down the road," the man said, smiling. "The Harrison Hotel. Not far from here."

"Could you call them and see if they have any rooms?" Dad asked.

"Nope, I can't do that," the clerk replied. "But I can tell you how to get there."

I could tell that my mom was about to give the guy a hard time. I mean, please! After all, how hard would it have been for the clerk to make a phone call? But knowing Mom, she didn't want to start off the vacation with an argument, so she jotted down the directions and we left.

"Well, he was weird," Mom muttered as we pulled onto the small road leading away from the motel. "Not to mention rude."

"What was with that mustache?" Seth asked.

"And that uniform?" I added. "He looked like a bellhop in an old black and white movie."

As Mom read off the directions, which called for us to

turn onto a small dirt road about a mile from the motel, we all noticed a thick fog rolling in. Dad flipped on his lights, but they barely cut through the dense white clouds hugging the road. After a short drive up a winding hill, a small three-story building came into view.

"That's got to be it," Seth said.

"I guess," Mom added, the disappointment obvious in her voice. The place looked very plain, definitely not the grand hotel she had been hoping for.

Grabbing our bags, we trudged up the walk, eager to get inside and out of the chill. A hand-painted sign above the front door said HARRISON HOTEL. Stepping into the lobby, we were amazed by the spectacle before us.

It was like an early-1900s exhibit at Epcot. The lobby was completely paneled in wood. The furniture was uphol-stered in rich velvet and stood on wooden claw feet. Women strolled through the lobby in high-buttoned blouses, long skirts, and lace-up boots, while the men wore shirt collars folded outside their jackets, with top hats on their heads.

Please tell me these actors make good money for putting up with this stupid costume idea, I thought.

"Yes, sir?" the desk clerk said as we approached. This clerk was dressed in the same dark blue uniform with brass buttons as the guy at the motel.

"We'd like two rooms for tonight, please," Dad said, shooting us a glance as he noticed the clerk's uniform. "One with a king and one with two twins."

"Two rooms, yes, certainly, sir," the man replied, pulling out two long, thin metal room keys attached to round wooden pegs. "Rooms 312 and 314, third floor. Fit for a king and his twins."

"Um, great," Dad replied, picking up a few of our bags. "Which way to the elevator?"

"Excuse me?" the clerk said, looking puzzled. He pointed across the lobby. "The stairs are right over there."

"I guess they don't have an elevator," Mom said, trying a little too hard to sound chipper.

"Lovely," Seth grumbled, gathering up his luggage.

We trudged up the three flights of rickety wooden stairs and found our rooms. The twin beds in both rooms were really short and covered in thick sheets topped by scratchy woolen blankets, and no pillows! The wooden doors had no peepholes or chains, just simple metal locks.

"Now I know why the other clerk couldn't call here," I said to Seth, starting to unpack my suitcase. "There was no phone at the main desk."

"Hey, there's no phone in our room!" Mom said, sticking her head into our room.

"I don't think there's a phone anywhere in this place, Mom," Seth replied.

"And no TV!" I moaned. "Not even a radio! This is roughing it! We might as well be camping."

"Looks like we're sharing a bathroom," Dad called from down the hall, "and it's as weird as everything else in this place."

We made our way out into the hallway. The four of us peered into the one tiny bathroom on the third floor. A tank full of water hung above the toilet with exposed pipes running down to the bowl. All the other plumbing was visible as well, connected to the free-standing sink and claw-foot bathtub. There was no sign of a shower.

"Well, you wanted someplace old, Mom," I said. "I'll see you guys in the morning."

We headed to our rooms.

To say I slept poorly would be a major understatement. I've spent more comfortable nights in wet sleeping bags outdoors. It was terrible. I wanted the night to be over, so I actually got up at 7:00 a.m. *on a vacation!*

"I've got to get a picture of this room," Seth said as he finished getting dressed. "It's too weird." He pulled out his phone and took a shot of me standing next to the bed.

Dad appeared in the doorway. "Great minds think alike, Seth!" he boomed. "I just took a shot of Mom in our room, since no one will believe that we actually stayed in a place like this."

I rolled my eyes. They were actually getting a kick out of this dump. "Where's my watch?" I asked, annoyed, as Seth and I finished packing. "I thought I put it right here on the dresser."

We searched the room but had no luck finding my missing watch.

"We'll tell the front desk and leave our address," Seth said. "They can mail it to us if they find it."

"No phone, no radio, no elevator. Let's hope they have *stamps* here!" I said. "They'll probably send it by Pony Express."

Looking forward to some French toast or waffles, I tried my best to cheer up as we arrived downstairs for breakfast.

"I'd like fruit and yogurt, please, and decaf," Mom said to the host, who was dressed in a formal suit.

"I'm sorry, madam," the host replied. "Today's breakfast is eggs with bacon. Your coffee will be out in a moment."

"Hello? What happened to choices? I'm a vegetarian!" I complained. "This sucks!"

The eggs were greasy, the bacon looked like it was swimming in fat, and the coffee—not decaf—was thick and bitter, with tiny grounds floating in the cup.

After our disgusting breakfast, Dad went to pay the bill. He pulled out his credit card.

"That will be six dollars and seventy-five cents for the two rooms and four breakfasts," the clerk said, staring in a confused manner at the rectangular piece of plastic in Dad's hand.

"Did I hear you right?" Dad asked. "Six seventy-five?"

"Yes, sir," the clerk replied.

"In that case, I'll pay, Dad," Seth said, waving some singles at the clerk.

"Of course," the clerk said.

"Well, say what you want," Dad said as we drove away from the hotel. "You can't beat the price."

"We saved so much on this place, maybe we can splurge and stay tonight in a place with *television*! Oooh, how fancy would that be?" I asked mockingly, still annoyed about my watch, my lack of sleep, and now my empty stomach.

The fog began to lift as we retraced our route back to the main highway.

"Wait!" Mom said when we reached the motel where we had first stopped. "I want to go back in there and see what they know about the Harrison Hotel."

As we pulled into the parking lot, the last of the fog vanished and the sun broke through a bank of clouds. The four of us walked into the motel lobby. This time the clerk was a teenage boy with a backward baseball cap, an over-sized T-shirt, and baggy shorts.

"Where's the other clerk?" Seth asked. "The one with the mustache?"

"Huh?" the boy replied. "No one with a 'stash works here."

"But we saw him last night," Mom insisted.

"My mom was working last night," the boy replied. "It's just me, my mom, and my dad. No one else works here."

"What do you know about the hotel down the road?" Dad asked.

"There's no hotel near here," the boy said. "No hotel for fifty miles."

Frustrated and confused, we slipped back into the car.

"You know we have to go back," Mom said.

"Let's go!" Seth shouted.

"Can't we just go home?" I groaned.

Following the route we had taken the previous night, we soon reached the spot where the hotel had been. We looked at each other in disbelief.

An empty, overgrown lot sat where fifteen minutes earlier the Harrison Hotel had stood.

"Are you sure this is the spot?" Mom asked.

"Positive!" Dad replied. "I marked the mileage. It's completely gone!"

We poked around the site and discussed what could have happened, but nothing made sense. Finally, we left and continued with our vacation, trying to put the weird incident out of our minds. About a week after we got home, Seth uploaded his phone's images onto our home computer.

"Hey, the weird hotel room shot's messed up!" Seth complained. "What happened? Dad, can you give me your camera so we can upload the rest of the photos?" he yelled down the hallway. "My shot of the weird hotel didn't come out."

We uploaded all Dad's images and clicked through them.

"How are they looking?" Dad asked as he poked his head in the doorway.

"All of them are great except for the shot you took of Mom in the room at that weird hotel. Her image is there, but everything else in the picture is gone, just a blurry swirl of color, like the entire background has been erased! Just like my shot of Abby!"

Seth quickly did a search on the Web for "Harrison Hotel," and up came a historical reference to an old hotel, right in the area where we'd found it. The hotel had been torn down eighty-five years ago!

One week later, an oddly wrapped package arrived in our mailbox. It was covered in waxy brown paper and tied with twine. The return address was that of the Harrison Hotel. Tearing open the package, I discovered my missing watch, with a note attached:

"The chambermaid found this while cleaning your room. We hope you enjoyed your stay. Please come again soon."

Looking back at the package, I saw that the postmark read August 17, 1903.

WASHINGTON
UFOs Welcome Here!

What I learned in history class: Mount St. Helens, a volcano approximately ninety-five miles south of Seattle, had lain dormant for 123 years before 1980. In the spring of that year, after a series of earthquakes, it began to spew ash and steam. On May 18, 1980, the volcano erupted. The explosion was heard as far away as Montana, Idaho, and California.

A story you won't find in your textbook: What is it about Washington State? It's like someone put up a giant sign that said: UFOS WELCOME HERE! More UFO sightings have been reported in Washington than in any of the other forty-nine Scary States. I've been collecting these cases and compiling a history of what should be nicknamed the Close

Encounter State. The earliest record I found of a UFO sighting in Washington State dates back to the 1930s. For a period of years during that decade, farmers near the town of Glenwood repeatedly reported seeing rectangular shapes in the sky, over a mile long and half a mile wide, blocking out the midday sun!

In mid-June 1947, a private pilot named Kenneth Arnold was flying near Mt. Rainier when he encountered nine metallic discs zipping through the air. In describing the incident, Arnold coined the term *flying saucer*. A few weeks later, the famous Roswell, New Mexico, incident occurred, throwing flying saucers into the consciousness of the American people. But even though Roswell got a lot of attention, Washington beats New Mexico any day in terms of sheer numbers. Since the 1940s, the U.S. Air Force has investigated over fifteen thousand UFO sightings in the state of Washington!

But the story that freaked me out the most came from ten-year-old Charlotte Jameson, who lives just outside Seattle. Here's the e-mail she sent me.

From: Charlotte Jameson (CJames@seattlenet.com)
To: Jspecter@scarystatesofamerica.com
Subject: Too many UFOs

Hey, Jason.

I really like reading the stories on your Web site, and I know you're trying to put together a history of all the UFO sightings in Washington. Well, I live in Washington, but I never thought I'd star in a UFO story myself.

It started a few months ago. My family lives in a small town outside of Seattle, and it can get really quiet after dark. One night I had just gotten into bed and was reading before I fell asleep. I heard a low humming sound that started off really soft and gradually got louder as I listened. Then a flash of bright white light shot through my window and right into my room.

I jumped out of bed and ran to the window, but by then the light had vanished. I thought about waking my parents, but they both get up early for work and were already asleep. Maybe I just dozed for a second and dreamed about the light. I got back into bed and tried to focus on my book, but the same thing happened a minute later. The bright light swept into the room. Again I jumped from my bed, only this time when I got to the window, I saw a shiny gold circle hovering just above the trees.

And that's when the weirdest thing happened. It was like the circle saw me! It zoomed to my window and a brighter light poured in, filling my room. I felt warm and a little dizzy. Then I got real scared.

"Mom!" I yelled as I ran from my room into my parents' bedroom. But somehow the white light followed me down the hall. When I got to my parents' room, I could see they were sound asleep.

"Mom! Dad!" I screamed. They didn't move. "Wake up! Wake up!" Still they didn't stir. My mom was usually a very light sleeper. Now I was really freaked out.

I ran to their bed and went to shake my mom—but my hand passed right through her! It was like she was made of light. "Mom!" I screamed. But I couldn't touch her, and she couldn't hear me. Was she even real? What had happened to my parents?

I spun around and the light shined directly on me. It had curved through the hallway and entered the room. It was like a giant snake, following me.

"What's happening?" I yelled, once again trying to shake my mom, and then my dad. My hand passed right through their bodies.

And then suddenly the light disappeared and I was standing in complete darkness.

The next thing I knew, I was waking up in my bed. It was morning and I had no memory of what had happened the night before. Now I remember everything. But then, it was like a normal morning. I was fine, my parents were fine. I got up and headed for school as if nothing had happened. Because in my mind nothing had.

Until that night. Again I was lying in bed reading when a bright white light shot through the window.

And that's when I remembered everything!

It's come back to get me!

Terror shot through my whole body. I jumped from my bed, but the light had already seen me. It bent toward me and I dove under my bed to hide.

Go away! Go away!

I was scared to call out for my mom because I didn't

want the light to find me. I was also terrified by what had happened to my parents last night. Maybe it would happen again. Maybe this time they would never wake up!

I peeked out from under my bed. My heart was racing.

I watched the light sweep across the room. It was definitely searching for me. It moved up the wall, then across and back down to the floor.

It was heading my way!

The light moved under the bed and slithered toward me. In a second it would see me.

I bolted from under the bed and ran to my door. The light saw me and followed.

"Help!" I screamed. But no one emerged from my parents' room.

This time I ran downstairs, hoping the light wouldn't be able to follow me there. I reached the bottom of the stairs. No light. *Maybe I got away? Maybe it will leave me alone?*

I stopped in the downstairs hallway and looked around. Still no light. I stepped into the living room.

The light blasted through the large living room window, just missing me. I screamed and ran into the kitchen. I saw flashes of white coming from the living room. I knew it was searching for me. I knew it would find me. Then the light disappeared and the house was dark.

I turned to check the kitchen window and the light caught me full in the face. Again I felt warm and dizzy. I ran back up the stairs, but it had found me and it wasn't letting go. I felt heat on my back as I rounded the stairs into the hallway and turned into my parents' room.

"Wake up!" I yelled, but they didn't move.

I was scared to touch them again, but I had to know. Again my hand passed through them like they were a mere optical illusion.

Then the room grew dark.

Once again I woke up in my bed with no memory of what had happened.

As I stepped from the shower that morning and passed the bathroom mirror, I caught a glimpse of my back.

"Mom!" I screamed in terror.

She came running into the bathroom.

"Charlotte! What happened?" she asked, her face pale.

"Look!" I cried, suddenly remembering everything. "Look what they did to me!"

There, on my back, snaked a long red scar.

"Oh my God, how did this happen?" my mom cried.

I broke down crying as memories of what had happened to me flooded my mind. A spaceship. A blindingly white room. The tiny, faceless creatures who held me down and cut me open as they poured images of my home and parents into my mind to prevent me from struggling. The chase. None of that was real. It was a virtual reality to keep me distracted and confused. That's why I couldn't touch my parents. I wasn't really in their room. They had tricked me at the time into thinking I was home, but now it all came rushing back to me, the whole horrible operation.

My mom called 911 and an ambulance rushed me to the hospital.

They say people can live with one kidney. But what if they come back for more?

WEST VIRGINIA

Mothman: Strange Creature, Alien . . . or Both?

What I learned in history class: Alderson Federal Prison Camp in Alderson, West Virginia, opened in 1927. Then known as the Federal Correctional Institution for Women, it was the first federal prison for women only. Famous inmates have included Tokyo Rose, Lynette "Squeaky" Fromme, Billie Holiday, and most recently, Martha Stewart.

A story you won't find in your textbook: My bud Creature-Fan is obsessed with collecting stories about all kinds of beasts, from Bigfoot to werewolves, and he's always careful to check out the facts. So when he IM'd me with this story, I knew it was for real.

CreatureFan: Yo, Para dude, got a mega-beast for you, man.

ParaGuy: You mean Mr. Jensen, my science teacher? I've already met him.

CreatureFan: Still with the jokes, huh, JS? Well, there's nothing funny about this guy. Does the name Mothman mean anything to you?

ParaGuy: NO way! You met Mothman? Is this your ghost IM'ing me, 'cause from what I've read, Mothman loves people . . . for dinner!

CreatureFan: I didn't meet him, dude. This kid in my school got lost in the woods and lived to tell the story.

ParaGuy: Details!

CreatureFan: First, how much do you really know about Mothman?

ParaGuy: A little. But I have the feeling that I'm about to learn a whole lot more.

CreatureFan: Here's what I know. The first sighting of Mothman took place in 1966 in this little town—Clendenin, West Virginia. It's actually not too far from where I live. Anyway, while digging a grave at a local cemetery, a group of men noticed what they thought was a large bird taking off from a tree. Looking up, the men realized that this was no bird! The creature looked more like a human being with wings. It appeared to be seven feet tall, with brown, leathery skin covering an unusually wide body. Large red eyes and what seemed to be antennae sprouted from its wide, bony skull. The creature flapped its batlike wings and soared into the sky and out of sight.

Over the next few days, the sheriffs' offices in Clendenin and nearby Point Pleasant were swamped with reports of sightings of the large winged creature, named Mothman by the local newspaper. One of the most chilling reports came from two young couples who were driving near an abandoned TNT manufacturing plant near Point Pleasant.

As they passed the large decaying building, their car radio inexplicably switched off. A few seconds later, their headlights went out. Then the car's engine stalled. Sticking his head out the rear window, one of the men looked up and saw a red point of light hovering just above the plant, hanging motionless in the sky. People came to believe that it was some kind of spaceship that delivered the creature to Earth—or something like that. But at the time, these four people didn't know *what* it was.

Before the guy could point it out to his companions, the

four friends were shocked by the sudden appearance of a large creature running right toward their car. The creature had large eyes that seemed to grow right out of its neck. It vaguely resembled a man but was at least seven feet tall. It had wings of some kind that were folded against its back.

Panic gripped the couples as the driver tried again and again to start his car. Finally the engine turned over. The driver floored the gas pedal, peeled out, and sped away. The man in the backseat glanced skyward and noticed that the red light was gone. Then the driver looked in the rearview mirror and saw the creature spread its enormous wings.

"Turn around!" he shouted. Everyone in the car watched through the rear windshield as the creature flapped its wings and took to the air.

The driver kept the pedal smashed to the floor, picking up speed. Tearing through the West Virginia night, he glanced at the speedometer and saw that he was zooming down the road at a hundred miles per hour. But the flying monster was matching their speed!

After a few minutes the creature flew away, but four other witnesses also reported seeing the flying Mothman that night.

People believe that the abandoned TNT plant has become the Mothman's lair. It's like a fortress, Jason. The building is surrounded by large concrete bunkers. A series of underground tunnels snake their way in all directions, making it easy for Mothman to hide or escape.

For years after the first Mothman sightings, lots of

reports of electric disturbances came in from houses near the plant. Passing cars continue to lose radio signals and headlights, or just stall out altogether. And many people claim to have seen the mysterious red lights hovering above the plant.

Anyway, told ya I know a lot!

◉◉

ParaGuy: You didn't find that out all by yourself!

CreatureFan: All right. Some of it I got from newspaper articles and books. So what? It's all true.

ParaGuy: Great. But what about the kid who got lost in the woods?

CreatureFan: Patience, Professor. Here's the story Todd Uptin told me about what happened to him.

◉◉

I like to hike in the woods. And I'm usually pretty careful— I'm out of there way before dark. But a couple of weeks ago, I must have lost track of time. Plus, I was exploring a new section of the woods. I can be pretty curious about stuff, and sometimes it gets me into trouble.

When I realized that it was starting to get dark and I should be heading back, I looked around and couldn't figure out which way to go. I got real freaked out, ya know? I tried to stay calm and hoped I'd recognize some sign of the path. So I switched on my flashlight and headed toward what looked like a building in the distance, figuring it was a ranger station.

Well, someone was there, all right, but it wasn't a ranger.

I scrambled down a steep embankment, crunching the dried leaves on the forest floor, and headed for the old brick building.

This is no ranger station, I realized when I saw how big and run-down the place was. It looked like an old factory. Weeds and vines climbed up the sides of the crumbling structure. A few years and the entire place would vanish back into the forest.

Moving as quietly as I could, I stopped at a smashed window and shined my flashlight inside. I wasn't really scared. The place looked totally abandoned. Through the window I saw a large, cavernous space—and not much else. I made my way around to the front door.

My curiosity got the better of me. I pushed the door and it swung in slightly, creaking like it hadn't been opened in years. I slipped through the narrow opening and swept the dank, dusty room with my light. I was shocked to find a round pile of twigs, leaves, and straw, about the size of a kiddy pool.

A nest! I thought. *This looks like a huge nest! But what kind of bird makes a nest big enough for a person?* It didn't make any sense.

And that's when the smell hit me. A sickly stench of rotting animal flesh stung my nostrils. There, next to the nest, was a pile of animal remains—a disgusting mound of the bones and insides of squirrels, woodchucks, and other forest rodents.

Covering my mouth and nose, I hurried across the cavernous room, where I encountered ragged sheets of brownish gray material. Kneeling down, I picked up a piece, then dropped it in disgust. I had touched a leathery chunk of skin, left behind as if a giant snake had molted. Yuck! I turned to leave, but froze in terror as a piercing whine filled the room.

The sound came from behind me. Holding my breath, I spun around. My flashlight beam revealed a tall, dark, winged creature staring down at me. Its bloodred eyes sprouted from a hideous misshapen head.

The thing towered over me, glaring and hissing, unleashing ear-shattering screeches as its two antennae twitched like those of a giant cockroach. Its wide body was covered with brown leathery skin.

As it shuffled toward me with small, wobbly steps, I realized that I was trapped. The hideous beast spread its enormous wings, which opened to a width nearly twice its height.

I backed away, moving toward the window, my light and eyes locked onto the terrifying creature before me. At that moment, I seriously believed I was going to die.

I considered leaping through the window, but the jagged shards of glass around the edges made me stop. The monster blocked my way back to the door. Ripped open by glass or torn apart and eaten by a monster—those are some grim options.

I quickly glanced over my shoulder and out the window, and spotted a red glow in the sky. The tiny, unblinking dot moved closer and closer, as if it were heading right for the building. Then my flashlight went out, and the room plunged into total darkness. Again and again I pressed the switch, trying to turn the light back on, but it was no use.

I squatted down, covering my head, preparing to be devoured. Through my fear, a bit of my natural curiosity surfaced and I snuck a peek out the window. The red light was now moving away. It quickly faded into the night sky.

"Yah!" I screamed, startled, as my flashlight switched back on by itself. I searched the room, but the creature had vanished.

I ran to the door and back out into the woods. I hustled through the woods faster than I ever had before. I soon came to a house near a road. I started to tell the people who answered the door what had happened to me, but they didn't seem shocked at all.

"Mothman," the old man said, nodding slowly.

"What is it?" I asked, trying to catch my breath.

"Alien, is my guess," the old man replied. "The red light people see is the ship. Not sure if it's visiting the creature, or maybe the ship keeps bringing new ones. Don't know. But there's some connection between the Mothman and that light."

I had heard enough. I called my mom, who came and picked me up.

On the ride home I told my mom about what happened. She looked at me kind of funny, like I was lying. She asked me what I was really doing in the woods. I insisted I was telling the truth, but she didn't buy it.

That's when the red light appeared in the sky above us. Our headlights went out and the engine stalled.

WISCONSIN
The Beast of Bray Road

What I learned in history class: Wisconsin is known as America's Dairyland. The dairy farmers there produce an average of 22 billion pounds of milk a year. Wisconsin is also known for its great cheese. The grass the cows eat has low acidity, which leads to a milder flavor.

A story you won't find in your textbook: Everybody thinks that werewolves only exist in the movies. But my IM buddy MonsterMavin, who lives in Milwaukee, knows better. Here's what he told me:

> **MonsterM:** My sister is so annoying.
> She just laughs when I talk about

werewolves and calls me a fantasy freak. I hope she gets attacked by one.

ParaGuy: That probably would convince her, but I don't think it's gonna happen.

MonsterM: Don't tell me you're a skeptic too!

ParaGuy: Dude, have you ever watched a werewolf movie? Some old guy jumping around, growling. It's so fake. And from all my time running this blog, I've never heard a real werewolf story. They're a Hollywood invention.

MonsterM: No way. Werewolf legends go way back, and there are still legit reports of them today. This TV reporter in my town saw one *himself*! And since I write for my school paper, I got to interview the guy. His name's Gavin McNally and he works at WSNI-TV. Check out my story. It ran on page 4 (it would have been front page if our teacher wasn't an unbelieving loser).

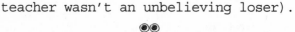

THE BEAST OF BRAY ROAD

by Gavin McNally

as told to Francis Stanton (aka MonsterMavin)

I sat down with WSNI-TV reporter Gavin McNally to talk about his frightening experience meeting the werewolf creature known as the Beast of Bray Road. Here's what Gavin told me during our interview:

I had been working at WSNI-TV in Milwaukee for three years before my fateful trip to Elkhorn. The small rural village may have only been fifty miles away from the city, but for me it was like traveling to another world.

I was pretty happy covering local stories for the evening news—the usual mix of local politics, crimes, and human interest in the Midwest. Then the stories from Elkhorn made their way to Milwaukee—tales of a monstrous beast, an animal that walked upright like a human. Witnesses described a big, hairy creature, with long, sharp teeth and powerful limbs, munching on roadkill and stolen chickens when it couldn't get its favorite food—human flesh.

Like most folks in Milwaukee, I laughed off the stories as blown-up Boy Scout campfire tales—until a newspaper reporter, whose work I really respect, wrote an article in the *Milwaukee Journal Sentinel* about her encounter with the Beast of Bray Road.

So I decided to see for myself. I couldn't convince my editor to send a camera crew along, but I figured I could still snoop around for any leads. If I found something worth putting on the air, I'd come back with a full crew. I did bring a digital camera along, in case I needed to present evidence to my boss.

After arriving in Elkhorn, I went straight to the county's office of animal control. The secretary let me look over a file labeled "Werewolf." It contained reports of a tall, hairy creature with long arms, a huge jaw, and pointed ears.

Some people reported seeing only weird-looking footprints. Others claimed to have seen a beast, running on two legs, chase down and catch a white-tailed deer. Grabbing the antlers with its powerful arms, the creature snapped the deer's neck and tore into its flesh with long fanglike teeth.

The reports had one thing in common. The sightings and attacks all took place on or around Bray Road, a winding two-lane country road that meandered through a thickly wooded area. My curiosity piqued, I contacted one of the people listed in the file.

Julie, a senior at Elkhorn High School, told me of a foggy night about two months earlier when she was driving home from a friend's house along Bray Road. The fog was so thick she could hardly see the road.

Then she felt her right front tire rise into the air as it bounced over something big.

Fearing she had hit an animal, Julie screeched to a halt and jumped from her car. Grabbing a flashlight and running back to the spot where the impact had taken place, she swept the fog-shrouded road with her beam but saw nothing. As she returned to her car, she caught movement out of the corner of her eye. Turning around, she saw that something was running toward her—and fast!

The thing, as she called it, had a big hairy chest. It stood upright and ran on two legs, its huge jaws gaping wide, its clawed hands outstretched. Terrified, Julie scrambled back into her car. Thankfully, the engine was running, but in her state of terror she lost precious seconds fumbling with the gearshift. Just as she managed to put the car in drive and slam on the gas, the thing grabbed hold of her rear bumper. Julie peeled out, hoping to dislodge the creature, but when she looked in her rearview mirror, she saw the beast climbing onto her trunk, crawling forward and digging its claws into the metal. Limb by limb, it inched forward along the outside of the car.

Panic swept over Julie as she realized

that the beast was heading right for the driver's door. If its claws could pierce metal, surely it would have no problem breaking her window.

Julie accelerated as the creature continued to claw its way toward her. Then the car's headlights illuminated the sign for Sitler Road, which veered off sharply to the right. Barely slowing down, Julie pulled the steering wheel hard to the right. Her tires squealed, and the smell of burning rubber mingled with the sickly odor of the hideous beast. The car spun into the turn, its back wheels skidding to the left.

Yanking the wheel hard to the left to narrowly avoid a ditch, Julie looked back over her shoulder just in time to see the creature fly from the car and tumble into the road. Her plan had worked. She sped home and called the police, but they were unable to find any trace of a mysterious attacker along the road.

Visibly shaken from telling her story, Julie said to me, "If I hadn't taken that turn when I did, I wouldn't be here talking to you right now. I know he would have devoured me." Then she showed me the deep gouges and scratches all over her car. I snapped a bunch of photos to show my editor.

I could tell from the way Julie had told her tale that she certainly believed it was true. And there didn't seem to be any other explanation for the damage to her car. Still, I had to find out for myself. As darkness fell over Elkhorn, I drove out to Bray Road. Pulling my car onto the shoulder next to a thickly wooded area, I hoisted myself onto the hood and sat there, digital camera and flashlight in hand.

The night grew still and deep as a million stars revealed themselves overhead and a chorus of crickets droned a steady rhythm. The sudden snapping of a twig cut through the air like a gunshot. I slid to the ground and switched on my light. I had walked about ten yards from the car, sweeping the woods with my flashlight, when I saw it, standing barely five feet away from me.

Part of me hadn't really believed the stories I'd been told, but there was no denying it now. I stood face to face with the Beast of Bray Road.

The creature rose to its full height, which must have been close to eight feet. Its body was covered with scraggly brown fur, and a scrawny but muscular chest led to a wolflike head. Its long snarling snout opened, revealing saberlike fangs and strings of blood-speckled saliva hanging from its lips. A deep, throaty roar shook the night air. Breath putrid with the stench of dead meat assailed my nose.

I knew that I could die, but I also knew this could be the opportunity of my career. I raised the camera slowly to my eye, surprised by my ability to function in the face of danger. I'd never been tested as a reporter like this before.

Flash!

The blinding burst of light from the camera momentarily startled the beast, which stumbled backward, squeezing its eyes shut and covering its face with claw-studded hands. I took advantage of the delay, turning and dashing back toward my car. But the beast recovered swiftly and gave chase. I knew I was no match for it. I was not going to reach my car in time.

As I forced my legs to go faster, I could hear the creature's growl behind me growing louder. It swiped at my arm, narrowly missing my wrist but knocking the camera from my hand. The camera tumbled into the dark woods, taking my evidence with it.

But I couldn't think about that now. I had to focus on survival. I raced ahead, only inches between my body and the beast's claws.

Looking up, I spotted an enormous tractor trailer barreling down Bray Road in my direction. *It's my only chance,* I thought. *If I can time it just right.* Cutting sharply to my left, I darted into the road, crossing just in front of the truck and diving to safety across the road.

Blaaaaaaa! The truck's horn blared and I turned back to see its taillights fade down the road.

Scrambling to my feet, I looked back across the road, desperately searching for the creature. I saw no sign of the beast. Was it smashed against the front of the truck? Had it vanished back into the woods to plan another attack?

I was certainly not about to stick around to find out. I slipped into my car and headed back to Milwaukee. Without the photos, I had no proof, and a follow-up crew was never sent to Elkhorn.

The Beast of Bray Road remains at large to this day.

WYOMING

Dead Man Talking

What I learned in history class: Wyoming's nickname is the Equality State. It was not only the first state to give women the right to vote, but it was also the first to elect a female governor, Nellie Tayloe Ross, in 1924.

A story you won't find in your textbook: I'm going to leave you with a tale that still haunts me some nights. I do a lot better these days coming face to face with the paranormal than I did that first time in the gym locker way back in fourth grade. Still, scary is scary, and weird is weird, no matter how many times you stare it in the eye. On a trip out west, I visited the Wyoming Frontier Prison in Rawlins, Wyoming. The prison closed in 1981 after operating for eighty years. Some of the prisoners, however, didn't seem to notice the closing. They decided to stay anyway. Of course, the prisoners I'm talking about died a long time ago. The Old Pen, as the prison is known, is now a museum—but as I discovered, it's haunted. Visitors can tour the cell blocks and Death Row. The prospect of that tour is what kept me going during a visit out west to some relatives.

◑◐

I had read about the Old Pen before our trip, so I knew that other paranormal detectives and ghost hunters had already recorded images of ghostly orbs, psychic energy fields, and disembodied voices.

Tour guides have reported seeing vague circles of light pass through solid walls. They told of hearing heavy footsteps after the museum had closed but finding no one when they traced the location of the sounds. Some guides said they had seen prisoners walking the halls and retreating into rooms. The guides followed them but discovered only empty cells. Of course, there have been no prisoners (no living ones, anyway) in the Old Pen for more than twenty years.

But none of these stories prepared me for what I found when I entered the large stone building. My cousin dropped me off—she had no interest at all in a haunted prison—and I told her I'd call her when it was time to pick me up.

I was part of an evening tour that began in pretty

typical fashion. The tour guide, Hillary Becket, outlined the history of the prison, beginning with its formation in post–Civil War, Wild West Wyoming.

She told us tales of lawless desperadoes, bold train robberies, women committing murderous crimes of passion, and inmates staging daring escapes. The tour was fun, but I saw or heard no sign of anything paranormal. Until we reached Death Row, that is.

This section of the prison felt especially dark and depressing. Hillary related stories of men awaiting execution, some for years. It was here that she briefly touched on the rumors that the spirits of the executed haunted the prison, but she ended her remarks with a dismissive "if you believe that sort of thing."

Resisting the urge to shout out, "*I* believe that sort of thing," I was startled to discover that one of the cells had a light on. "Why does that cell have a light on?" I asked.

"Well, that's odd," Hillary replied. "I really don't know." She reached through the bars of cell number 485 and switched off the light.

As the tour rounded a corner and left Death Row, I glanced back at cell 485. To my astonishment, I saw that the cell was once again lit. Falling behind the group, I quietly walked back to the cell and peered through the cold metal bars. There was no one around, and no one behind our tour group who could have turned the light on.

As I stared into the gray cell, which contained nothing

more than a cot and a toilet, I heard a voice. A strained, plaintive cry drifted out of the cell. "Innocent!"

I jumped back, shocked by the sound. I looked around. There was no one near me. And there was definitely no one in the cell. I stepped back up to the cell. "Innocent!" cried the desperate voice again.

Where was it coming from?

"Young man!" boomed a voice from behind me. I nearly hit the roof, I was so startled. I turned around to see Hillary Becket glaring down at me. "You'll have to keep up with the tour. And you should not have turned that light back on. Were you the one who turned it on the first time?"

"No!" I cried. "And I didn't turn it on this time either."

"Then why is it on?" she asked, again switching off the light. She gave me a look that clearly said, "I don't have time for childish pranks."

"Whatever," I whispered, the hair on the back of my neck still standing. I knew what I had heard, but I decided it was best not to bring it up with a skeptic like Hillary.

The tour ended and I browsed the museum's gift shop, trying to look like I was really interested in the postcards, key chains, and books.

I wasn't. I was just killing time. I had no intention of leaving the prison before I checked out that cell again. My cousin could wait. I had to find out what was going on here.

Shortly before the museum closed, I slipped out of the gift shop and hurried off to a dark corner of the prison.

Squatting in the deep shadows, I heard the last visitors leave and the door slam.

Panic seized me. I felt trapped. I was being locked inside a prison. I couldn't shake the feeling that I had sentenced myself to a horrible night in this terrifying, depressing place. But I had to go back to that cell.

When the place had been totally silent for a few minutes, I stood up and made my way quietly through the empty prison. My scuffling footsteps echoed off the grimy cinder block. Mixed in with the echoes, I could just make out whispering voices—sad, angry, desperate voices, pleading for mercy.

I pressed on, and the smell of human waste and filth washed over me, mixed with something else that was putrid and unfamiliar. The smell of death?

I rounded the corner and stepped back onto Death Row. The din of hopeless voices grew louder. The dark hallway was lit by only a handful of dim bulbs. I moved slowly along the line of cells.

I was almost back at cell 485. As I moved to step in front of the cell, the light blazed on.

I jumped back, keeping out of the yellow glow pouring into the gray hallway. The moment the light came on, all the voices fell silent. Now the quiet was eerie, almost unbearable.

Glancing back over my shoulder to make sure I was totally alone, I stepped into the light in front of the cell. Once again I surveyed its cold stark emptiness. And then I heard the voice again.

"Innocent!" it cried, thin but clear.

I pressed my face between two of the bars, the chill of the metal shooting into my cheeks. "Wh-who are you?" I stammered.

"Innocent!" it repeated, louder now, more agitated.

I stood there for a few minutes, listening to the same sad voice repeat that single word. I had to learn more. Hurrying down Death Row, I turned the corner. Then I paused and peered back around.

The light in cell 485 was off again. The hallway was dark.

I made my way to the prison's lowest level, where I remembered Hillary pointing out the old records office. Luckily, it was unlocked. The night watchman must not have made his rounds yet. I slipped inside.

It took me a few minutes to shuffle through various boxes and cabinets, but then I came upon the prisoner records. Looking up cell 485, I found my answer right away.

Cedric Malcove was the last prisoner to occupy cell 485 on Death Row. He was also the last person executed at the Wyoming Frontier Prison before it closed. Pulling Malcove's file from the drawer, I began reading.

Cedric Malcove, age forty-one, was convicted of the murder of George Jeffries and sentenced to death. He was executed at Wyoming Frontier Prison on January 22, 1981. Malcove maintained his innocence up until the moment of his death. He claimed that he had been framed and that the real killer still walked free.

"Maintained his innocence." That phrase bounced around my brain. Apparently, Cedric Malcove is still claiming his innocence, even after his execution. I closed the file and put it away.

Then I stepped from the office and bumped right into the museum's night watchman. I fell back in fear. I was caught!

"Well, what have we here?" the man asked. He was an elderly gentleman with white hair peeking out from beneath his cap. He wore a blue security uniform. "Anxious to get a taste of what it's like to spend the night in prison? You wouldn't be the first curious visitor to stay behind after we close. I was about to lock you in the records room!"

"I'm sorry," I said. "I didn't mean to break any rules. I just heard something in cell 485 and I—"

"Old Cedric, huh?" the guard said, smiling. "He doesn't speak to just anyone. You must be special. Oh, I've heard him, but I never could convince the museum directors that he was real. But he's real, all right. And I know he's innocent."

"Am I in trouble?" I asked nervously.

"I think we can avoid executing you this time," the guard said, smiling again. Then he introduced himself as Sam Cliveson.

I thanked him and headed out of the prison. I dialed my cousin to come pick me up, certain that I had encountered the ghost of Cedric Malcove. My trip out west ended a couple of days later, but I couldn't get that voice out of my mind.

Back home, over the next few months, I kept up with

the online edition of the *Daily Times*, the Rawlins news-paper. There were mentions from time to time in the paper of the mysterious light in Death Row cell 485, and of the ghost of Cedric Malcove crying his innocence. Then one day about six months after my visit, I was stunned to read the huge one-word headline blazing across the front page of the *Daily Times*:

INNOCENT!

The story went on to reveal that new DNA evidence had come to light in the Cedric Malcove murder case, proving the claim that Malcove had made all along. He was innocent. The DNA evidence connected another pris-oner with the murder of George Jeffries and also with a second homicide—the murder of the prison's night watch-man, Sam Cliveson!

I fell back in my chair and rolled halfway across the room. It was impossible. I'd met Sam Cliveson six months ago. How could he have been murdered in the early 1980s? I decided to call the prison and ask for Sam.

"Is this some kind of joke?" said the man who answered the phone. "If it is, it's in very bad taste. Sam Cliveson was a friend of mine. And he was murdered over twenty years ago! They just found his killer. It's in the paper."

I dropped the phone, my heart pounding in my chest. Sam Cliveson was not the first ghost I had met during my travels, but learning that I've had a conversation with a dead man always creeps me out.

A sidebar to the *Daily Times* cover story said that the light in cell 485 had stopped coming on, and the mournful cry of "Innocent!" could no longer be heard. Apparently, Cedric Malcove was finally resting in peace.

I only hope that Sam Cliveson is as well.

A FINAL WORD

I never set out to be the clearinghouse for the paranormal in this country. But once it started, my collection just kept growing. I'm glad I could share these stories with you. It was tough to select just one for each state, because I've uncovered so many more.

But what about *you*? Do you live in a scary state? Let me know. I'd love to hear about your encounters with the creepy, the bizarre, the unexplainable, and the just plain scary. Drop by my Web site, www.scarystatesofamerica.com, and share your stories with me.

I can't wait to read them.

Jason Specter

HOW THIS BOOK
CAME TO BE

I first "met" Jason Specter a few years ago when I began to read the stories on his Web site. I always liked tales of the unexplained, and I have to admit I was hooked right away.

I wrote to Jason and challenged him to pick his favorites—no easy task, as it turned out. I told him I'd like him to choose one story from each state and that I'd help him organize it into a book. I then used my contacts in the publishing world to see if I could help get his stories into print. One thing led to another, and you now hold the result of those efforts in your hands.

I hope you enjoyed your journey through a world beyond that which we take for granted—the world of undead spirits, unearthly creatures, and unexplained lights in the sky. A world filled with out-of-body experiences and past lives recalled, or, as Jason likes to call it, the Scary States of America.

This book would not have been possible without the hard work and commitment of Michael Buckley, Alison Fargis of the Stonesong Press, and Marissa Walsh, Joe Cooper, Stephanie Lane, and Beverly Horowitz of Delacorte Press. I thank them all, but more importantly, Jason thanks them all.

I also thank my wife, Sheleigah, who held my hand through the scariest sections of this book. And Jason also thanks all his e-mail and IM buddies around the Scary States who pointed him toward the true but terrifying.

A final word of thanks from me to my friend and your host on this journey through the shadowlands of America—Jason Specter.

Michael Teitelbaum
New York City, 2007